THE SUMMER BRIDE

SEASONS OF CHANGE
BOOK THREE

ANNEMARIE BREAR

SEASONS OF CHANGE SERIES

Book 1 The Winter Widow
Book 2 Whispers of Spring
Book 3 The Summer Bride

CHAPTER ONE

range Lea Estate
Lincolnshire
March, 1854

CAROLINE LAWSON KNELT at the edge of the garden bed closest to the house, pulling out old weeds between spring bulbs. Yellow heads of daffodils stood proudly amongst the overgrowth of the abandoned gardens. The winter snow had melted away and the days grew longer. She had great plans for the garden, beds full of lush plants and swathes of green lawn.

Along the next garden bed, Dickie, a youth employed by Max, was turning over the soil around the ancient roses Caroline had trimmed into shape after years of neglect. The bright green growth on the roses matched the opening buds on the trees lining the long drive and boundary stonewalls. The drab greyness of the cold months was slowly receding into brightness. The sun shone from a pale-blue sky, the clouds fluffy and white, the breeze held a hint of warmth and Caroline breathed in the scent of damp earth and clean air.

The new year had brought in many changes. A fresh start for her and her dearest friend, Trixie Wilkes and Trixie's sisters, Elsie and Bertha. They'd moved from Yorkshire to Grange Lea in Lincolnshire, an estate given to Caroline's new fiancé Maxwell Cavendish from his aunt, and they'd all taken on new roles, accepted changes and embraced a future none of them assumed they'd ever have.

Caroline never expected Max to propose marriage or for herself to agree to it. She would become mistress of this house, a wife again. Would she be as happy with Max as she was with her first husband, Hugh? She liked to believe so. Max loved her, and she loved him. Yet, she knew sometimes love wasn't enough when the harsh world crept inside the front door and brought difficult challenges to face.

But they had been through a lot already and she took strength from that. If they could survive what life had previously dealt them, then surely, they could survive anything else that might come their way?

'This bed is done, madam,' Dickie said, coming towards her carrying a shovel. 'Shall I start on that large bed by the trees?'

'That'll be enough for today, Dickie. We've made good progress.' Caroline got up from her knees and shook out the sacking apron that she wore to protect her old dress. 'Jacob might be needing you now.' She spoke of another dear friend who'd come with them from York. Jacob had lived all his life in the same tenement building as Trixie within the slums of York. He'd helped Caroline and Trixie and the girls to flee York when their lives were in danger from the thug Victor Dolan. Jacob had joined them in the country at Hopewood Farm and remained a loyal friend. He also had feelings for Trixie.

Dickie banged some soil off his spade. 'Rightio. Shall I take your tools back as well?'

'Yes, thank you. They need a good scrub.' She handed him the mud-caked digging tools she'd been using. 'We'll do some more gardening tomorrow if we have time.'

Dickie surveyed the huge front garden and the two beds they'd been working on. 'It'll take all summer, madam.'

'That's fine.' She smiled. 'Once the worst of the hard work is completed, it means each year from now on won't be as onerous.'

'Onerous? What does that mean?'

'Difficult.'

'Aye.' Dickie nodded thoughtfully. 'I don't mind gardening.'

'We've the kitchen garden to sort out as well. It's Trixie's domain, but she'll need our help.'

'That's my favourite job. Knowing the seeds we plant will be something we'll be eating soon.' He rubbed his lean stomach. 'We'll never be hungry if we grow our own food, madam.'

'Correct, Dickie.' She dusted off her hands and pulled off her gloves. 'We'll make a farmer out of you yet.' She smiled and walked towards the house, slipping around the back and into the yard.

She entered the scullery and took off her apron and hat. As she tugged off her boots, Trixie came to the doorway leading into the kitchen.

'You'll be wanting a cup of tea?' Trixie asked, tucking a cloth into the waistband of her white apron. Employed as the cook, Trixie was in charge of the kitchen, and Rosanna, the kitchen maid.

They'd shared a filthy room in the poverty-stricken slums of York, been through the worst of times together and were more like sisters than friends. However, Caroline's marriage to Max, a gentleman, meant Caroline would be higher in class than Trixie and Caroline hoped it wouldn't change their close bond.

'That'd be lovely.' Caroline put on her house shoes and followed her into the warm kitchen. Rosanna was cutting vegetables at the large pine table in the middle of the room.

'Did you get much done out the front?' Trixie asked, pouring boiling water into the porcelain teapot to warm it.

'We've made a good start on two of the beds closest to the drive, which are now weed free. Visitors will be greeted with tidy edges and hopefully beautiful roses instead of knee-high weeds. But I told Dickie that we will help you in the kitchen garden before we do anymore out the front.'

'I'd like to get more planting done. If we've seen the last of the cold weather, we can start planting the salads. The tomato and cucumber seeds are growing well in the barn. We can bring them out into the garden beds soon.' Trixie poured out two cups of tea and sat beside Caroline at the other end of the table.

Caroline sipped her tea. 'Lincolnshire seems warmer earlier in the year than Yorkshire, don't you find? I'm glad we've managed to get the potatoes planted and the onions and carrots.'

'Enough talk of vegetables.' Trixie grinned. 'I want to talk about the wedding. Elsie and Bertha won't stop going on about it.'

Rolling her eyes, Caroline grinned. 'I only get peace from them while they are at their lessons. I've promised them new dresses for the day.'

Trixie's expression fell. 'They are missing Mussy so much. The wedding is taking their minds off his death.'

'We all are missing him,' Caroline murmured. Their dear friend, Mussy, had died of tuberculosis three months ago and he'd left a large hole in all their lives.

'Elsie is struggling to teach Bertha,' Trixie added. 'Bertha isn't as interested in books as much as Elsie. Mussy was so good at teaching Bertha and getting her involved, but she just ignores Elsie.'

'I wish I could afford to pay for a governess for them.'

'No, don't be silly,' Trixie tutted. 'They're working-class girls, Caro, not daughters of a gentleman. They don't need a governess.

They've had more learning than most girls of their class. It's enough.'

Although she knew that to be true, Caroline saw potential in Elsie who she'd taught to read last year. 'You can never be educated enough.'

'Working-class girls can be. It'll give them high expectations.'

'I see nothing wrong with that,' Caroline argued. 'It's a shame the local village school won't take girls and only boys.'

Trixie drank some of her tea. 'Girls aren't important. They marry and stay home. Boys need to be educated to rule the world.'

'It won't always be that way, I hope.' She sighed, disliking that the education system lacked for girls, especially in the country. 'Girls need to be educated as well as boys. They are left widows and need to learn how to run businesses and such things.'

'Or they just remarry.' Trixie shrugged. 'Anyway, Elsie and Bertha will manage with the education they get from you. Now, let's talk about this wedding.'

Caroline played with her teaspoon. She didn't want to talk about the wedding. 'Why are you getting so excited? It's months away and it'll be a small occasion at the village church.'

'And the wedding breakfast?' Trixie prompted.

'Hardly anyone is coming.' She finished her tea. 'We want to keep it intimate. Just us here at the farm.'

'Your wedding is a happy occasion, and we should celebrate it.' Trixie frowned. 'We deserve a bit of a do. Why you had to make us all wait six months since Mr Cavendish proposed, I'll never know.'

'I told you I wanted a summer wedding,' she lied, not willing to tell Trixie the truth. 'June will come soon enough.'

'Another two and a half months away,' Trixie scoffed. 'At least let us have a party. We can invite the villagers, have some music, perhaps hire a brass band from Lincoln?'

'Goodness, a brass band? That's a bit much.' She chuckled. 'A fiddler is more than enough.' She rose from the chair, ending the conversation. 'Is Jeannie upstairs?'

'Aye, madam,' Rosanna answered before Trixie could. 'She's dusting the bedrooms.'

Caroline clenched her teeth in annoyance at the girl. For the three months since Max employed Rosanna and Jeannie, Rosanna had been quick to speak when it wasn't her place to, despite both Trixie and Caroline warning her to hold her tongue. The girl was too bold. Rosanna's saving grace was that she worked well, when she applied herself, which, frustratingly, wasn't all the time.

Leaving the kitchen, Caroline headed along the service corridor to the front hall. She glanced into the drawing room and checked the fire was still burning. Although the day was pleasant outside, the house's upkeep had been neglected for decades and it needed fires burning in all the rooms to keep the damp at bay. Max and Jacob had been working on repairing roof slates that had slipped or broken over the years, but the damage had been done and the house required a lot of restoration. A new roof was on the top of Max's very long list.

Across the hall, Elsie and Bertha were in the library, and raised voices greeted her as she opened the door. 'What is all this noise?'

Nine-year-old Elsie wiped her wet eyes. 'Bertha won't listen to me.'

'I don't want to do numbers!' Bertha, nearly seven, pouted stubbornly, arms folded.

'Now then, let's calm down.' Caroline strode to the desk where the girls sat. 'Bertha, I want you to write your numbers from one to ten.' She pulled another armchair closer to the desk. 'Elsie, what are you doing?'

'I was reading this book and writing out any words I don't recognise. That's what Mussy told me to do. Then he used to help me learn the words I'd not seen before.'

'Very good. Let's continue doing that,' she encouraged with a smile, while turning to Bertha and helping her.

The afternoon sped by as she aided the girls in their learning endeavours until the door opened and Max walked in with a loving gaze.

'Is it time for a bit of fresh air and a walk in the fields?' he asked, lifting Caroline's hand and kissing it. He held her hand as the girls packed away their books and papers.

'Was your journey into town successful?' she asked him once they were walking amongst the sprouting crop fields surrounding the house. Elsie and Bertha ran ahead with Caroline's two dogs, Prince and Duke and Max's dog, Princess.

Max took off his hat and ran a hand through his dark hair, his blue eyes serious. 'I managed to obtain a loan from the bank using the estate as security.'

She stopped and stared at him. 'Was that what you wanted to do?'

'I had no other choice. I have nothing to use as collateral that is of any worth except the estate. I need the loan to invest in more livestock and better farming equipment. We must pray that the harvest is good, and that the animals sell well when they go to market at the end of the year so I can meet the repayments and still make a profit.'

She tucked her arm through his, sensing he needed her support, her comfort. Since his proposal she'd been keeping him at arm's length, a chaste kiss every now and then was all she could give him, but when they were alone together, she made certain she listened to him and discussed with him his plans for the future, their future. Max wanted her involved in everything he did, and she adored him for including her, but she held back from giving him all of her. She didn't want to delve into the farm and really make it her home when she was still uncertain as to whether it would be.

Keeping her distance from him was becoming more difficult

to do. One look from his loving eyes, a smile from his handsome face, a touch of a hand in passing, all melted her heart, sent shots of awareness through her body. She wanted Max in every way a woman wants a man. However, the past still haunted her and made her doubt any decision she made.

Thankfully, amazingly, Max was patient with her. He knew her rape last year by his cousin, Wayland, was still a concern, a trauma she hadn't fully accepted. What Wayland did to her caused her anguish in quiet moments and lingering doubt that Max would want her after his cousin's defilement. It was one of the reasons she'd put off the wedding until summer. She needed Max to be completely sure she was the woman he wanted as his wife, in all ways. Would he be able to see her as desirable and ignore the thoughts of Wayland's brutality? He said he could, and a part of her believed him. Yet, a hidden voice inside her head told her to wait, to be doubly certain the next man she married would love her unconditionally as Hugh had done. She wanted the happiness of a pure love again. The pain of anything less would destroy her.

'We'll work hard to ensure Grange Lea is a huge success,' she said softly.

'Hard work is not always the answer. We cannot control the weather, or the diseases animals can succumb to, or accidents, or market prices...'

'This is unlike you to be so negative.' She glanced up at him with a frown.

'So much is depending on this estate making money. I want to give you a good life, Caroline. I will work myself to the bone to give you everything you want, for you to never regret marrying me.'

She turned to him. 'No, stop. I'll not be responsible for you killing yourself with worry just to make me happy. Your love and care are all I want. I could live in a tiny house in the middle of... of anywhere, I wouldn't care, as long as you are by my side and

Trixie and the girls are safe and well. I don't need to be a mistress of an estate.' She swept her arm wide, indicating the property. 'All this is a bonus, Max. You must believe me?'

He bowed his head. 'I do not want you to *simply settle* for me as a way of security. I want you to be happy with everything in your life, happy with *me*.'

She stepped closer and cupped his cheek, forcing him to look at her. 'You doubt my love for you?'

Uncertainty flickered in his eyes. 'At times, I wonder if you care for me as much as I care for you.'

Her hand dropped from his face. 'You know I care.'

'Then why did you want a six-month engagement? We could have been married at the beginning of the year, three weeks after Mussy died.'

'That wasn't the right time.' She turned away and started back towards the house.

'You say you love me, but you have made no plans for the wedding, Caroline. I never see any excitement from you about it when the day is mentioned,' he said sadly.

Her footsteps faltered. In the distance, the girls laughed, and the dogs barked, only she felt cold and lonely.

'Are you marrying me for security?' he asked, his tone low. 'Answer me with honesty, please?'

She spun on her heel and faced him. Only yards separated them, but it might as well have been miles. 'No. I'm marrying you because I love you.'

'Are you sure about that? I do not always feel it. You say the words, but are they empty of true meaning?' He shrugged and walked away in the opposite direction to her or the girls, his shoulders slumped.

Caroline watched him, her chest tight with emotion. She'd hurt him. She had to fix that, but how? How could she speak of what was in her head? Being a widow had given her independence, and she liked it. Then, there was also the problem of her being barren. Max would want children. She hadn't fallen with child with her first husband or when Wayland raped her. She had to be barren.

Those issues were difficult enough, but she was also tormented by the thought Max might not be able to touch her intimately, that his mind might be full of his cousin's actions, of what that monster did to her. All that gave her much to consider. How would Max react when he saw her naked for the first time on their wedding night? Would he imagine Wayland's hands on her body?

Would she?

And if it altered how they felt about each other, it would be too late. They'd be married, joined for life, and she didn't consider she could cope with being in a marriage of convenience. She'd rather stay a widow.

CHAPTER TWO

The tense mood between Caroline and Max grew more and more as the days rolled by. Neither could stomach a sincere conversation about what really mattered, so they spoke only pleasantries and avoided each other as much as possible. Max stayed out on the farm until late each day, helping Jacob and Dickie assist the ewes with the lambing of the flock, as well as attending to the calving of the dairy cows and the small beef herd. When he wasn't out in the barns and fields, he spent the evenings in his study, while Caroline kept occupied supervising the running of the house and the nights in her room reading, or trying to, instead of sitting alone in the drawing room.

After a week of barely speaking, Max told her he was going to Oxford to visit his brother, Thomas. He'd be gone for some weeks, leaving Jacob and Dicky to see to the farm. Spring was such a busy period on the farm and for Max to be leaving at such an important period showed her how much he needed to be gone from her presence.

Frustrated, and annoyed at the situation, Caroline refused to speak of it with Trixie, who looked at her with raised eyebrows.

The morning he was to leave, Max found Caroline in the

laundry shed, lighting the fire beneath the large copper pot that was filled with water.

She faced him, hating the edgy atmosphere between them. She didn't know how to make it right. 'You're ready to go?'

He stood stiffly in the doorway, dressed in a dark-grey suit, hat in hands. 'Yes. All the lambs have been safely delivered and most of the calves. Dickie can monitor them. Jacob can start ploughing in the east field. Dickie will also repair the roof on the hen coop. They have their instructions for what needs doing while I am away.'

She nodded.

Max cleared his throat. 'I have left a purse of money in my desk drawer in the study for any expenses that arise. Jacob will take you into Lincoln should you wish to go.'

'Thank you.'

'You should not be washing the clothes. Get one of the maids to do it.'

'Sometimes I do, but Rosanna and Jeannie are not laundry maids.'

'Nor are you! It is bad enough that you work in the dairy.'

'I enjoy the dairy, you know that. Milking, making butter and cheese is a chore I take pride in.'

He tapped his hat against his leg. 'As my future wife, I do not wish for you to be performing such manual labour. We must employ a laundry maid and a dairy maid.'

She crossed her arms. 'Money for those two wages would be better spent elsewhere when I can manage perfectly well. You do not have the wealth of your late uncle at Misterton Abbey. This place can't be managed as the abbey was with abundant staff to do everything. There isn't the money for it.'

'I am doing my best,' he defended.

'That wasn't a slight against you not being wealthy enough, Max.' She huffed. 'I'm being practical.'

It was a discussion they'd had many times before, one which was never resolved.

For a long time, they stared at each other.

'Well, I had better be going. I do not want to miss my train.'

She glanced away, wanting him to go and yet also to stay. 'Of course.'

'I expect to be gone a fortnight.' He took a step towards her, and she took one to him. Max lifted her hand to his lips. 'If I am staying longer, I will write.'

'Take care.' She wished he would keep holding her hand.

'You, too.' His hand fell away and let out a sigh. 'Reflect on our future while I am gone.'

'What do you mean?'

'I mean, think very deeply about what you want, Caroline. We can talk about what you decide to do when I return.'

'What *I* decide to do?' What was he saying?

'You are having doubts about us marrying. I can see it plainly.' His blue eyes turned sad. 'I would not wish you to marry me when it is not what you want.' He looked dispirited as he left her without another word spoken and it took great effort not to call him back, but she stilled her tongue, knowing they needed time apart to consider everything, or at least she did.

Taking a deep breath, she returned to her task of the weekly washing, but the day had become duller without Max in it. His parting words lingered on the air, echoing in her mind.

What exactly did she want? Max? Marriage? She honestly didn't know. She loved him, she was sure of that. Yet, the walls she'd built around her heart after Hugh died were difficult to bring down.

* * *

IN THE PAST, hard work proved her salvation and Caroline

plunged into tasks that kept her occupied from dawn until she fell into bed exhausted each night.

Some days, Caroline worked alongside Trixie, creating a well-organised kitchen garden filled with vegetable seedlings and salad and herb plants. She took the dogs with her walking the fields to check on the ewes with their skipping lambs and the cows and their bashful calves. Other days she worked with Jacob, ploughing in the fields, or with Dickie in the barns, cleaning, sorting, arranging tools and farming equipment.

The dairy had become a priority since the cows had calved and there was plenty of milk to be had. She spent back-breaking hours churning butter and making cheese. She cleaned the dairy each day, swilling the floor, washing the stone sinks, the butter churn, and the milk urns.

When it rained, she stayed in the house, giving each room a thorough once over with Jeannie's help. They moved furniture into better positions to catch the summer light to read by. They washed curtains and rehung them, cleaned windows, rolled up the carpet rugs and took them outside to be beaten. The wooden floors were mopped and polished. Every surface was dusted or polished until it shone.

The first week of Max being away passed rapidly as Caroline worked non-stop, but the second week dragged endlessly. The evenings grew lighter, the days longer, so she took longer walks with the dogs, venturing into the villages of South and North Carlton, meeting the locals and learning her way around the area.

Mr and Mrs Todd, the elderly couple who Max bought chickens from when they first arrived, always welcomed Caroline when she called. Mrs Todd would make a pot of tea or pour glasses of elderflower cordial, and Caroline would sit with her on a stool outside the old woman's cottage and listen to her tales of farming or village life in this quiet part of Lincolnshire.

After one such visit to Mrs Todd and two weeks after Max

had left, Caroline returned home, entering the kitchen to the delicious smell of freshly baked bread.

Trixie, red-cheeked from tending to the hot oven, wiped her brown curls from her eyes. 'Oh, good, you're back.'

Caroline unpinned her straw bonnet. 'Is something wrong?'

'Rosanna and Jeannie have been whispering and disappearing all morning, and I'm fed up with it.'

'Have you spoken to them about it?'

'I've told Rosanna to get on with her work, but then she leaves the kitchen again the minute my back is turned.' Trixie tucked a cloth into the waistband of her apron. 'I just sense something isn't right.'

'I'll get to the bottom of it. Where are they?'

'No idea. I've not seen Jeannie for hours and Rosanna has hardly said a word to me, which in itself is odd, for the girl never shuts up normally.' Trixie stirred the contents of a simmering pot. 'It's not good enough, Caro.'

'No, it isn't.' Caroline headed for the door to the corridor. 'Where's Elsie and Bertha?'

'Out with Dickie. Some chicks hatched this morning, and the girls won't leave the chicken coop. Jacob is spreading manure on the crop near the drive.'

Caroline nodded and moved along the corridor, her gaze flicking to Max's empty study, half wishing he was sitting in there and half relieved he wasn't. She checked every room downstairs and then proceeded up to the bedrooms, but they were empty as well.

She glanced at the narrow stairs leading up to the attics. Were the two maids up in their room in the middle of the afternoon? Intrigued, she climbed up the steep stairs, holding her skirts high so as not to trip. At the top, she opened the door and walked along the tight passageway between the slope of the roof and the small bedrooms. One of the bedroom doors was open slightly. On hearing voices, she stopped and listened.

'You'll be all right, Jeannie, I promise.' Rosanna's frightened tone caused Caroline to lean closer to the door.

'I'm going to die, Ros,' Jeannie's wail ended in a moan.

'No, you're not. I'll not let you.'

'I *want* to die!'

'Don't talk such rot!' Rosanna snapped.

'But what are we going to do?'

'I'll tell Miss Wilkes you're sick and she'll tell Mrs Lawson. It'll be fine.'

'Fine?' Jeannie screeched.

'Shh! For God's sake, Jeannie, be quiet.'

'It hurts so much, Ros,' Jeannie cried. 'How can I have it without anyone knowing?'

'You'll have to bite on something, a pillow or the blankets. They can't realise what's going on downstairs, Jeannie, or we'll both be out on the streets.'

'And what about the baby?'

'Once it's born, I'll slip out when it's dark and take it into Lincoln and leave it somewhere, at a church door. Someone will find it and take care of it.'

Caroline blinked in shock. *A baby?* She jerked her hand out and pushed open the door. On the bed, sweating and crying, lay Jeannie while Rosanna hovered over her with a damp cloth.

They both turned to her with expressions of guilt and fear.

Before Caroline could speak, Jeannie drew her knees up and groaned deeply as a contraction gripped her body.

Once the pain passed, Jeannie rested back against the pillow, eyes closed, silent tears slipping down her cheeks.

Rosanna straightened and faced Caroline. 'Madam, we—'

'Whatever you're going to say next, Rosanna, it had better not be a lie.' Caroline glared at her. 'I want the truth, *all of it.*'

'It's all my fault,' Jeannie muttered miserably.

'No, it wasn't,' tutted Rosanna before staring boldly at Caroline. 'I'm sorry, Mrs Lawson.'

'For what? Lying to me, to us all?' Caroline crossed her arms in disappointment. She liked the girls, especially Jeannie, and felt betrayed by their lies.

'I didn't realise I was with child when we came here before Christmas,' Jeannie confessed. 'I promise!' She began to sob.

'Jeannie only realised a few weeks ago when she couldn't fasten up her skirt that she was having a baby,' Rosanna spoke for her friend. 'I just assumed she was getting fat from all the good food Miss Wilkes cooks.'

Caroline stared at Jeannie's stomach, which wasn't very large, not that Caroline had any experience of women with child.

'It's the truth, madam,' Rosanna added. 'Jeannie didn't tell me until a few days ago.'

'And you didn't think to come to me?' She was hurt the girls didn't trust her. Was she unapproachable? Had she been too focused on her own problems to see what was happening right under her nose?

'We were worried you'd throw us out.' Rosanna rubbed her forehead, the worry clear in her eyes. 'You've every right to do that, madam.'

'Yes, I do,' she snapped with annoyance. 'An unmarried maid secretly giving birth in the attic... Yes, that is grounds for dismissal.'

Jeannie arched her back as another contraction tortured her. 'It's coming!'

'Oh Jesus!' Rosanna's scared expression implored Caroline to help.

Springing into action, Caroline pushed aside the unknown circumstances that lead to the current situation. That discussion would come later. 'Rosanna, strip the bed of the blankets and sheets. We need to protect the mattress.' She glanced around the room and spotted the newspaper and wondered fleetingly which one of them read it. 'Spread the newspaper under Jeannie and get her into a nightgown. I'll go downstairs and fetch some hot water and towels.'

Jeannie gasped. 'I need to push it out.'

'What?' Caroline spun around to her. 'No, not yet!'

'I can't help it...' Jeannie moaned.

'How long have you been having pains?'

'She started suffering twinges yesterday,' Rosanna supplied guiltily. 'The proper pains started last evening.'

'Last evening? That long ago?' Alarmed, Caroline ran from the room. Lifting her skirts high, she raced down to the kitchen, frightening Trixie as she dashed through the door.

'Good God, what it is?' Trixie held a spoon mid-air that dripped stew onto the floor.

'Jeannie. She's having a baby. Now.'

'What?' Trixie stared. 'Oh no...'

'You need to help us. Hot water, towels and what else?'

'A midwife?' Trixie suggested. 'I'll get Jacob to go into Lincoln.'

From the cupboard, Caroline took out two large jugs. 'There's no time for a midwife. It'll take hours to get one here and I don't think we have that long. Jeannie wants to push.'

'Push? Already?' Trixie's eyes widened. 'Is this what's been going on all morning?'

'She started her pains yesterday.'

'Yesterday? How did we not know?'

'I've no idea, but then, why would we expect our housemaid to be secretly with child? I need hot water.'

'Caro, we need a midwife. None of us have delivered a baby before.' Trixie poured the kettle of warm water into the first jug. 'There must be a woman in one of the villages who can help?'

'I've helped deliver animals on the farm...' Her mind shifted in different directions at the enormity of what was about to happen.

'It's hardly the same,' Trixie murmured.

19

'We don't have time to find a midwife.'

'I'll send Dickie, anyway.'

'No.' She faced Trixie in a panic. 'The gossip. The villagers already consider it strange that I live here with Max, and we're not married yet. They'll think the baby is mine.'

'Don't be silly.'

'Or yours. All of us are unmarried on this farm,' she argued. 'And now there's a baby in the mix.'

Trixie blew out her cheeks. 'I'll go out and tell Jacob what's happening and ask him to keep our Elsie and Bertha with him. Then, I'll come up and help.' She took the stew off the heat and refilled the kettle. 'We'll need more water.'

'Why?' Caroline asked, pulling old towels from a cupboard in the scullery.

'To wash the baby and Jeannie?' Trixie shrugged. 'Jacob will know, his sister Sarah is a midwife back home in York.'

'Right, yes. Ask Jacob.' Then Caroline had a concerning thought. 'Heavens, Trix, I pushed Jeannie hard last week. We were moving furniture and all sorts, and *she was with child*.' Guilt riddled her.

'Well, how were you to know she carried such a secret? She wasn't showing as far as I could tell. She always wears that huge apron.'

'Now we know why.'

'What's done is done.' Trixie poured water into a pot. 'Did Rosanna know?'

'Not until recently.' Caroline's hands shook, spilling some of the water out of the jug. 'I'd best get back up there.'

'You'll do just fine.' Trixie nodded encouragingly.

Upstairs in the attic, Caroline paused before entering the bedroom. She needed a moment to take a deep breath and clear her mind. From somewhere, she found the courage to open the door and walk in and face the ordeal of delivering a baby.

'I've done all that you said to do,' Rosanna whispered pale-faced, coming to her side. 'I can see the head.'

'Good.' Ignoring the sweat beading her upper lip, Caroline gave Jeannie a false smile. 'Right then, let's get this baby born, shall we?' She laid a towel over Jeannie's stomach and hitched up her nightgown. 'I'm just going to have a look, Jeannie, and see what's happening.'

Nervously, Caroline peeped between the girl's parted legs and frowned as she made sense of what she saw. Dark hair and blood. The baby's head half emerged.

Jeannie raised herself up to grip her knees and push.

In amazement, Caroline watched as the baby's head appeared a little more. 'That's it, Jeannie. Well done. I can see the baby has dark hair.'

'I don't care,' the girl growled, straining again to expel the baby.

For once, Rosanna said little, just held Jeannie's shoulders with silent encouragement.

For another twenty minutes Jeannie pushed, panted and rested, and pushed some more. Finally, the head was fully out and having helped sheep give birth to their lambs in the past, Caroline knew to wipe its little face of mucus as she'd done with the lambs. The shaking of her hands lessened as she concentrated on clearing the baby's tiny nose. Jeannie pushed again and Caroline held the baby's head when the shoulders appeared.

With a loud scream, Jeannie gave one final push, and the baby slithered into Caroline's hands just as Trixie came in with another jug of hot water.

'It's done!' Caroline rejoiced, quickly wiping the baby clean.

'You did it, Jeannie!' Rosanna kissed the top of her friend's head.

Caroline loosely wrapped the baby girl in a clean towel and then tied off the cord, knowing that was important.

'Here.' Trixie handed her a pair of scissors.

Deftly, she cut the cord, separating mother and daughter. The tiny baby girl stared at her without crying, flexing her little fingers.

'Is it dead?' Jeannie mumbled without looking.

'She's very much alive and perfect,' Caroline declared with relief. 'Would you like to hold her?'

'No.' Jeannie turned away into Rosanna, eyes closed.

Rosanna stroked Jeannie's head. 'Have a rest.'

'Take it away,' the new mother whispered. 'I don't want to see it.'

With tears in her eyes, Rosanna looked at Caroline and Trixie. 'She doesn't want it.'

'She'll need feeding.' Trixie glanced at Jeannie. 'You'll need to feed her.'

'I won't.' Jeannie sobbed into the pillow. 'Let it die.'

Alarmed, Caroline cradled the baby close to her chest. Innocent dark-blue eyes gazed at her. The baby's skin turned pink as Caroline rubbed her gently.

'Will I take her down to the kitchen?' Trixie asked.

'Give it away!' Jeannie cried. 'I don't care what happens to it.'

Stunned, Caroline glanced at Trixie. 'Take the baby downstairs. I'll need to deliver the afterbirth.'

When the door closed, Caroline's hands began to shake again as she realised what she'd done. Somehow, unbelievably, she'd delivered a baby and the enormity of it made her tremble.

However, as she began to tidy away the soiled towels, she knew there was more to do. 'Jeannie, there's the afterbirth to deliver. Once that's done, you can have a sleep.' She silently prayed that she could manage to do the last bit successfully as well.

Thankfully, a short time later, the afterbirth came away with some pushing from Jeannie. The girl was spent. Rosanna bathed her with warm water.

Caroline made the bed up before she and Rosanna settled

Jeannie under the blankets and let her rest. The maid hadn't spoken. Tears leaked from her eyes, but she said not a word.

'We'll make you some tea and toast, Jeannie. Rest now.' Caroline grabbed a bundle of stained towels. 'Come with me,' Caroline ordered Rosanna.

Downstairs, Trixie sat in a chair by the fire, the baby asleep in her arms.

'Is the baby well?' Caroline asked, dumping the towels in the scullery sink.

'Aye, she's been asleep.' Trixie looked at Rosanna. 'But she'll need feeding when she wakes.'

'Yes, miss, but Jeannie doesn't want anything to do with her.'

'She doesn't have a choice,' Trixie reasoned.

Rosanna's face crumbled. 'I'll walk into Lincoln with the baby and give her to an orphanage.'

Caroline stared at the girl. 'Do you think it's that simple? The baby will be hungry. She needs her mother. She's not an unwanted puppy.' It broke her heart that this innocent little mite was being carelessly tossed away when Caroline couldn't have a child and had longed for one for years.

'Who is the father?' Trixie asked.

'He's not important.' Rosanna's expression turned hard.

'I disagree.' Caroline raised an eyebrow and waited.

'He doesn't know that Jeannie was with child.'

'Can he marry her?'

A broken laugh escaped from Rosanna. 'Him? Huh. That's a joke.'

'He has a child he should be made aware of,' Caroline continued calmly. 'I want his name and where he lives so I can write to him.'

'Nigel Orville will not even remember Jeannie or what he did to her,' Rosanna scoffed with hatred in her eyes.

'What do you mean?'

'He raped Jeannie, and that baby is the result of it, madam.' A tear slipped over Rosanna's lashes.

Caroline's chest tightened. A wretched memory of Wayland holding her down as he lifted her skirts flashed in her mind.

Trixie sighed deeply and rocked the sleeping baby. 'Tell us what happened.'

'Orville's a mean, evil drunk, madam. He'd come to London because his mother, our mistress, was dying. He drank every night and was always pushing me into corners, touching me. He wanted me to visit his room. I refused. He would try to kiss me at every opportunity.' More tears fell over her lashes. Rosanna brushed them away angrily. 'Then, on the night of Mrs Orville's funeral, he got very drunk and leery. I knew he'd not take no for an answer, so I escaped the house and hid in a park. I waited there all night until dawn. When I came back to the house and crept upstairs, I went to mine and Jeannie's room...'

'He had attacked her?' Caroline supplied.

'I didn't think he would turn to her because he'd not even looked in her direction before, it was always me he was after, always me...' Rosanna's face crumpled. 'If I'd known he'd go to Jeannie I'd have never left her alone... She's like a sister to me.'

A familiar fury filled Caroline; one she'd often felt since Wayland held her down in the stable. Once again, a man had taken what he wanted, abused and punished, just because he could.

Rosanna wiped her wet eyes with the back of her hand. 'Orville left the next morning after his attack on Jeannie. The house was put up for sale, but no one bought it. A few months later, Orville returned to live in it and that's when I told Jeannie we'd leave and go far away, go somewhere nice, like the country. We got on a train and ended up in Lincoln and then Mr Cavendish offered us a position here. I wasn't aware Jeannie was carrying Orville's baby, I promise you, madam.'

The three of them looked at the tiny bundle in Trixie's arms with its mop of dark hair and little pink face.

'And Jeannie truly doesn't want the baby?' Caroline asked.

'No. She hates it. It reminds her of Orville and what he did to her, not just once but twice that night.' Rosanna shivered. 'When I found out she was with child, I promised her I would give the baby away, otherwise Jeannie said she'd kill herself, and it's no idle threat, madam. I believe she would do it.'

'What a mess,' Trixie whispered.

Rosanna held out her arms. 'I'll take the baby somewhere.'

Letting out a long breath, Caroline glanced at Trixie. 'No, I'll go. I'll get Jacob to hitch the carriage. I'll take the baby into Lincoln. There's bound to be an orphanage where we can leave her.' She glanced at Rosanna. 'Go upstairs and ask Jeannie one final time if she wants to keep her.'

'I know the answer, madam,' Rosanna replied with a show of her usual confidence.

'Just ask her, will you, please?' Caroline insisted. 'This is an enormous decision for her.'

'And nothing has to be decided today,' Trixie added.

Caroline sucked in a breath. 'No. She can take her time to decide what to do with the baby. Tell her that.'

'Madam, Jeannie will never hold that baby,' Rosanna stated.

When Rosanna had left the kitchen, Trixie turned to Caroline with a wry smile. 'Our lives were becoming too quiet. We've gone months without anything happening out of the ordinary. We were due to be shaken up.'

Caroline grunted. 'I like the quiet and normal.'

'What will Mr Cavendish say? You will tell him, won't you?'

'Yes, I'll tell him. We can't have any lies between us.'

Trixie rocked the baby gently as it stirred. 'Do you miss him?'

Considering the question, she realised that she did miss him, a great deal, which only made her decision whether to marry him or not harder to make.

CHAPTER THREE

*H*olding the baby in her arms inside Max's small black carriage, Caroline glanced from the baby to the passing buildings as Jacob sat up front steering the horses through Lincoln's narrow streets.

Dickie, a Lincoln native, told her there was an orphanage on Sewell Road and gave Jacob directions to it. The sun was setting as they turned into the stone pillar gates and passed a sign that read, Saint Giles Orphanage. They travelled down the drive to a large brick house shaded by mature birch trees.

Jacob helped Caroline down from the carriage. 'Do you want me to go in with you?'

'I should be fine. Stay with the carriage.' She took a deep breath and stood before the solid black door and rang the bell. The baby moved her head a little but remained quiet and asleep, so trusting in the adult who held her, and Caroline's heart twisted. Was she doing the right thing? Was there another option?

A tall man answered the door wearing severe black, his lined face didn't smile a welcome. 'May I help you?'

'Yes. Er… well… I have a baby to give to the orphanage,' Caroline faltered over her words. How did you give a baby away? What were the correct words she needed to say?

'Come in.' He opened the door wider, and the faint noise of crying babies filtered down from the wide staircase. From another part of the building came the sound of children singing hymns.

Caroline followed the man down a long corridor and then he tapped on a door. When bidden to enter, he opened the door for Caroline, but didn't step inside.

'Mrs Fleetwood, there is a woman here with a baby for adoption.'

'Thank you, Mr Grisham.'

Caroline stepped through the door with her head held high. She had nothing to be ashamed of and refused to be cowered by the enormous building and the people in it. She faced the elderly Mrs Fleetwood who rose from her chair behind the wide desk. 'Thank you for seeing me.'

'Welcome to Saint Giles.' Mrs Fleetwood walked around the desk and held out her hand for Caroline to shake. Her gaze raked in Caroline's well-made summer dress of green-sprigged cotton and her lightweight short cloak in the colour of oatmeal that matched her hat. 'I'm Mrs Fleetwood, owner of this establishment, and you are?'

'Mrs Caroline Lawson. I've recently moved to Lincolnshire from York.'

'Please, take a seat, Mrs Lawson.' Mrs Fleetwood indicated to the chair near the desk and returned to her own on the other side. 'So, you are unable to care for your baby?'

'The baby isn't mine.'

Mrs Fleetwood paused in placing her spectacles on her nose. 'Not yours?'

'No. My maid, a girl of sixteen was taken by force at her previous employment. I only found out about her secret when

27

she went into labour today. My maid refuses to have anything to do with the child.'

'As is often the case.'

The baby stirred and whimpered, the first noise she'd made since leaving Grange Lea.

'She needs feeding. I have nothing with which to do so,' Caroline explained.

Mrs Fleetwood nodded and stood and tugged a bell pull beside the fireplace. Instantly the door opened and the tall man in black waited for instructions. 'Bring Ida to me please, Mr Grisham.'

'Immediately, madam.' The door closed behind him.

'We employ wet nurses, Mrs Lawson. We'll have the baby fed shortly.' Mrs Fleetwood sat down again and opened a ledger. 'May I have some details of the child?'

'Yes. She was born today.'

'Where?'

'At Grange Lea, a small estate north of Lincoln owned my… my betrothed.' Caroline hesitated to say the word, betrothed. 'Do you need such details?'

'All details are important, Mrs Lawson, I assure you. Now the mother's name and age?'

'Jeannie Booth, aged sixteen. Originally from London.'

'And the father?'

'As far as I've been told it's a man by the name of Nigel Orville. I have no more details about him.'

'He definitely wants nothing to do with the child?' Mrs Fleetwood kept writing.

'He wasn't aware Jeannie was carrying his baby. Jeannie left his employment soon after his attack.'

'A tragic, and sadly, a repeated tale of woe.' Mrs Fleetwood glanced up as the door opened and a young, working-class woman came in. 'Ah, Ida. We have a new baby for you to feed, a little girl born today. She's not had a feed and will be ravenous.'

'Yes, madam.'

'Take the child to the chair in the corner.'

Ida gave Caroline a timid smile as she reached for the baby. 'I'll see to her, madam.'

Reluctantly, Caroline released the baby, alarmed by the instant wave of protection she felt towards her. She watched as Ida settled herself on the wooden chair in the corner and unbuttoned her blouse, pulled aside her shift and forced her nipple into the baby's mouth which opened instinctively.

'Mrs Lawson, does the baby have a name?' Mrs Fleetwood drew Caroline's attention back to her.

'No.'

'Would you like to give her one? Of course, her new family might change it if we are successful in finding her a placement. Babies are easier to find homes for than older children so I'm certain this little one won't be with us for very long.'

'I see...' Caroline looked back at the baby feeding contentedly and was relieved that she'd no longer be hungry. 'She'll be well taken care of?'

Bristling slightly, Mrs Fleetwood nodded. 'Naturally. I run a respectable establishment with a board of patrons who insist on cleanliness and education for the children. Their donations would stop if they found any evidence of foul conduct by myself or my staff.' The older woman removed her spectacles. 'Many places such as this are prone to mismanagement and cruelty. The managers usually skim off the money donated to line their own pockets and leave the children starving and dirty, totally uncared for like unwanted kittens. That is not my business practice, Mrs Lawson. I can give you a tour if you wish?'

'That won't be necessary.' Caroline's gaze drifted to the baby still feeding. 'I'd like her name to be Rachel.' A name she'd always liked to give her own daughter if she'd had one with Hugh.

'Rachel.' Mrs Fleetwood nodded in agreement. 'Rachel Booth.'

Impulsively, Caroline opened her reticule and gave Mrs Fleetwood fifteen shillings. 'For Rachel's upkeep. I will call every week with money until Rachel is taken by a new family.'

'Would you like me to write to you when that occurs? You can be consulted on the couple if you wish?'

'I would like to meet any potential couples who are interested in Rachel.' Caroline shook Mrs Fleetwood's hand. 'Thank you.'

With another glance at the baby, she walked out of the office. Mr Grisham escorted her back to the front door where Jacob waited for her.

'How did it go?' Jacob helped her up into the carriage.

'Better than I'd hoped.'

'You've done a good thing today.' He closed the carriage door.

Caroline sagged against the seat as Jacob drove the carriage down the short drive. Had she done the right thing? Should she have waited a few days before coming here? Would Jeannie regret giving away her baby? She didn't have the answers, but hoped Jacob was right.

When Caroline entered the kitchen, Trixie and Rosanna came straight to her. 'It's done,' she told them. 'The baby is settled, and it seemed a nice enough place.'

Rosanna's shoulders relaxed. 'Thank you, madam.'

'Go up and tell Jeannie where the baby is,' Caroline said to Rosanna. 'Is there tea in the pot?' she asked Trixie.

'I'll pour you a cup. Oh, and Mr Cavendish has returned home, about half an hour ago.'

'Max is home?' Caroline's stomach somersaulted in joy and trepidation.

'He asked for you. I said you'd gone into Lincoln, but I didn't tell him why.'

'No, you did not.' Max stood in the doorway leading from the corridor. 'Is it a secret?'

Caroline's heart twisted at the sight of him. 'Welcome home.'

His blue eyes gazed at her, the expression on his handsome face questioning. He came to her side. 'I am glad to be home.'

'I can bring a tea tray to you,' Trixie said quickly, taking cups and saucers from the dresser.

'Not Jeannie?' Max lifted an eyebrow in question.

'There is something I need to tell you about Jeannie,' Caroline said.

'Let us go and sit down.' Max took Caroline's hand and led her through the corridor into the drawing room. He closed the door behind them and faced her. 'How are you?'

'I'm well. Did you have a successful visit to Thomas? How is he?'

'I did and Thomas is fit and healthy as always.' Max paused. 'What is this information about Jeannie?'

'She's had a baby. She was raped and the child is the result.'

He blinked in surprise. 'I was not expecting you to say that.'

'I delivered the baby today, and have just returned from leaving her at an orphanage in Lincoln.'

'I saw that girl every day and I suspected nothing.'

'You weren't the only one. We were all shocked.' Caroline sat on the sofa. 'Jeannie didn't realise what was happening to her. She only told Rosanna a few days ago. Will you dismiss her?' Caroline watched his reaction.

'Dismiss her? Do you think I should?' He frowned. 'The maids are under your control. You must do whatever you think is correct.'

'None of this was her fault. She was taken against her will.' Caroline's anger flared. 'She has been punished enough. She doesn't deserve to be put out on the streets for what another did to her.'

'I agree.'

Caroline sighed, pleased he was of the same mind. 'Then she will stay at Grange Lea and this situation will be forgotten as best we can.'

'As you wish.'

The door opened and Trixie brought in the tray, gave Caroline a small smile of encouragement and then closed the door behind her.

Needing something to do, Caroline began to pour out the tea, but her hands trembled so she put the teapot back on the tray.

'I had plenty of time to think about things while I was away.' Max finished pouring the tea for her.

'Oh?' She stared at him, trying to read his expression.

'About us.'

Dread landed heavy on her. 'That sounds worrying.'

'It need not be. That depends on you.' He walked to the window, his hands clasped behind his back. 'Have you thought about us?'

She was ill at ease, hating the awkwardness between them. 'Yes.'

'We have both had days to think while I was away.'

Caroline waited, not knowing if she should speak or let him continue to talk.

'Do you love me, Caroline?' Max asked, turning to her. 'I mean truly love me, the kind of love that poets write about, the kind that swamps you whole, leaves you breathless?'

She took a moment to absorb his words. They were strong words. It was an important question, one she couldn't take lightly.

'You hesitate,' he murmured sadly.

'I hesitate because of the significance of the question.'

'Whatever your answer is, I would appreciate the truth from you. I can take it.' Max lifted his chin as though ready for a blow.

Her heart melted. This fine man had been nothing but kind, generous and caring towards her since they met. He'd been patient while she held him at arm's length for months. 'Yes, I love you. I have told you that once before.'

'Yet, I do not always feel it.' He frowned. 'I see how you are around the people you love. They way you act towards Trixie and the girls, the warmth, the light in your eyes when you laugh with them. You don't act that way with me.'

'No.' She bowed her head in sorrow for hurting him.

'Will you ever act that way with me?' His voice was soft, wondering.

'I wish to, very much.'

'Then what holds you back?' he implored.

'The past, the future...' She shrugged, finding the words to explain difficult thoughts that tortured her.

'The past is gone, Caroline. It is behind us.'

'But it affects our future.' She looked at him, hoping he'd understand.

'In what way?'

'In every way!' Suddenly she was tired of second-guessing everything, of walking on eggshells, of trying to put a brave face on her worries.

'Explain it to me.'

'How can I when I can't explain it to myself? All I know is that I'm frightened!'

He jerked back. 'Of me?'

'Of all of it.'

'I would *never* hurt you.'

She flung out her hands. 'You could, without knowing it you could, as I might do to you.'

'I am willing to take the risk. Can you not?' he implored.

'How will you know how you truly care about me after we are married and can share a bed?'

He was puzzled. 'What do you mean?'

Fired up, she advanced on him. 'All we have done is kiss, but what happens on our wedding night, when your hands touch my naked body? Will you feel revulsion for the violation I suffered, by the disgusting treatment Wayland inflicted upon me? That he has used my body before you?'

'No!' Max reared back as though she'd slapped him.

'Are you certain about that?' she challenged. 'You might look at me and think only of him and what he did.'

Max held up his hands, his face in torment. 'Caroline, this is nonsense.'

'Is it? Because these are the kinds of thoughts that are in my head, that keep me awake at night.'

'You have no need to be worried about such things. I love *you*. I *want* you.'

'And another thing,' she flung at him. 'I can't give you children.'

'What?'

'That's right. I'm barren.' She nodded vigorously. 'I was married to Hugh for two years and no babies, not even a hint of a baby, and then Wayland's rape, he left me with no child either. The problem must be with me. How can I marry you when I can't give you children, a son to carry on your name, to inherit this estate?'

'Christ above, Caroline.' He rushed to her and gripped her arms. 'Children would be a blessing, of course, but if we were not fortunate in having any, it would not alter my love for you.'

'You say that now, but in five or ten years or even twenty when we are old and infirm and there is no one to take over the farm, you'll curse me then.'

'Stop it!' He shook her gently. 'Stop this utter madness.' He crushed her to him and when she tried to squirm away, he held on tighter. 'No, you are not walking away from me. I shan't let you give up on our future before it has even begun,' he whispered into her hair. 'You are my world, Caroline.'

Chest tight, Caroline closed her eyes and rested against him, weary and deflated.

He cupped her chin and raised her face to his. 'With children or without, I will never want to be anything but your husband. Your past haunts you, I realise that, but when I look at you, I only see my Caroline, my beautiful, sweet woman who makes me tremble with want, who makes my heart beat out of my chest. You delight me in every way. I am no poet and declaring words of love is not a talent I possess with any great authority, but I will strive to make you happy for the rest of my life if you will allow me? Can I make myself any clearer?'

Emotion clogged her throat. 'I just want you to be sure. I can't stay here if you have any doubts. I am not like other women. My past with Victor Dolan, Wayland... It defines me, makes me different to some gentle daughter of a gentleman that you should marry.'

'I have no ambition to marry a gentleman's gentle daughter.' He kissed her softly, his lips barely touching hers. 'You are everything I want and need, but I must have the same in return, Caroline. I cannot live with you walking like a ghost around the house, barely engaging in life, not willing to trust me to make our future together worth the gamble. I need your heart and soul, Caro.'

She reached up and placed her hands on either side of his face, seeing the love, hearing his honesty and she knew he meant every word he said. 'Then you have it.'

Max closed his eyes and let out a deep breath. 'Promise me you will rid your mind of your doubts. I want us to be married, to be blissfully content with our life, but you must want that as much as I do or there is no point to any of it.'

She nodded. 'I do. I realise that now. I'm sorry I have caused you pain.'

'If *you* are happy, *truly* happy, then that makes me the luckiest man on earth. Do you understand?' he asked earnestly. 'Trust us, Caro, please.'

'I will.'

He kissed her then with a depth of longing that left her in no doubt of his feelings and desire and she returned the kiss equally, wanting him, needing him.

His hands roamed her body, pulling her closer into him. He

murmured something against her lips she didn't catch. When his lips touched her neck, his hand on her hips she arched against him, needing him like she'd never needed anyone before.

When they finally pulled apart, he stared into her eyes, panting slightly. 'Now, can we start getting excited for our wedding day and plan it with enthusiasm, yes?'

She smiled, her body pulsing with need. 'Trixie wants a band to play so we can dance the night away.' She kissed him again.

'I want a band!' He laughed, holding her tight, kissing her repeatedly. 'Our wedding will be the best day of my life.'

Joy filled her at giving him such happiness. The doubts she'd harboured for months floated away like snowflakes on a breeze.

* * *

BY THE LIGHT of the lamp Trixie had placed on the scrubbed table, she concentrated on reading Eliza Acton's cookbook, *Modern Cookery for Private Families*. A gift Caroline had bought her for her last birthday. The book, like the one Mussy had bought her last year, was one of her most prized possessions. She'd never owned much of anything when growing up in the slums of York. Earning money as a prostitute for food to feed her sisters and to be able to pay the rent was all that mattered, personal items, especially objects to treasure, were unheard of in her past. Until she met Caroline, and everything changed.

Unable to read, Mussy and Caroline had taught her letters and that in itself was the most valued skill she had learned. A new and exciting world had opened for her. Being able to read, she could follow recipes and develop her natural talent to cook good food. That flair of providing decent meals gave her confidence, but it also gave her the ability to gain purposeful employment, a position of responsibility. Something to be proud of, to earn money and be respected helped to wipe away the stain of her former work.

Now, in the quietness of the kitchen, with a small fire glowing in the grate and everyone asleep, Trixie, despite being tired, was spending precious minutes alone in peace.

She sipped her tea, squinting at the word she'd stumbled over and silently cursed her lack of knowledge of bigger words, especially the French cookery words, but then she remembered how far she'd come in such a short period of learning to read and write. Her ability to do both of those things was a testament to Mussy and Caroline's teaching, and her own determination to better herself. Elsie and Bertha could read very well now, and Trixie refused to be an embarrassment to them by being illiterate.

The door to the scullery opened and Jacob stepped in with a smile. 'I assumed someone was up, I saw the light through the window.' He glanced at the book. 'Sorting out the week's menu?'

'Something like that. Want some tea?'

'Aye, I'll grab a cup.' He took a cup and saucer from the dresser and sat opposite her at the table. 'Everyone else gone upstairs?'

'Aye, ages ago.' She poured tea from the pot into his cup. 'There are scones if you want any?'

'I'm fine with just tea.'

'Why aren't you in your bed?' Trixie closed the cookbook. 'You're late doing your last walk around.'

'I just wanted to double-check the chicken coop. That damn fox is killing a couple a night and at that rate we'll have no chickens by next week. The dogs are at the door waiting for me.' He sipped his tea.

'Those dogs spend more time with you than Caroline.'

'They're farm dogs. They need to be on the farm not inside with Caroline. Although when it's raining, I think they'd rather be inside with her.' He grinned. 'Rosanna told me this afternoon that Jeannie is out of bed now.'

Irritated that Rosanna was spending time with Jacob, Trixie

sipped her tea. 'Aye. Today was her first day downstairs since having the baby last week. Caro has her doing small things, nothing too heavy, a bit of dusting, that sort of thing.'

'Mr Cavendish hasn't said much to me about the situation.'

Trixie shrugged. 'Apparently, he was shocked that some fellow took advantage of Jeannie, but he couldn't lay any blame on the poor girl. He knows she is a young lass who was frightened. He's a good man. Some masters would have thrown both her and Rosanna out.'

Frowning, Jacob leaned back in the chair. 'Mr Cavendish does seem a lot happier since he came back from Oxford.'

'He and Caroline have sorted things, cleared the air so to speak, and I'm glad. They are both finally coming to their senses and talking. Caroline has definitely come alive more in the last week than I've ever seen her.' It pleased Trixie so much to see her dear friend happy and seemingly at peace, which was all she deserved after everything she'd been through.

'So, Caroline won't be wanting to leave?'

'No, she's settled and happy, so she tells me. The wedding plans are happening and she's excited. We can all relax at that.'

'Would you have left with her if she'd gone?' Jacob stared down at his tea.

'Of course. Me and the girls are her family.'

Jacob jerked to his feet. 'Thanks for the tea.'

Surprised by his sudden change in manner, Trixie watched him take the cup to the sideboard. 'Is something wrong?'

He hung his head for a moment and then slowly turned to face her. 'I wouldn't have wanted you and the girls to go.' He waited a moment then continued. 'If I'd asked you to stay, for me, would you have?'

'None of us are going anywhere,' she stalled, uncomfortable with the turn of the conversation.

'That's not what I'm asking, Trix.' His gaze held hers. 'Would you have stayed for me?'

'There's no point talking like this, Jacob. Caroline isn't leaving. I'm not leaving.' She stood and picked up the book. 'We are all staying here.'

'Am I being a fool?'

The question made her raise her eyes to him. 'You're not a fool, Jacob.'

'I deem myself a fool. Wasting my life, hoping you might think of me as someone you could ever want. But I'm not Thomas Cavendish, am I?'

'Stop it. Stop talking of him as though he is who I want.'

'But he is. You're waiting for him to come to his senses and come back for you.'

'I'm not!' She flared. 'Thomas and me will never be together.'

'Yet, you still don't see what is right under your nose.' He walked out and she heard him whistle to the dogs.

Rubbing the tiredness from her eyes, Trixie placed her book on the dresser shelf. Was she unknowingly waiting for Thomas? Had her feelings for him not died as she supposed? Thomas had been here at Christmas, and they'd barely spoken a word to each other. Her past came between them. Being a former prostitute was never going to be accepted by Thomas, and she didn't blame him. However, her heart still skidded when she thought of him, remembered the kiss they shared last year when he didn't know of her shameful secret.

Jacob wasn't the fool, she was. She had a good man wanting to be with her even though he knew everything about her, had even saved her life when she'd been beaten and left for dead.

Why couldn't she give her heart to Jacob as he had earned? What was holding her back? He was kind and caring and adored Elsie and Bertha. She should be eager to marry him, to wipe away the stain of her past. Caroline was doing it so why couldn't she?

Disheartened, she lit a smaller lamp to light her way up to her bedroom and turned down the wick of the bigger lamp dousing the kitchen in midnight gloom, a gloom that reflected the despair of her mind.

CHAPTER FOUR

*I*n the bright April morning sunshine at Lincoln's cattle market, Max rested his arms on the wooden railing of one of the holding pens. He watched as a dozen prime heifers were guided out of the gate and along the walkway to the waiting farmer who'd outbid Max.

Three times he had been outbid that morning. The successful bidders had paid a lot more than Max had been willing to pay and he turned away disappointed. Building his cattle herd was a priority. The sheep flock was expanding well, most of the ewes had born healthy lambs, some even had twins, and they grew fat on the spring grass, but he wanted a larger cattle herd. He had his eye on leasing land to the north of Grange Lea and he intended to move the herd to that new pasture. Yet without beasts, the land would have to be put under plough, and he didn't have the manpower to do that at the moment.

He wound his way through the gathering of farmers wanting to find Caroline who he'd left shopping in the main street.

'Bad luck on missing out there,' an old man suddenly spoke to Max.

'It has been that kind of morning,' he replied good-naturedly.

'Those beasts sold for more than they were worth.' The old man scratched his whiskery chin.

'I assumed so as well.' Max gave him a nod and took a step.

'Better luck next time, Mr Cavendish.'

Max faltered and turned back to the old man, who was dressed in a worn suit and a shabby hat. 'Are we acquainted, sir?'

'Nope. Folk around here always learn about newcomers. Every man in this market has been talking about you.'

'Why?'

The old man shrugged. 'As I said, you're a newcomer.'

'I was born in Lincoln,' Max defended.

'Aye, but you left and now you own Grange Lea.' The old man cleared his throat. 'Folk like to gossip.'

'I am not worth their efforts.'

'Happen so… Time will tell.'

Dismissing the old man's words, Max headed for the edge of the market where Jacob and Dickie waited, sitting on the cart with the dogs. If he'd been successful in buying some cattle, the dogs would have been used to help Jacob and Dickie drive the cattle along the roads to Grange Lea. Instead, all he'd bought was a crate of young chickens and a sleek ferret for Dickie to use when he went rabbiting.

'How did it go, Mr Cavendish?' Dickie asked.

'No good.' Max patted each of the three dogs as they came to the side of the cart for his attention. 'Jacob, you and Dickie might as well head home. I will hire a hansom for Caroline and myself when she has finished her shopping.'

'Right you are, Mr Cavendish.' Jacob collected up the reins.

'Have either of you two heard anyone speaking about me this morning?' he asked.

'No, sir,' Dickie replied over the clucking of a chicken in the crate.

'Nothing came to my ears, sir.' Jacob stared down at him from the seat. 'Has something been said?'

'I am not sure. It is probably nothing.' Max nodded to them and walked away.

He didn't want to be the fodder for gossip. Yes, he was a new face to many, especially in the farming circle of Lincoln. People would want to learn what kind of man had returned to own Grange Lea. Many would be watching to see if he succeeded or failed after the estate had been left to ruin for so long. However, Max would show the gossipers that he could prove himself to be a successful farmer. He'd managed the much larger and grander Misterton Abbey Estate and the surrounding Melliton village for his uncle, Lord Stockton-Lee, and he had no doubt he could make Grange Lea a thriving farm as well.

He found Caroline coming out of a haberdashery shop on the high street and his heart squeezed as it always did at the sight of her loveliness. How had he been so fortunate to find someone like her? He watched her for a moment as she spotted something in the window next to the shop's door.

Max sidled up next to her. 'Are you going back in?'

She grinned up at him. 'No. I saw those gloves as I came out and they are prettier than the ones I've bought.'

'Then we shall return inside and change the gloves.'

She slid her arm through his. 'I can't be bothered, honestly. I've visited so many shops now, I've had enough.'

'Did you buy all that you needed?'

'Yes. I shall be expecting parcels to arrive at the house every day for a week at this rate. I have bought Bertha, for her birthday, a doll and a little box that plays music when you open the lid. It's very sweet.' She chuckled and the sound delighted him. He couldn't get enough of her. Everything about her made him happy.

It chilled him whenever he thought of how close he was to losing her when she left York last year because of his revolting cousin, Wayland. A chance meeting at Doncaster train station had given him the opportunity to help her with Mussy, who'd become ill. He'd offered them refuge out of the cold winter weather at his farm, Grange Lea, and he had no intention of letting her slip away from him again. She made his life worth living.

They sidestepped a beggar and Max threw a few pennies into the man's battered hat on the ground.

'I have my wedding trousseau completed. Last week the seamstress measured Elsie and Bertha for their new dresses and Trixie's dress is finished.'

'And your dress?' he asked, steering her around a pile of horse manure as they turned into Silver Street where he knew hansom cabs were lined up ready to take passengers.

'I still need another fitting for my dress.' She smiled sweetly. 'I'll do that next Friday.'

'In six weeks, we will be married.' He hardly dared to dream such a magical day would happen. The woman he adored would be his for life.

'It will come around quickly.' Caroline climbed up into the first cab lining the street.

Max gave directions to the driver and pressed coins into the man's hand.

'Oh, and I've sent an invitation to Annie to attend the wedding,' Caroline told him as the cab pulled into the street to join the other horse-drawn vehicles.

Annie Aspall had become a mother-like figure to Caroline, Trixie and the girls while they lived at Hopewood Farm. Max knew how much they missed the old woman who lived in Melliton village. 'I hope she can come.'

'The girls miss her, and so do Trixie and I, but it's a long way for a woman of her age to travel and she's never been to Lincoln before. I worry she'll decline the invitation because of the journey she'll have to make.'

'If she considers the travel is too much for her on her own, I will send Jacob to fetch her.' Max took Caroline's hand. 'Would that ease your mind?'

She squeezed his hand gratefully. 'That would be wonderful, thank you. Jacob could visit his sister, Sarah, in York, as well while he's passing through to Annie's.'

'Who else have you invited that I do not know about?' He smiled at her.

'No one else. You know I've invited Matthew. He was such a good friend to us, especially to Mussy. I'd like him to attend if he can get some days away from the hospital. Matthew's previous visit was full of sadness when Mussy died. I'd like him to visit again on a happier occasion.'

Max thought of the fine doctor from Doncaster who'd become a friend to them all. 'He is a good man. Let us hope he can attend.' Max glanced out at the people walking the streets as they headed up the hill out of the town's centre. A man stood on the street corner near a tree, his eyes watched Max as they passed by. Max stared at him in return, wondering if he knew the face, but the man didn't seem familiar and was soon gone from sight.

'Did you buy some beasts?' Caroline asked.

'No, unfortunately.' It still irked him that he'd been unsuccessful in the bidding. He wasn't used to losing or not getting his way when it came to purchasing animals. Only he didn't have the wealth of his uncle this time.

Being a land agent for his uncle had taught him a way of life that he was not only good at but which he loved. Now he had the chance to make Grange Lea, the place his dear Aunt Lucille had given him, something to be proud of, something that would be his legacy. However, as a land steward for his uncle he hadn't known the pressure or the responsibility of paying back debt, not like he did now.

The bank loan he took to restock the Grange Lea land and to make the house comfortable weighed heavy on his shoulders. He'd never been in debt in his life and now he truly knew the significance of good stock breeding and the fear of crop failures because the results completely affected him this time. Before he had his uncle and then his cousin's wealth to cover any shortfalls. Yet now he had to stand on his own and a failure of the farm would have far more reaching consequences.

'Could we stop at the orphanage, please?' Caroline asked.

Max gave her a cool look. 'Is that wise?'

'If I don't go today, I'll only go tomorrow instead.'

Max leaned out to the driver and told him the change of plans. As the driver turned the horse into the next street, Max glanced at Caroline's stubbornly set chin. 'I do not understand why you are doing this. Jeannie wants nothing to do with the baby.'

'The child is an innocent. I told Mrs Fleetwood I would call once a week to check on the baby and to give her some money for her upkeep.'

'Is Jeannie aware that you visit the baby every week and pay for its keep?'

'No. Only you, Trixie and Jacob.' Caroline gathered her skirts as the hansom slowed in front of the black door of the orphanage.

Max climbed out and then helped Caroline down. He didn't understand her need to visit the child. She needed to forget about it. What was done was done.

Caroline introduced him to Mr Grisham and Mrs Fleetwood. The matron seemed pleased to see Caroline and accepted the money with gratitude.

'How is Rachel?' Caroline asked, sitting on a chair in the matron's office.

Max stood behind her. The office was clean, sparsely decorated. Mrs Fleetwood appeared to be a woman of austerity by the look of her prim black dress devoid of any adornments.

'She's no trouble to anyone.' Mrs Fleetwood moved behind

her desk. 'She drinks her milk and sleeps and hardly ever cries. The perfect baby.'

'And she is thriving?'

'See for yourself.' Mrs Fleetwood nodded to the door as it opened, and Mr Grisham carried in a bundle wrapped in a shawl. He bent and placed the baby in Caroline's arms.

Caroline smiled lovingly down at the little face. 'She's putting on some weight.'

Something twisted in Max's chest as he stared down at Caroline holding the little baby. He moved to the side to watch Caroline carefully unwrap the sleeping baby and checked her little body. He'd never seen Caroline with a baby before and the vision shocked him. He could imagine her holding their own child, and desperately wanted that to come true, but Caroline had warned him she was barren, and he quickly squashed any hope of having children.

'Look at her legs,' Caroline crowed happily. 'She has grown since last week.'

'A little, yes.' Mrs Fleetwood agreed. 'A couple came to view her yesterday. Unfortunately, they left undecided. The husband wanted a baby boy.'

Caroline's head shot up. 'The arrangement was that I would vet all potential couples who were considering Rachel.'

'I'm aware.' Mrs Fleetwood handed Caroline a sheet of paper. 'I expected you to arrive today or tomorrow and I told the couple you would wish to meet them before anything was finalised. Here are their details.'

'Thank you.' Caroline blushed. 'I didn't mean to sound harsh, but I want the right people for Rachel.'

'It is our shared ambition, Mrs Lawson. I promise you, Rachel will go to a good family.'

Twenty minutes later, Max helped Caroline up into the hansom, who he'd asked to wait, and they were once more heading out of Lincoln. He sensed Caroline was deep in thought about the child. 'You are becoming too attached to the baby, sweetheart,' he said softly, taking her hand.

She sighed heavily. 'I'm trying not to be, but I grew up an orphan in a convent. I understand what it's like to be without a mother and father. The nuns were kind, mostly, some could be cruel when we didn't do exactly as they asked, but on the whole, my life wasn't too uncomfortable. I never knew anything different. Only, I never received the soft embrace of someone who loved me, not until I married Hugh. I don't want to witness Rachel being taken by people who will not love her.'

'Then we will do everything we can to make sure she goes to a good family.'

'Thank you for supporting me in this. I understand it is unconventional.'

He smiled. 'Nothing much you do is conventional, my love. I am used to it.'

She grinned at him, and he couldn't help but kiss her. He kissed her at every opportunity he could find. It was becoming achingly difficult to sleep down the hall from her every night and not visit her bedroom. He'd lie awake at night imagining her lying in bed, her soft skin, the delicate touch of her fingers on his body, the scent of her…

Being a gentleman tested his patience.

When they reached the Grange Lea gates at the beginning of the drive, Caroline asked the hansom driver to stop.

'What's wrong?' Max frowned.

'Let us walk up the drive. We'll have another few minutes of being alone,' Caroline suggested.

He grinned. 'A perfect idea.'

He helped her down, and they strolled along the drive arm in arm in the warm midday sunshine. Birds flew between the avenue sycamore trees and Max gazed about the fields. The healthy flock of sheep and the small herd of cattle he was trying to build up in number were something to be proud of and they gave him joy.

The dogs, sensing their presence, came racing along the drive towards them. Prince the fastest, beat Duke with Princess shortly behind.

Max made a fuss of Princess, his sweet girl, while Caroline laughed as Prince and Duke wagged nearly their entire bodies in the rapture of their mistress being home.

'I was only gone a few hours.' Caroline petted them.

'Imagine how they will react when we return from our honeymoon!' Max took Caroline's hand so they could continue walking.

'Honeymoon?'

'Of course.' He looked at her questioning expression. 'Do you not wish to go somewhere after the wedding? Just the two of us?'

'I'd like nothing more. Can you spare the time from the farm?'

'Jacob and Dickie will cope. It is what I pay them for, after all.'

'I haven't met anyone who has been on a honeymoon before. I didn't have a honeymoon with Hugh. We had no money for things like that.'

'My wish is to give you the finer things in life, Caro.' He brought her hand up to kiss the back of it.

'I don't need fine things, Max. I just need you and my family. Everything else is just extra.'

He stopped and gathered her into his arms, aching to share a bed with her and make love to her for hours. 'You'll always have me.' He kissed her deeply, needing to show her how much he wanted her.

'Caroline! Max!' Elsie and Bertha dashed out of the house to run to them.

Reluctantly, Max drew away from Caroline, his body rigid with need.

'Girls, slow down,' Caroline called, laughing, but she gave Max a secret smile that twisted his loins in yearning.

Max noticed Jacob and Dickie standing by the barn and a man with them. 'Who is that?'

Elsie glanced over her shoulder. 'A man looking for work. Jacob had to put Prince and Duke in the kitchen for they wouldn't stop growling at the man.'

'They don't like strangers,' Caroline said, looking at the newcomer.

'I had better go and speak with him.' Max walked away, the girls' voices chattering away behind him.

'Mr Cavendish.' Jacob stepped forward. 'This chap was on the road earlier, and we gave him a lift in the cart on the way back from the market. He's wanting work. I said for him to speak to you.'

Max gave the fellow a quick once over. He appeared neat, clean, arms strong in his thin jacket, but the man's gaze didn't quite meet Max's eyes and that was a failure in Max's mind. 'I am Mr Max Cavendish, owner of Grange Lea. Your name?'

'Herman Grover.' The fellow slowly extended his hand for Max to shake.

Max shook his hand. 'What work do you do?'

'Field work, mostly, but I can turn my hand to anything.' Grover shrugged in an uncaring way. 'I do whatever I can to put a few shillings in my pocket.'

Max folded his arms, not taking to the fellow. Something about him seemed shifty.

Grover glanced around the yard instead of looking at Max.

'Unfortunately, there is no work here at the moment,' Max told him. In truth he could do with a couple more labourers but not this man.

'None at all?' Grover squinted at him.

'Not until the harvest.' Max stared him down. 'Good luck in finding a position elsewhere.' He gave him a curt nod and walked into the barn, ending the conversation. 'Jacob, Dickie,' he called over his shoulder.

'I thought you wanted another labourer?' Jacob asked once he was inside the barn.

'I do, but not him.' Max couldn't explain it. He always knew when he liked someone and when he didn't. 'Right, we need to discuss the shearing of the ewes next week.'

'And the lambs will be docked?' Jacob asked.

'Yes. I met a fellow this morning, Seth Dockerty, at the market who will bring his team to shear the ewes on Tuesday. We only have him for the day, and I was lucky to get him as he and his team are in great demand. But having only a small flock he could fit us in between the bigger estates. We will need to build a temporary sorting pen out behind the barn and on Monday evening we will separate the ewes from their lambs ready for Dockerty arriving at dawn on Tuesday.'

'Right you are, sir.' Jacob nodded.

'Good, let us make a start.' Max rubbed his hands together in anticipation of the work to come, knowing it would advance the farm. 'I will go and change my clothes and meet you out the back of the barn shortly. We can use those timber posts that are stacked near the piggery.'

Walking back across the yard to the house, Max was looking forward to the shearing on Tuesday. The sale of the wool would be a much-needed financial boost to his coffers. It would be his first income from the farm after months of constant spending.

He smiled at Bertha as she skipped past swinging an empty egg basket on her way to collect eggs. In the garden, Elsie was picking flowers from beneath the chestnut tree at the side of the house, and through the kitchen window he saw Trixie hard at work. Coming out of the scullery door was Rosanna, the maid bobbed her head to him. He wondered again for the hundredth time how lucky he was to have a such a lovely home such as this for his own.

Although he could have used the side entrance, he liked to go through the kitchen, where he could sometimes grab a tart cooling on a tray or simply just stop and say a few words with Trixie.

Making sure his boots were clean, he smiled at Trixie as he entered.

'Ah, Mr Cavendish. There's some post for you.' Trixie waved to the silver platter on the sideboard by the door. 'I was going to put them on your desk once I'd finished this mix.' Her hands were covered in flour.

'If I was a wealthier man, Trixie, I would hire a butler.' He grinned. 'He would see to the post and such things.'

'Maybe one day, sir,' she replied.

Max certainly hoped so. He walked into his study and noticed one of the letters was from his aunt. He sat at his desk and opened it.

Dear Maxwell,

An alarming report reached me today from Wayland. He writes that he has been convalescing from a terrible beating. A beating that YOU gave him. How is this possible?

You would appreciate my shock and my concern to read such news. Could this be true? Pray tell me it is not!

Wayland writes that the attack upon his person was unprovoked and unwarranted and that you fled the abbey in disgrace!

I must strongly communicate my displeasure, my anger and my great disappointment that you, of all people, would do this to my son.

I trusted you to guide him, to be his teacher in all things, for I held you in such high esteem, but you have failed me. That you would be so brutal to your own cousin astonishes me.

After all I have done for you since your parents died, I am betrayed in this way!

I fully understand that Wayland can be difficult at times, and a law unto himself when he chooses. However, I never expected you would ever take matters into your own hands.

I require a full report on the events leading up to your attack on my son. I want the whole truth on your side of the shocking incident. Spare me no details.

I have sent this letter to Grange Lea, since that is where you said you now lived in your letter to me at Christmas, a letter which made no mention of the circumstances leading to your departure from the abbey. Why would you keep something so monumental from me? I have so many questions, Maxwell.

I beg you to answer me promptly with an explanation.

Yours sincerely,

Aunt Lucinda.

MAX READ the letter three more times, the words burning into his brain. It upset him greatly to have hurt his aunt. He paced the room, trying to work out what action he could take with causing more damage.

Max returned to his chair, words circling his brain as he gathered his thoughts. How could he write such a letter to his aunt? How could he put pen to paper and reveal Caroline's torment and what Wayland did to her?

He couldn't.

CHAPTER FIVE

*F*our weeks before the wedding, and after taking breakfast in the morning room by herself as Max was out on the farm early, Caroline folded the letter with a sigh and left the drawing room to speak to Trixie in the kitchen. Trixie was alone, preparing a leg of mutton to roast. 'Where is Rosanna?'

'Helping Jeannie with the ironing in the laundry shed.' Trixie wiped her hair away from her face with a forearm. 'I'm worried about Jeannie. She's nowt but a skeleton. She eats less than a bird. Have you noticed?'

'All I've noticed is the shadows beneath her eyes. She works non-stop.' Caroline frowned. 'I merely have to mention something needs doing and she is doing it.'

'She's not been right since she had the baby.'

'Is it any wonder?'

'She's been through a lot and she's only young.'

Caroline passed a large roasting pan across to Trixie so she could place the mutton into it. 'I'll have a word with her.'

Trixie nodded, adding water to the bottom of the roasting

dish and then quickly consulting the open cookbook on the table. 'Are the girls at their lessons?'

'Yes. They are reading the newspaper and learning about the British Empire and why Britain and France have joined forces against Russia and about the current war in the Crimea.'

'Goodness, that's a bit horrid for young minds, isn't it?' Trixie's eyebrow's rose in surprise.

'They need to learn what is going on in the world.'

'They are both under the age of ten, I'm not sure they need to know about that yet.'

'It's only for an hour, then I'll have them reading something more pleasant. Perhaps they can write to Annie. I received a letter from her in this morning's post.'

'Annie would always enjoy letters from the girls. I need to write to her as well, it's been a fortnight since I last sent her a letter.' Trixie began to peel some onions, popping them into the dish beside the mutton.

Caroline waved the letter. 'Annie says she can't come to the wedding. She had a fall a couple of weeks ago and her hip hasn't been good since. She deems the journey would be too much for her. I'm sad she won't be here.'

Trixie glanced at Caroline. 'A fall? That's not good.'

'She'd have no one to care for her in Melliton,' Caroline mused. 'I wish she was closer to us so we could look after her.'

'Wouldn't it be lovely if she had a cottage in the village here? We could walk across the fields and see her every day. The girls would be made up at that.' Trixie smothered the leg of mutton in lard. 'Do you think Annie would consider it?'

'No.' Caroline shook her head. 'To move to a new place at her age? I doubt she'd want to do that.'

'Wouldn't hurt to ask though?'

'Are there any empty cottages in South Carlton? I don't think there is even if she did agree to come here.'

'She could bunk in with Jacob in his cottage.' Trixie chuckled.

'Oh, I'm sure he'd like that!' Caroline grinned. She turned as the back door opened into the scullery and Max came through wearing a furious expression.

'What's wrong?' Caroline went to him.

'The lambs! They are all dead except for half a dozen.'

Caroline gasped. 'How?'

'Wild dogs I am assuming, we cannot be sure yet. Jacob found them this morning. The ewes have been standing over their offspring, but it is too late, they have succumbed to their injuries. We have been walking the fields looking for clues as to what might have happened but have found nothing.' He rubbed a hand over his face. 'Twenty-three lambs. Dead. I cannot believe it.'

'That's awful,' Trixie murmured.

'And they were growing so fat and well,' Caroline added. 'It's so dreadful. Dogs did this?'

'A wild pack I would think.' Max seemed to switch between being distraught and raging.

'I've never heard of such a thing.'

'I have seen it once at Melliton, but the pack was only three wild dogs. This pack must be larger in number to kill so many.'

'What can you do?' Caroline asked, wishing she could wipe away the worry from his blue eyes.

'Jacob and Dickie and myself, with Prince, Duke and Princess, will patrol the fields tonight in case the dog pack come back to finish off the others. Thankfully, they left the calves alone. I do not suppose they would take on an irate mother cow.'

'And you're sure it were dogs and not foxes?'

'Foxes would not kill that many, not in one night. Not in a pack, anyway. Foxes are usually solitary animals. One fox could decimate a hen house, but I doubt it could manage to kill so many lambs.' Max accepted the cup of tea Trixie poured for him. 'I cannot tell you how much of a blow this is. The value of those lambs...'

'Can we do anything?' Caroline asked. 'Can Trixie and I patrol as well?'

'There will be enough with us men, but thank you.' His smile was fleeting. 'I am going to ride into the village and talk to others and see if they saw anything or were affected. I will ride along Ermine Street and call on the neighbouring farms. The Cuthberts and others. Someone might have seen something.'

When Max had left the kitchen Caroline looked at Trixie. 'I feel so useless. How can I help him?'

'You can't, none of us can. Things happen on farms, don't they? Crops fail, livestock die.' Trixie placed the mutton in the oven.

Restless, Caroline grabbed her bonnet and stepped out into the May morning sunshine. Birds flew above her head, and the chickens scratched around the yard. Bright green leaves had replaced the blossom and the gardens around the house were bursting into colour from months of care and attention.

She heard chatter coming from the laundry shed where Jeannie and Rosanna worked but skirted that building and strode through the gap between two barns and to the smaller yard behind where the pigsty and storage barns stood at a right angle to the main outbuildings.

On the slight breeze came the mournful sound of the ewes bleating for their dead lambs.

Jacob was backing the plough horse between the shafts of the old cart. 'Morning, Caroline,' Jacob said sadly.

'Morning. Max told me the news.' She bent to stroke Prince and Duke's ears as they bounded out of a barn on hearing her voice. Princess was missing and would have gone with Max into the village.

'Tragic, isn't it?' Jacob tied the straps between the horse and the shafts. 'We're off to bury the lambs now. They're too little to make use of their meat...'

Caroline nodded. 'Do you need my help?'

'Dickie and me will have it done soon enough. We're digging a pit near the midden to bury them. Hopefully, being near the midden the dog pack won't be tempted to dig them up again if they return.'

'Do you think they will return?' She patted Prince's head who refused to let her hand hang idly by her side. Duke sniffed at the cart's wheels.

'They might have a taste for blood now.'

Caroline shuddered. 'But to kill such a number? It must have been many dogs.'

'Aye, and I heard nowt! My cottage is just on the other side of the last barn, closest to the fields and I heard *nowt*.' His expression clearly showed his puzzlement. 'How could I not have heard anything?'

'It's not your fault, Jacob. To hunt their prey, they'd have to be quiet. You wouldn't have heard anything unless they were barking.'

'I should have heard the lambs bleating.' He sighed heavily. 'I could understand the dogs killing one or two lambs, but that many?' He shrugged. 'It's a sorry state of business for sure.'

'And a costly one,' Caroline said angrily. 'Potential meat and wool lost and for what? The dogs killed all those lambs and didn't even eat them!'

Jacob nodded. 'Aye, Mr Cavendish said the same thing, but was a lot more heated in his choice of words.' Jacob took the horse's bridle. 'Keep the girls inside if you can. They don't need to see this.'

'Of course. Elsie and Bertha took such delight in watching them being born. This will upset them.' Caroline stepped back as he turned the horse around and guided it through the open gate into the field.

Dickie came alongside her carrying two shovels. 'Mr Cavendish is upset, madam, we all are.' He continued on into the field, head bowed.

Seeing the pile of tiny lamb corpses, their white wool covered in red blood was disturbing. Caroline turned on her heel and left them to the grim job.

'Caroline!'

She turned back at Jacob's call. 'Yes?'

'Come and have a look at this.' He held a dead lamb up by the back legs.

'What am I to look at?'

'See this?' He tilted the lamb's head so she could see the throat where it had been cut. 'See the slit?'

'Yes?' She frowned, not understanding.

'That's a clean cut, Caroline. No dog would kill so neatly. That's a knife being sliced through the neck.'

'No, it couldn't be…' She peered closer.

'Dogs would have torn the flesh,' Dickie added.

A cold shiver passed across Caroline's skin, despite the warmth of the day. 'Are they all like this?'

'No, some have puncture wounds, which we thought were the dog's biting, but actually I think they might be stab wounds now I've seen this one with its throat cut.'

'Check them all!' She bent to the next lamb lying on the grass. She squatted down and inspected the lamb. It had puncture wounds in its stomach.

'Here, another throat is cut cleanly.' Jacob pointed one out. 'How did we miss this?'

'Because we were shocked to find them dead,' Dickie said, bending over another lamb. 'We just collected them up. We didn't look too closely, did we? We were just upset that it'd happened, and Mr Cavendish was angry.'

'So, someone has purposely killed our lambs,' Caroline whispered and saying the words out loud scared her. 'Max needs to be informed immediately. Don't bury them until he can see for himself. Dickie, go to South Carlton, if Max isn't there try North Carlton and come back along Ermine Street. This needs reporting to the police.' She thought quickly. 'Jacob, go into Lincoln to the police station. I remember Max telling me the station is located on the corner of Lindum Road and Monk's Road.' She glanced at Dickie for confirmation since he was born and raised in Lincoln whereas she and Jacob were new to the city.

'City Sessions House,' Dickie told him as they walked out of the field.

'Aye, I've driven past it.' Jacob closed the gate. 'I'll get changed and head there to report it.'

'We need a constable to come here. Don't let them fob you off with an excuse for them not to come out and inspect the lambs.' Caroline marched across the yard. 'Dickie, we need to find Mr Cavendish quickly.'

Going back into the kitchen, Caroline told Trixie what they'd found.

Trixie's eyes widened, and she stopped stirring the sauce she was making. 'Killed on purpose? Why?'

'I've no idea.' Caroline's stomach somersaulted.

When Max trotted into the yard twenty minutes later, Caroline went out to meet him. 'Did Dickie find you?'

'Yes. He found me on the road between South and North Carlton.' His grim face matched his tone. 'I cut across the fields and inspected the lambs myself. How did I not see it straight away?'

'Why would you look for knife wounds? Of course, you would only think a fox, or dogs, would have caused the destruction.'

He led his horse, Queenie, into the stables. Princess was panting from the adventure but put up with Prince and Duke nuzzling and sniffing her in welcome.

Caroline watched him unsaddle Queenie, a task he did quickly, his movements jerky, his expression hard, unreadable.

'Why would anyone want to do that to innocent lambs?' she asked.

Max's hands stilled, and he turned slowly to face her, his blue eyes like chips of ice. 'I do not know, but I intend to find out. Whoever did this will pay, trust me on that.'

Caroline hadn't seen this side to him before. She'd heard how he'd fought Wayland when he found out what Wayland had done to her, but she hadn't seen any of that. Now the anger oozed out of him, his body tense with rage. 'Did I do right sending Jacob for the constable?'

'You did.'

'I'll go and make sure a tea tray is prepared for him.'

'Caroline.' Max came and kissed her lightly on the lips. 'Thank you.'

'We're in this together, Max. The good and the bad.' She squeezed his hand and left the stables.

Later, when the constable and Max had finished inspecting the lambs and the fields, Caroline poured them fresh tea in the drawing room.

Constable Wells took the teacup and saucer from her. 'Thank you, Mrs Cavendish.'

'Oh, we aren't married, not yet. In four weeks, we will be,' Caroline told him.

'My mistake, apologies.' Wells gave her an admiring glance.

'Mrs Lawson is making me wait,' Max said, trying to lighten the sombre mood. 'But she is worth waiting for.'

Caroline grinned at Max, wondering if he was staking his claim on her in front of the younger policeman.

Wells smiled at Caroline as she sat at the other end of the sofa to him. 'You are not from these parts, Mrs Lawson? I'd heard that Grange Lea had been taken on by new people. I understand Mr Cavendish is Lincoln born and bred.'

'I'm from York.' She offered him a lemon curd tart from the

plate, which he accepted. 'As is the rest of my family, who you met in the kitchen, and Jacob outside.'

'I hope you will soon consider this area as your home.'

'That depends on whether we have any more nasty incidents like the one that happened last night.'

'As I said to Mr Cavendish, I expect this is a one-off event. Mr Cavendish says he has no enemies in Lincoln and the farm is legally his, so there are no land disputes, and the boundaries are set and well-defined so that would eliminate hostile tensions with neighbouring landholders. With those situations taken out of the equation, I see no reason why someone would commit such an assault as the one that's been done to your livestock.'

'Then who could have done such a thing and why?'

'I will report back to my fellow officers, and we'll investigate. This will take some weeks, I must warn you, Mr Cavendish. We have no motive, no witnesses to the attack.'

'I need answers, Constable.' Max gave him a steely look. 'Overnight I have lost a great deal of money.'

'I understand, Mr Cavendish.' The constable rose and placed his cup and saucer on the small occasion table beside the sofa. 'I will call again in a couple of days with an update, if any.'

Caroline saw him to the door where outside Dickie waited, holding the man's horse.

'They shan't find a thing,' Max declared when Caroline rejoined him. 'No motive or witnesses. You heard him. This will not be high on his list of priorities.' He headed for the door. 'I will go into Lincoln and visit a few public houses. Sitting at a bar you can sometimes hear things.'

She touched his arm as he passed by. 'Take Jacob with you. Two sets of ears are better than one.'

He nodded. 'How clever you are.' He kissed her and left.

Caroline sensed his anger and despondency. Losing the lambs were a blow, and it pained her she couldn't help him.

CHAPTER SIX

A week before the wedding, Trixie worked long hours in the kitchen, preparing the wedding breakfast menu, sourcing ingredients from Lincoln and having Rosanna and Elsie scrubbing the kitchen, cleaning the glassware, the best crockery and the small number of pieces of silver plate ware that Max had bought.

Beyond the kitchen, she knew Caroline and Jeannie were airing bedrooms for Thomas and Matthew Gibb and also giving the downstairs rooms a good *going over* as Caroline liked to call it.

Jacob strode into the kitchen, carrying a crate of vegetables fresh from the market to add to the supply from their own garden. 'Here you go.' He placed the crate on the floor by the table where she worked kneading bread.

'Thanks for going to the market for me. I just don't have time.'

'I'll fetch the other crates.' He gave her a wink.

'And I'll have a cup of tea ready for you.' Trixie set the loaf of bread in the proving dish and placed it on the windowsill where the sun streamed in. She wiped the flour off her hands and set about making two cups of tea.

'Where's Rosanna? She should be helping you,' Jacob asked, returning with two bulging crates of vegetables.

'She's in the dairy turning the cheese rounds for Caroline.' Trixie poured the boiling water into the teapot to mash the tea. 'Did you buy a new suit for the wedding?'

'No, Mr Cavendish gave me one of his suits that he's grown tired of wearing. It looks hardly worn.'

'You'll look handsome in whatever you're wearing.' The minute she spoke the words, Trixie blushed. Why had she said that to him? Although it was the truth, she had no right to say it.

She plonked the teacup in front of him, slopping some over the rim. 'Mr Cavendish is a good man to gift you a suit,' she spoke hurriedly and moved back to the range to check on the tray of date pinwheels cooking.

Jacob sipped his tea and leant his hip on the side of the table. 'I used my money to buy a new pair of boots. I picked them up this morning while at the market.'

'Another pair of boots? Didn't you get some in winter?'

He grinned. 'Aye, but a man can never have enough boots. I've a pair for working, a pair for driving the cart into town and doing business for Mr Cavendish and now a best pair for special occasions and church.'

'Goodness. Such riches,' she joked.

'And to think a few years ago I had nowt. Old boots that were held together with string, ragged trousers and a torn jacket. Hungry, cold, turning my hand to anything just to earn a few pennies.' Jacob frowned. 'I thank the fates every day for leaving York to find you and Caroline at Hopewood Farm. That decision changed my life.'

Trixie turned to him. 'Leaving York and trusting Caroline that her father-in-law's farm would be better for us changed all our lives. I dread to think what my life would be like if I hadn't met Caroline.' She shivered, remembering the horrid nights plying her wares as a prostitute just to keep a roof over her sisters' heads.

'I would've taken care of you,' Jacob murmured.

'How? You could barely look after yourself and you had your sister, Sarah, and her young ones to care for.'

'I would've found a way.' He shrugged. 'I wanted to ask you to marry me years ago, but I had nowt to offer you.'

Trixie stared at him. 'Years ago, I was a barefoot kid taking care of two other barefoot kids and a sick mam.'

'You know what I mean.' Jacob put the cup down on the table and came to her. 'Would you consider me, Trix?'

Her heart softened because he was Jacob, her kind and dear friend who had stuck by her, knew her history, and still wanted her. 'Can I think about it?'

Hope flashed in his eyes. 'You would?'

'Aye. There's a lot to consider, it's not just me but the girls.'

He took her hands. 'I love Elsie and Bertha. I have the cottage and Mr Cavendish said I can improve on it in any way I wish to, so I could add an extra room on, for the girls.'

'Slow down.' She smiled at him.

'I could make you happy, Trix. I'll work hard every day to show you that I'm worthy.'

'You are worthy, Jacob.'

'Then you'll consider marrying me?'

'I will give it some thought. There's no rush, is there?'

When his lips lightly touched hers, a longing to be touched and held came over her. She kissed him for the first time and enjoyed it.

The sound of voices outside drew them apart and moments later, Dickie and Rosanna came into the scullery chatting with Elsie and Bertha. Trixie took the pinwheels out of the oven and couldn't stop smiling. She had just kissed Jacob. Who would have thought it? She certainly didn't. He'd only ever been her good friend.

She turned back to the table and her smile dropped. Behind Elsie and Bertha stood Thomas Cavendish and her silly heart flipped and the fine hairs on the back of her neck stood on end. She dragged her stare from him to Jacob, who was carefully watching her reaction to the handsome Thomas, and the sadness in Jacob's eyes made her remorseful of her response to Thomas. No matter how hard she tried, how often she thought of the harsh way he rejected her at Hopewood Farm, she couldn't shake the attraction she felt towards Thomas.

'It is good to see you, Miss Wilkes.' Thomas bowed his head stiffly.

'And you, Mr Cavendish.' She couldn't summon a smile for him and turned away to order Rosanna to set out a tea tray. 'Our Elsie, Bertha, go and find Caroline and Mr Cavendish. Dickie take Mr Thomas's luggage upstairs to the green bedroom, the one he had at Christmas.'

She gave out orders, her head and heart at war. Jacob and Thomas. One was offering his soul to her, and she'd be very foolish to ignore that, especially when the other one had turned his back on her and was ashamed of her past, yet she still craved *him* like air.

Angry with herself she marched into the larder and stayed in there until there was only Rosanna left in the kitchen. How in God's name was she to cope for a week with Thomas in the house? She'd kissed Jacob, promised to consider his hand in marriage. Only, her mind remembered other times when she had kissed Thomas back at the farm in York, when he had declared his love for her, his wish for them to be wed. Until he found out about her past.

Everything had been ruined after that, not that she'd really believed she could marry Thomas, a gentleman's son, not her, a slum whore.

That evening while Caroline and the Cavendish brothers ate in the dining room, served by Jeannie, Trixie kept busy feeding the others in the kitchen. She didn't sit with them at the large pine table, but instead told them to start without her while she made sure the pudding she had prepared for the dining room was ready to be served.

As always, Dickie and Rosanna dominated the conversation around the table and Trixie could tune out to them all laughing and chatting. Even Elsie and Bertha's contributions to the conversation didn't take her focus from stirring the custard and trying not to think of Thomas.

'You're very quiet,' Jacob said, coming to stand beside her.

'I'm busy. I didn't expect a guest for a few days yet.' She took the apple pie from the oven, the delicious smell filling her nose.

'Does *him*, Thomas, being here change everything?' Jacob stayed by the range, his voice low so the others wouldn't hear.

'He changes nowt,' Trixie snapped, wishing she didn't react to Thomas in any way.

'Good.' Jacob returned to his chair at the table as Rosanna asked him to explain something to her. Usually, Rosanna's domination over Jacob didn't bother Trixie but now it did since he'd asked her to consider him as a husband. Did the stupid girl not realise Jacob didn't want her?

Jeannie came in with a tray of empty plates and unloaded them in the scullery.

Trixie cut the apple pie and placed portions in delicate glass bowls. 'Rosanna, if you've finished eating, pour that custard into a jug, no, not that jug, the crystal one over there.'

'Before, we used the porcelain jug,' Rosanna sniped.

'And this time we're using the crystal one as we have a guest.' Trixie put the bowls onto a silver tray as Jeannie waited to go back into the dining room to serve.

'Mr Thomas told me to pass on his compliments. He enjoyed his meat very much and said it was tender,' Jeannie told her. 'They all enjoyed it.'

Nodding, Trixie took the jug of custard from Rosanna and

added it to the tray. She didn't want to hear if Thomas liked her food or not. His opinion meant nothing to her. Or so she told herself.

She glanced at Jeannie. 'This is ready to go now. Then come back and have your own meal. It's warming in the oven.' She turned to Rosanna who was laughing at something Dickie had said. 'Rosanna, clear the table if you want your pudding.'

'Elsie, help me clear away,' Rosanna said, stacking plates from the table. 'Dickie, pour us another cup of tea, will you? I'll give you the biggest piece of pie.' Rosanna smirked.

'That makes a change from Jacob always getting the biggest piece,' Dickie joked.

Trixie didn't hear the reply and kept her back to the table, cutting pie for everyone else. She was hot and bothered and wanting her bed where she could curl up and hope sleep would save her from her questioning mind and troublesome heart.

* * *

CAROLINE LOOKED AROUND THE CHURCH, delighted by the arrangements of the white flowers by the altar and the pink satin bows tied to the end of each pew.

'I've tied the last of the white satin ribbons on the front door, Caroline.' Matthew Gibb walked down the aisle, frowning at the half dozen flowers he held. 'I think I've broken some stems.'

She smiled at him. 'We'll stick them in the middle of the other bouquets, no one will realise.'

'Except you and I.' His expression was concerned.

'Well, I'm the bride and if I don't mind then it doesn't matter.' She gave the small church another glance. 'We did so well. Thank you for helping, and you only arrived a few hours ago. It would've taken me a lot longer to do on my own as Trixie and the girls have enough to do.'

'It was a pleasure. I am honoured to be a guest at such an

occasion. Tomorrow you will become Mrs Maxwell Cavendish,' Matthew said softly. 'How happy Mussy would have been to see you marry.'

'He would have walked me down the aisle,' Caroline whispered, eyes filling with tears. She gave Matthew a watery smile. 'He would have enjoyed the day, ordered a new suit and cravat.'

'In the colours of sky blue and canary yellow, no doubt.' Matthew chuckled, but it was tinged with sadness.

'Mussy would've insisted on a huge party. He knew how to celebrate anything with full vigour.'

Matthew grinned. 'How lucky we were to have known him.'

'He was the best,' she added, tucking her arm through Matthew's.

By mutual instinct they walked out of the cool church and into the warm sunshine over to Mussy's grave. Prince and Duke laid in the sun, panting, but came to her side immediately.

In silence, Caroline and Matthew gazed at Mussy's plain limestone headstone paid for by his father. Caroline would have liked the headstone to have some detailed carving to it, something to represent Mussy, but the stonemason had his instruction from Mussy's cold-hearted father, and the result was basic writing on an unadorned stone. It annoyed Caroline every time she looked at it.

Matthew touched the top of the headstone. 'I knew him for only a short while, yet his impact on me was immense. He was unique.'

'He certainly was that.' Caroline plucked a few weeds from the base of the headstone. 'I miss him terribly.'

'Mussy told me once that you would marry Max.' Matthew gazed up into the trees and the white fluffy clouds beyond. 'I think it was when you were all staying in that hotel in Doncaster when Mussy was ill. You had given a short answer in a blunt tone to an innocent question from Max. I'd whispered to Mussy that I didn't think you liked Max Cavendish very much, and he snorted and said you were madly in love with him, but wouldn't acknowledge it.'

Caroline tossed her head with a smile. 'Mussy knew me better than I knew myself!'

'How fortunate you were to have such a friend, that we were all fortunate to have him in our lives.'

'Even if it was for too short a time…' Caroline walked away, feeling the sadness rise. Tomorrow she was to be married to the man she loved, but Mussy would be missing, and it hurt.

'Shall we walk back?' Matthew took her arm again.

'Yes, I should be getting back to the mayhem. Trixie is determined to make this the greatest wedding ever.' She laughed.

Matthew shut the churchyard gate behind them. 'I hear there will be a band of sorts playing in the front garden?'

Caroline watched Prince and Duke run ahead, sniffing in the hedgerow. 'Yes, to entertain our guests.'

'How many people are coming?'

'Too many in my opinion. Our neighbour farming families, like the Cuthberts and Forbes and so forth. Plus, all of South and North Carlton have been invited, and I barely know any of them, but Max insisted as he has met most of them. My thoughts are he's buttering them up so they will agree to help bring in the harvest at the end of summer,' she joked.

'He's a clever man.'

'The hired marquee will be going up this afternoon, Jacob and Dickie have strung yards and yards of lanterns through the trees. Max has hired entertainers for the children, the band for people to dance to and there was talk of fireworks…'

Matthew chuckled. 'It will be a fabulous day.'

'It will be exhausting.' She sighed happily.

'But it's what you want?'

'I only want to be married to Max,' Caroline admitted. 'I'd have been content to have a quiet wedding, but that's not fair on everyone else. It's been a tough few years for us and as Trixie said, we deserve a bit of a do.'

'She's right. Life can't be all about struggles and surviving. When we can, we should grab whatever happiness comes along, even if it's only fleetingly.'

'You are very wise, Doctor Gibb.' She squeezed his arm in affection.

Back at Grange Lea, Matthew left her to help the men set up the marquee and tables while Caroline searched for Jacob. She found him polishing the harness in the tack room of the barn.

'There you are.' She watched him rub the oil into the leather while the dogs reunited with Princess, the three of them ran out of the barn and into the yard.

Jacob looked up at her from his seat on an upturned crate. 'Aye, I wanted to give the harness a polish and check the paint is dry on the cart. I want it looking smart for tomorrow. Are you looking for Cavendish? He's in his study with Constable Wells. Apparently, Wells is finishing up the investigation of the lamb slaughter. He found nowt about it. Mr Cavendish isn't best pleased.'

'I don't imagine he would be, but it wasn't Max I was looking for but you.'

'Do you need me to do something?'

'No, only to ask you a question.'

'Oh, aye?'

'Would you do me the honour of walking me down the aisle in the morning?'

'Me?' Jacob's eyes widened in surprise. 'I'd be honoured, Caro...'

'Wonderful. You'll be in the carriage with me, Trixie and the girls. Max and Thomas will ride, and Dickie can drive Matthew, Rosanna and Jeannie in the cart.'

'I never expected you to ask me,' he said in awe.

'You're like a brother to me after all we've been through, and I have no family of my own, except Trixie and the girls and you.'

'Well, I'm proud and honoured, Caro, truly I am.' He resumed his polishing with vigour. 'Thank you for asking. And, don't forget, come tomorrow, Mr Cavendish and his brother will be your family.'

'Yes. I'm very lucky.' She paused. 'Trixie told me what you'd asked her.' Caroline acknowledged it was a delicate subject, especially with Thomas back at Grange Lea.

'Aye, for what good it did me. Thomas Cavendish walked through the door a moment later and I saw her face, Caro. I saw the way she looked at him.' Misery filled his eyes.

'She was caught by surprise.' Caroline put a hand on his shoulder. 'Don't give up on her. Thomas means nothing to her. You are the one for Trixie and she knows it.'

'I'm not too sure she does, actually.' Agitated, he jerked to his feet. 'I'm a bloody fool, hanging about waiting for her...'

'No, you're not. Just be patient for a little bit longer. Thomas will be gone in a few days. He's been offered a position in Cumbria, on a large estate. We shan't see him for a couple of years I wouldn't think. So, all you have to do is grin and bear the next few days and he'll be gone.'

'Aye, but will he be gone from her head?' Jacob tossed the polishing rag into a bucket. 'That's what's worrying me.'

Returning to the house, Caroline found Max escorting Constable Wells to the door and she waited by the stairs for him to close the door. 'What did the constable have to say?' she asked, walking with him into the drawing room.

'Nothing of any use.' Max ran his fingers through his hair. 'Wells does not seem to have a sense of urgency about finding the culprits. He has made enquires around Lincoln and the farms along Ermine Street, the same as I did, and he has found no news or leads. He is closing the case.'

'You mustn't be happy about that?'

'No, I am not, but there is no more I can do. Wells has done little enough, but his superiors agree with him that with no evidence other than dead lambs, they have nothing to go on.'

'What can we do now?'

'I shall keep the patrols going for another week. Hopefully, no more kills will occur.' Max came to her and grasped her hands. 'Did you finish decorating the church?'

'Yes. Matthew and I did a wonderful job of it. Mrs Todd is going to check the flowers in the morning before everyone arrives to make sure none have drooped.' She placed her hands on his shoulders, rubbing her fingertips over the fine material of his jacket.

'Kiss me,' he whispered.

She needed no second bidding and touched her lips to his. As always, the passion quickly ignited between them. Max gathered her in closer, their kiss deepening. She was hungry for his touch and could feel his response to her body pressed against his.

'Tomorrow night cannot come soon enough, my darling,' he murmured, nuzzling her neck. 'You will be mine and I will yours for the rest of our lives.'

She cupped his face to bring his mouth back to hers. 'And we'll never be parted again.'

'Only in death and may that be fifty years or more from now.'

Caroline held him, never wanting to let go, but she heard Matthew and Elsie talking in the hall and reluctantly drew away. 'Tomorrow night…' she whispered sensually in his ear before stepping away as the door opened.

CHAPTER SEVEN

*T*he soft cream silk was cool against Caroline's skin as Trixie adjusted the wide skirt over her petticoats.

'You look like a princess!' Bertha declared, sitting at the edge of the bed in her pretty new dress of apple green.

'Thank you, sweetie.' Caroline smiled, her stomach full of nervous flips.

'There's a carriage coming up the drive,' Elsie stated, sitting on the window seat.

'Who could that be?' Trixie murmured, arranging tendrils of Caroline's hair until they were just perfect. 'I'll pin your hat on now. The cream roses look so real. That milliner in Lincoln did a splendid job of it.'

'I can't see who it is.' Elsie knelt up on the window seat.

'Elsie Wilkes, get down before you spoil that dress with creases!' Trixie demanded. 'Those dresses cost a fortune, and I'll not have folk saying my sisters look like street urchins.'

Chastised, Elsie stood and smoothed down the dress of peach satin which she adored.

'They both look adorable, Trixie.' Caroline smiled at the girls.

'Why don't you both go downstairs and have a drink before we leave for the church.'

'Not too much, mind. I'll not be leaving the ceremony to take you to pee behind a bush!' Trixie warned as the girls left the room.

'Calm down.' Caroline took Trixie's hand. 'Everything is perfect and will continue to be so.'

Tears welled in Trixie's eyes. 'I don't want anything to go wrong. This is the best day of our lives, Caro. You're marrying Max Cavendish, a gentleman. You'll be the mistress of this house. We'll be safe now.'

'Safe?' Caroline was confused.

'I'm being silly, but well, as a married woman, to Max, we don't have to worry about losing the roof over our heads, of being on the road, hungry, needing work and—'

'Heavens, Trix.' Caroline hugged her. 'You've been worrying about all of that? Why? We've been here for over eight months now.'

'After living in the Water Lanes' slums, being evicted from the farm, all the danger and uncertainty we've suffered in recent years... It doesn't leave me. Then you were wavering in your decision to marry Max, and I worried we might leave here, be with nothing again...'

'I didn't mean to worry you.' Caroline hadn't realised the stress she'd caused.

Trixie wiped her eyes. 'You marrying Max saves us from being homeless, jobless. I can relax now. The fear has gone.'

'And I thought I was marrying Max because of love,' Caroline joked to lighten the mood.

Trixie snorted. 'Well, there's that as well.'

'Come on, let's go.' Caroline gave one final look in the mirror. The dress was lovely. The cream silk fitted her shape beautifully, and the cream lace of the bodice and sleeves matched the lace hemming the bottom of the wide skirt.

'You are beautiful, Caro.' Trixie stood beside her. 'Nothing at all like the scared widow I found locked in a brothel's attic a couple of years ago.'

Caroline gazed at Trixie's reflection. 'And no one from the Water Lancs would recognise you now in your finery.' She admired Trixie's soft rose-coloured gown, before kissing Trixie's cheek. 'Thank you for being my dearest friend.'

'Stop it, you'll have me blubbering like a baby next.' Trixie grinned and hand in hand they walked out of the bedroom.

Downstairs, they walked into the kitchen to find the girls chatting away to a woman dressed in dark green, who, when she turned around, cried in delight at seeing Trixie and Caroline.

'Annie!' Trixie ran to her and hugged her tightly.

Caroline waited for her turn to hug the older woman, who they'd sadly left behind in Melliton. 'We didn't think you were coming.'

'I changed my mind at the last minute.' Annie wiped the tears from her eyes. 'I simply had to come, though the journey nearly killed me. Those trains! I'm so stiff from sitting so long and I've not slept. I must look a mess.'

'You look wonderful,' Trixie said.

Jacob came in through the scullery, appearing splendid in his suit and new boots and freshly shaven. 'We need to be going, ladies. Mr Cavendish left for the church fifteen minutes ago.'

Everyone was giddy with excitement. Out in the yard they climbed up into the cart and carriage, laughter and chatter filled the air as the morning sun shone from a clear blue sky.

'It's a beautiful day,' Jacob declared as the carriage trundled out of the farm.

'Who is driving?' Caroline asked.

'A lad from the village. Wouldn't even take any payment from Mr Cavendish either.'

'Weddings bring out the best in folk,' Trixie said, smiling at Elsie and Bertha. 'We're going to have a fabulous day.'

Caroline's nerves grew once they turned into the village road. In what seemed only a few heartbeats, they were climbing down and straightening skirts, tweaking bouquets and lifting chins in readiness to walk into the church.

'This is it!' Trixie gave Caroline the biggest smile and included Jacob in her joy, before she turned and whispered to the girls to start walking as the organ played.

'Ready?' Jacob asked, slipping her arm through his.

Caroline glanced at Mussy's grave and gave it a slight nod, her chest bursting with equal happiness and sadness. Then she faced the church door. Inside Max waited, and she longed to stand by his side and say her vows to the man she loved. 'Ready.'

The ceremony passed in a blur. Max stood tall and handsome in his dove-grey suit, Thomas standing proudly beside him. Max's blue eyes shone as he watched Caroline walk down the aisle on Jacob's arm.

'You are beautiful,' he whispered, when she joined him.

She beamed at him, feeling beautiful and special and loved.

The sun shone through the stained-glass windows of the small church, highlighting the dust motes in the air and the gold plates sitting on the altar.

In no time at all, Caroline was back out in the sunshine on Max's arm, smiling and receiving their guests' best wishes.

'Oh, I want to leave my bouquet for Mussy.' Caroline excused herself from the milling guests and walked across the grass to the grave. She knelt and placed her flowers beside Mussy's headstone and then kissed her fingers to rest them on his engraved name.

She straightened and Max took her hand with a gentle smile. 'He is watching over us,' he said.

She nodded and smiled. Today was one of happiness. No sad thoughts.

Max turned to her, the love evident in his blue eyes. 'So, Mrs Cavendish, shall we go home?'

Her heart swelled in her chest. 'Yes, my husband.'

'Husband. How grand it is to be called that.'

Max kissed her all the way back to the farm, the two of them secluded in the carriage. 'I am impatient for tonight, my beautiful wife.'

She sighed against his lips. 'Me, too.'

'I'm the luckiest man alive.' He cupped her cheek, his thumb rubbing gently against her bottom lip.

His passionate kisses ignited a longing deep inside her. She was his woman, and he was her man. She wanted to show him how much she loved him, and she wanted to experience all the love he held for her. But that would have to wait for the front of the house was filling up with guests piling out of carts and gigs, wagons and carriages.

Max gave her one last kiss before he opened the carriage door. 'Welcome home, Mrs Cavendish.'

For hours she and her new husband mingled with guests, receiving their good wishes and words of advice in the light-hearted manner in which it was given. Food flowed from the kitchen out to the tables, Rosanna and Jeannie were run off their feet. Dickie and Jacob supervised the drinks table and glasses were repeatedly filled. The band played, their music drifting over the gardens while a juggler entertained the children.

Sometimes, Caroline would search the crowd for Max, and they'd catch each other's eye and share a secret smile.

It was while she was talking to Mrs Todd and some other women from South Carlton that she noticed Trixie talking to Thomas by one of the refreshment tables. She quickly glanced around to see if Jacob was close by, but she couldn't see him. In amazement, she watched as Thomas touched Trixie's hand. Trixie pulled her hand away quickly and ducked away.

'Excuse me, ladies, I need to check on the food.' Caroline made the excuse, determined to find Trixie, but after several minutes of looking gave up when Reverend Trott tapped his glass and brought everyone's attention to him.

'If I may be permitted to make a small speech?' he asked the crowd.

Max came to her side. 'What is it? You look worried?'

'I saw Trixie and Thomas talking, Trixie seemed upset.'

A muscle clicked along Max's jaw. 'I thought all that was over and done with?'

'So did I,' she whispered back.

'Thomas will be gone to Cumbria soon. No harm can be done in a few days.'

'I hope you're right.' Caroline turned her attention to Reverend Trott.

'Ladies and gentlemen, friends,' Reverend Trott spoke to them all. 'It was my great pleasure earlier to solemnise the wedding of our dear neighbours, Mr and Mrs Cavendish. I can safely say on the behalf of everyone gathered here today, at your home, that we all wish you both a long future of wedded bliss. Shall we toast to the happy couple?'

Cheers rang out and Max and Caroline smiled at their guests who raised their glasses.

Max took Caroline's hand and led her to stand beside the reverend. 'May I express that my wife and I are extremely grateful for all your good wishes and for sharing our special day with us. We are not long of this parish, but I speak for both of us when I say we are fortunate to have been so welcomed and we now consider you all as our friends as well as neighbours. Thank you.'

More cheers erupted and glasses were raised again.

Caroline was soon caught up in new conversations with village people she'd waved to when passing, or greeted at church on Sundays, yet now they were celebrating her day with kindness and gladness in their hearts and it gave her much joy to know she was part of a community.

It was long into the night when Caroline realised she'd not seen Trixie for hours. Although the June weather was warm, fires were burning in iron tubs situated around the garden, the lanterns lit up the trees like a fairyland and the food and drink continued to stream from the kitchen out to the marquee. The band became livelier and played reels and jigs. Those who enjoyed dancing were flattening the grass with their partners in energetic abandonment.

Caroline waved to Elsie and Bertha who were playing chase around the trees with some of the village children. Max was deep in conversation with a farmer from North Carlton while Matthew was being dragged into the dancing area by a laughing Rosanna.

Visiting the kitchen, Caroline smiled her thanks at Jeannie who carried a tray of clean glasses back out to the marquee. Trixie was slicing more ham from the large leg she'd cooked earlier in the week. 'Rosanna should be helping you,' Caroline told her.

'She's drunk too many glasses of ale and is of no use to me.' Trixie wore an apron over her rose dress. 'Annie has been helping instead.'

'Let Jeannie do this, come back out to the party. I can get some of the women to come in and do a bit. Many hands and all that.'

'It's my kitchen.' Trixie placed the ham slices on a platter next to the slices of tongue and roast beef.

'I haven't seen you dancing yet,' Caroline cajoled.

'I've never danced in my life!' Trixie scoffed. 'There wasn't much call for it in the Water Lanes.'

'I'm sure Jacob would like you to partner him.'

Trixie gave the platter to Jeannie who returned with an empty tray. 'What else do we need?'

'I'll take some more bread out and we're low on pickles and boiled eggs.'

'Right.' Trixie walked into the larder.

Caroline followed her. 'Why are you hiding inside? You

wanted a big party for the wedding, and everyone is out there enjoying themselves. Why aren't you?'

Taking a large jar of pickles down from a shelf, Trixie pushed past Caroline and went back to the table.

Caroline knew something was wrong. 'What's happened?'

'I've made a right bloody fool of myself that's what,' Trixie snapped.

Annie came into the kitchen carrying a stack of dirty plates. 'That lot out there are hungry and no mistake. What else can I do?'

'Can you slice the fruit cake, please, Annie?' Trixie forked pickles into glass bowls. She glanced up at Caroline. 'Go back out and enjoy the party. I'll be along in a minute or two once I've sorted out more food.'

Caroline knew she was lying, and she wouldn't leave the kitchen. 'Don't be long.'

Outside in the yard, Thomas stood in the shadows. Caroline crossed to him. 'I thought you'd be dancing.'

His face creased into a welcoming smile. 'Perhaps I was waiting for my new sister-in-law to join me?'

She gave him her hand. 'I'd be delighted.'

A cheer rose as they joined the circle of dancers. It'd been years since Caroline had danced, not since she met her first husband Hugh at a fair. Hugh, light-hearted and young had swept her off her feet in a wild dance, and that had begun their friendship and ultimately their courtship. After they were married, they often danced in their little cottage to no music but to Hugh's humming. How innocent those times were, and they seemed a lifetime ago now.

With Thomas she sensed he wasn't as joyful as he usually was and while he swung her about in time with the enthusiastic band, she could tell he wasn't his vivacious self.

'Have you and Trixie had words?' she asked him as they twirled.

'Why would you ask that?'

'Because she's in a foul mood and you are less than jovial.'

Thomas took her hands, and they made a turn and parted. When they came back together his sober expression confirmed her thoughts.

'Do you want to talk about it?' she prompted.

'No.' He twirled her around. 'This is not the time nor place.'

'Oh, Thomas,' she sighed.

Max stood on the side of the dancers with a smile. Thomas guided Caroline to him. 'Dance with your husband.' Thomas kissed her hand and left them alone.

'May I dance with my wife?' Max took her in his arms.

'You may.' She caressed his shoulder as they moved closer together.

'No one seems ready to leave,' Max whispered in her ear. 'It is late.'

'Everyone is enjoying themselves.'

His hold tightened. 'I want to enjoy myself as well, in other ways.'

Her legs weakened at his suggestive words. 'Then why don't we sneak off?'

He pulled back in surprise and then laughed. 'An excellent suggestion, my delightful wife.'

Grabbing her hand, they quietly walked away from the dancers and into the shadowed garden. With a spurt of laughter, then ran, hand in hand, around the side of the house and slipped in through the French doors of the dining room which, thankfully, weren't locked.

In the darkened dining room, Max whipped her around to him and kissed her deeply. Desire flooded her veins, and she gripped him tightly, eager for his body. He kissed her neck, arching her over the table, his hands clasping her hips against his.

Suddenly, he gathered her up in his arms and carried her out of the room. She kissed him all the way up the staircase, laughing as he stumbled slightly.

But once in their bedroom, she became serious as he lowered her onto the bed. 'I love you, Max, more than I thought I could ever love anyone.' She meant every word. After all her indecision, she knew he needed to hear that.

He leaned over her and kissed her reverently. 'You are my entire world, Caroline Cavendish, and tonight is only the start.'

'Show me,' she whispered against his lips.

CHAPTER EIGHT

*L*oud bellowing had Caroline sitting bolt upright in bed. Dawn crept grey light across the bedroom. Max lay spread out asleep beside her, and she melted inside at the memory of the night of shared passion, of exploring each other, of soft whispers declaring their love, their desires. It had been the best night of her life.

A cow bellowed again, and it sounded close, too close. Caroline scrambled out of bed, naked, and peeped through a gap in the curtains. Below, trampling through the garden beds and across the lawn were the dairy cows and their calves.

'Blast!' She ran to the set of drawers and pulled out her under clothes, her linen shift, bloomers, stockings and chemise before searching for one of her corsets.

'What are you doing?' Max drawled, one eye opening. 'Come back to bed. The sun isn't up yet.'

'The cows are in the front garden. They're loose.'

'Dickie and Jacob will get them.'

'They have their calves with them!' Caroline explained. 'Which means no milk for us today.'

Max rubbed the sleep from his eyes and leaned up on one elbow. 'Someone must have left the gate open.'

'Both gates, the one for the cows and the one for the calves. I had Dickie separate them as usual last night during the party.' She turned to Max for him to tighten her stays. 'Hurry.'

'I would much rather you returned to bed, and we can continue on from last night,' he said cheekily.

'And have the cows ruin every plant I've put in the garden?' She stepped away as he finished and quickly donned a service-able navy skirt and bodice.

'We need to employ a dairy maid,' Max said with a yawn. 'I do not want my wife waking at dawn to milk every morning. I have other plans for an early morning activity.'

'I'm sure you have,' she flashed him a smile, 'but I am a farmer's wife, Max, not a genteel lady. I will have my dairy.'

'A milkmaid will be of great use to you, my love.'

Another bellow had Caroline dashing to the window to see Annie limping about the garden trying to shoo the herd back across the lawn.

'Where is my morning kiss?' Max grinned.

She kissed him quickly and then fled the bedroom, gathering up her hair with combs as she hurried downstairs and out the front door.

'Oh, Annie, I'm so sorry.'

'Nay, lass, it's not your fault.' Annie tapped the backside of one of the cows to get it moving. 'I didn't want to wake you. I tried to wake the lads, but everyone is deep in slumber, sleeping off the drink. I think some only went to sleep a few hours ago. The garden is littered with drunken guests.'

'Buttercup, Clover,' Caroline called to her prized cows. 'Dan-delion, get out of my irises!' She pushed the large beast away from her flower beds which had looked so splendid yesterday for the wedding, and which now resembled a ruin. 'Blossom, get away from there!' She nudged the side of Blossom to guide her away from the yellow roses.

It took some doing, but she finally managed to herd them back onto the drive and closer to their own field.

'What a sorry state they can make with their great hoofs,' Annie called from the end of the garden, leading Tulip along with the promise of a nub of bread.

Opening the gate, Caroline and Annie encouraged the cows and their calves back into the field behind the barns where they happily grazed in innocence.

Annie secured the gate latch. 'Folk can be plain stupid at times. They should know better than to leave gates unfastened.' She waved towards the wagon of sleeping band members. Some of the villagers hadn't made it home either and were asleep on the grass or on chairs in the marquee. 'Likely it was one of those lot.'

Something about the cows being out didn't sit right with Caroline. 'The calves were separated from their mothers into the holding pen last night. Dickie told me he'd done it before the festivities got underway properly.'

'Aye, but no doubt people wandered about last night, drunk and forgot to shut the gates.'

'They had no need to be near the holding pens.' Caroline tapped her fingers together, trying to grasp what was tormenting her.

'Well, apart from trodden flowers and no milk, the crisis is over.' Annie hobbled back towards the house.

'Thank you for helping.' Caroline walked beside her, noticing Annie wince with each step.

'I was awake, anyway, enjoying a cup of tea in the kitchen. My hip doesn't allow me to sleep for long.'

'About that,' Caroline said as they entered the kitchen where Trixie was up and stoking the fire in the range. She bade them good morning.

'Morning, Trixie, lass,' Annie said, washing her hands in the sink. 'What do you want me to do first?'

'No, Annie, sit and rest.' Trixie indicated to a chair at the table. 'Rosanna will be down in a moment. I've already been up and knocked on their door.'

'Annie, do sit,' Caroline said. 'I want to talk to you about something.'

'What would that be?' Annie had aged in the months since they last saw her and it worried Caroline.

'What would be your thoughts on moving here to live with us?' she suggested to the older woman.

Annie blinked in surprise. 'Move here?'

'Yes. If you sold your cottage, you'd have money to live on which would save you having to have a market stall and sell your beeswax candles as you do. I'm sure Max would hire someone to build a cottage onto Jacob's.'

'That's a great idea,' Trixie said. 'Then we could look after you. We've missed you so much. The girls would be mad with excitement if you came to live here.'

'Nay, that's a big move for someone my age.' Annie's grey eyebrows drew together. 'Melliton is my home.'

'Home is wherever you are loved, and you are loved here,' Caroline added. 'If we build a cottage next to Jacob's, you'd have your independence to do as you pleased, but we'd all be here to care for you as you grow older.'

'We'd hate you being so far away and us not knowing how you are faring.' Trixie poured tea for them.

'What would Mr Cavendish have to say about it?' Annie asked.

Trixie rolled her eyes. 'He's newly married. Caro could ask for the moon, and he'd try to give it to her.'

They laughed and said good morning to Rosanna and Jeannie who came in from the hallway and, as the back door opened,

Jacob and Dickie entered rubbing sore heads, looking worse for wear.

'Too much to drink last night?' Caroline inquired with a raised eyebrow.

'I'm never drinking again.' Dickie's face held a green tinge to it.

Trixie snorted. 'You'll not be wanting some eggs then?'

Dickie shook his head and winced at the motion. 'Tea will be fine, thanks.'

Caroline poured it for him. 'The cows and calves were out. Tell me the truth, did you separate the calves from their mothers last night and secure the gate to both pens?'

'Aye, Mrs Lawson, er, Mrs Cavendish.' The lad frowned at the question. 'Blossom kicked out at me, and I only just got out of the way. I didn't want her ruining my new suit. She can be a mean beast at times.'

'Aye, she can,' Rosanna said, slicing bread. 'She kicked me a time or two when I've tried milking her.'

'You squeeze the teats too tight, that's why,' Caroline commented before turning back to Dickie. 'All of them were out this morning in the front garden. Calves and cows together.'

Rosanna groaned. 'So, no fresh milk then?'

Caroline gave her a sharp stare. 'Obviously not. The calves have been allowed to drink from their mothers before we had a chance to do the milking. You'll have black tea like everyone else.'

Trixie nodded to the cellar door. 'There's a jug of milk in the cellar. Our guests will be able to have milk in their tea. Speaking of which, Jeannie, you'd best get the dining room ready for breakfast. Rosanna warm the serving containers, the bacon will be ready in a moment, and I need to start cooking the eggs.'

Annie rose and stirred the porridge. 'You see to the guests, lass, I'll manage the breakfast for us in here.'

'Thanks, Annie.' Trixie smiled. 'It's good to have you here.'

'Dickie,' Caroline brought his attention back to her. 'You are certain you secured the gates?'

'Aye, Mrs Cavendish, I did. I'm a stickler for making sure gates are fastened.'

'He is,' Jacob agreed. 'Perhaps one of the wedding guests unlatched the gates.'

'For what reason would they need to be behind the barns in the holding pens?' Caroline sipped her tea. How strange it was to be called Mrs Cavendish.

'Lass.' Annie held up her hand. 'It's done now. Don't let it spoil your first day as a married woman.'

Relaxing slightly, Caroline took a deep breath. 'You're right.'

'And about what you were saying earlier…' Annie hesitated.

'Yes?'

'If I can sell my cottage for a good price then yes, I'll come here to live with you all, and only if Mr Cavendish allows for a cottage to be built next to Jacob's.'

The kitchen erupted with cheers, and everyone began talking at once, filling in Elsie and Bertha on the news as they came into the kitchen, sleepy-eyed. The girls squealed and ran to Annie.

'I'll speak with Max.' Caroline left them to their breakfast and entered the dining room, where Jeannie was setting out the table. 'I'll finish that, Jeannie, you go and bring in the warmers.'

'Very good, madam.'

'Jeannie?'

'Yes, madam?'

'How are you feeling?'

'Oh, I didn't drink last night, madam.' The maid grinned. 'I don't like the taste of any alcohol.'

'No, I mean in general, yourself. How are you coping with all that happened to you?'

Jeannie's expression fell. 'Sad. Embarrassed. Guilty… I gave her away.'

'You've no need to feel guilty at all. You've done what you thought was best for the baby.'

'No, madam, I did what I thought was best for me. I don't want her. I never will. She needs to be cared for by someone who will love her.' Jeannie stared down at the carpet. 'I'm guilty of putting myself before her.'

'You're only sixteen, Jeannie, no one blames you for any of it.'

'They don't need to. I blame myself, madam. I should have fought him, shouted my head off, but I froze. I couldn't move while he was on me. I daren't even breathe. Rosanna would have fought him. I laid there with my eyes closed praying he'd just go away.'

Caroline placed her arm around the thin shoulders. 'You're a little slip of a girl. How could you have fought him? Don't let those type of thoughts rule your life. Promise me?'

Jeannie nodded. 'I'll try.'

'You have a lifetime ahead of you to make yourself happy and content. Don't let that one man, this one incident, spoil your life.'

'I'm trying to forget about it, about *him*... about *her*,' Jeannie whispered, eyes cast down.

'She's doing well at the orphanage.'

The girl's head snapped up. 'How do you know?'

'I visit every week. I have to, I'm sorry, but my conscience wouldn't let me walk away without knowing she was being taken care of. She is an innocent.'

'Thank you, madam...'

'She's called Rachel.'

'Rachel...'

'Rachel Booth.'

'Booth? My name?' Jeannie's eyes widened.

'She is your daughter. Obviously, that will be changed if she is taken by another family. But I told the matron I wanted to have final approval of the family who apply for her, so I can be sure Rachel will be looked after. Do you agree?'

'I've no say in it, madam. I gave her up.' Jeannie turned away to pick up a tray.

'Yes, for the chance to be given a lovely home with parents who will care for her.'

'If you say so, madam.' Jeannie looked desperate to leave the room.

Caroline sighed. 'Be kind to yourself, Jeannie. You were placed in an awful situation. Both you and Rachel are not at fault for any of it. Don't punish yourself over it, I beg you.'

With the maid gone back to the kitchen, Caroline finished setting the dining table. Max always sat at the head of the table, and she smiled as she set a cup and saucer out for him. Her husband. She could barely take it in. Yet, last night, she'd seen another side to him, a side she adored. He had shown her such passion, such tenderness, sharing his most intimate thoughts and desires and loving her freely without any restraint or guardedness.

She had given him the same in return, knowing he wanted her heart, body and soul. She had no reservations about giving him everything she had. They were man and wife, lovers, friends and partners. There'd be no secrets between them about anything, Max had promised her that and she believed him.

Rosanna entered the room, wheeling in a trolley carrying food warmers and the portable kettle warmer and stand for both tea and coffee. Behind her, Jeannie held a tray filled with small crystal bowls of marmalade, plum jam and Caroline's own butter as well as little jugs of milk and cream.

Caroline set the bowls and jugs on the table while the two maids set up the sideboard before going back to the kitchen to fetch the food. Grilled ham, bacon, scrambled and boiled eggs, cold lamb cutlets and stewed tomatoes filled the warmers.

Matthew entered with a warm smile. 'Good morning.'

Rosanna bowed her head at him but managed to give him a

coy smile. 'Good morning, Doctor. Would you care for some toast?'

'That would be marvellous, thank you.' He took a plate from the sideboard and began to fill it from the food warmers.

'Did you sleep well?' Caroline asked him.

'Wonderfully well.' He nodded to Jeannie to pour him a cup of coffee.

Max, cleanly shaven and dressed in a dark-brown suit, came into the room and before serving himself, he kissed Caroline's cheek. 'Good morning, my wife, and everyone.' He smiled at Jeannie. 'I am starved.'

'Tea or coffee, sir?' She gave a slight smile in return, nervous of any man who paid her direct attention.

'Tea, please.' Max added bacon and eggs to his plate just as Thomas entered. 'Are the cow and calves safely put away?' Max asked Caroline.

She gave him a saucy look. 'Yes. Your help was much appreciated.'

He grinned at her sarcasm. 'I pay enough people to herd cows without having to do it myself on the morning after my wedding.'

'It was only Annie, and me who got the cows in the field.'

He had the grace to bow his head in sorrow. 'Forgive me, I should have helped you.'

'Not a good way to start married life, Brother.' Thomas chuckled, filling his plate. 'You are already disappointing your wife…'

'I will make it up to her,' Max replied. 'I will spoil her for the entire honeymoon.'

'Just for the honeymoon?' Caroline joked. 'Does the spoiling end once we are home again?'

'Absolutely not!'

'Where are you going for your honeymoon?' Thomas asked, sitting at the table.

Rosanna brought in racks of toast and slices of bread, which she placed before Matthew while giving Thomas a sidelong glance.

Caroline's teeth clenched. The girl was too forward. Did she honestly expect either Matthew or Thomas would pay her the attention she clearly wanted? The girl was mad for men. Caroline would need to speak with her and nip such behaviour in the bud.

'It is a surprise for Caroline,' Max answered with a wink. 'Jacob will drive us to the train station mid-morning.'

'I think I'll head home as well,' Matthew said, though he didn't sound enthusiastic about it.

'You can stay here as long as you like,' Max told him. 'Treat this house as your own home. We do not have to be in residence for you to be our guest.'

'I appreciate the offer, but I should get back to the hospital.'

'You must visit as often as you can,' Caroline added, knowing Matthew had no family in Doncaster.

'That is most generous of you both, thank you.' Matthew nodded happily.

Halfway through breakfast, Rosanna hurried into the room and stood beside Max's chair. 'Sir, Jacob wishes to see you and it's urgent.'

Everyone looked at the girl.

Caroline swallowed her mouthful of toast. 'Urgent?'

Max dabbed his mouth with a napkin and rose. 'Where is he?'

'Waiting in the yard, sir.'

Leaving via the French doors in the dining room, Max was gone in an instant.

Caroline rose and halted Rosanna in the doorway as the maid took a tray of dirty plates back to the kitchen. 'What's happened, do you know?'

'No, madam. Jacob had gone out to see to the animals, but minutes later, came tearing in, scaring us all and told me to fetch the master urgently.'

Caroline glanced back at Thomas and Matthew, both were

staring at her. As one they rose and joined her, and they all left the dining room to find Max.

The yard was empty, and they strode between the barns into the smaller yard beyond. Near the pigsty, Max stood with Jacob and Dickie. He looked dazed.

'Brother?' Thomas was the first to reach him.

Max swore and raised his face to the blue sky above.

Caroline's footsteps slowed as she smelt the blood, heard the buzz of flies. She didn't want to look into the pig pen, but she had to and then wished she hadn't. The sows and their piglets had been slaughtered. Throats cut, bodies left in the morning sun.

'God Almighty,' Matthew whispered behind her.

'This is no pack of wild dogs,' Jacob stated furiously. Caroline knew how much he loved the pigs. He'd spent endless hours watching the sows give birth to their large numbers of piglets and he cared for them with devotion.

'Fetch the constable, Jacob,' Max's tone was icy. 'This is no accident! I will have the police make this an urgent investigation!' He turned and marched away. They followed him as he headed for the front of the house. The band members were loading up their cart and some of the villagers were waking up and heading home.

Max raised a hand and shouted. 'Wait, all of you. I need to speak to each and every person here. No one is leaving.'

Thomas glanced at Caroline. 'I am assuming you may not be going on your honeymoon today.'

'No.' She watched her husband as he spoke to the lingering wedding guests, his shoulders tight, his face a mask of controlled anger. 'A honeymoon can wait. We need to find out why our animals are being killed for no reason.'

CHAPTER NINE

*S*itting in front of the mirror wearing her nightgown and robe, Caroline brushed her long hair. Max said it was the colour of chestnuts when he ran his fingers through it the night before. She doubted they would share a relaxed night tonight, not after the day they'd endured, which had been tiresome and sad.

Constable Wells had arrived and questioned everyone at the farm, including those of the band, the juggler, who was found snoring under a tree down the drive, and those villagers who didn't go home and were waking up after sleeping off their drink. He'd then left to ride to both South and North Carlton to speak to all the guests who'd attended the wedding.

While Jacob and Dickie performed the unsightly task of burying the sows and piglets, Max and Thomas had ridden out to visit the local farmers along Ermine Street to ask their own questions. They returned in despair. No one had seen nor heard anything, nor had any other farms been targeted.

Dinner had been a sombre affair. Matthew had left to catch the train home to Doncaster and Caroline already missed his calming presence in the house. Max spent the evening prowling the drawing room, going over the incident. He alternated between raging and sullen silence as he tortured himself over who could be causing this destruction.

She turned to look over her shoulder as the bedroom door opened. 'I didn't expect you to come to bed for hours yet,' she said to Max. She'd left him and Thomas talking and drinking brandy.

Pulling off his cravat, Max threw it on a chair and came to her. 'Jacob and Dickie are taking the first watch. Thomas and I will take over at midnight.'

'Do you think the scoundrels will return?'

'Possibly, but likely not tonight. Still, until they are caught, we must patrol the grounds and fields. We cannot afford to lose any more stock.' He kissed the top of her head.

Caroline rose from the chair and took his hand. 'Come to bed. Sleep if you can.'

'I doubt I shall be able to.' He sighed heavily, undressing. 'Constable Wells is making us a priority in his investigations, but I am not confident in his ability or that he will be successful.'

Taking off her robe, she hung it on the chair near her side of the bed and pulled back the bedcovers. 'It is a mystery as to who would want to do this to us. A neighbour, possibly. Someone who wants the land?'

'I agree.' Naked, Max joined her in the bed and gathered her close. 'While Grange Lea lay empty, the land was grazed by the neighbours. Most of the farmers have told me that to my face. They did not hide it from me.'

'And Constable Wells is certain the previous manager has left the country? He would be the only one to hold a grudge against you.'

'Yes.' Max stroked her waist, his finger lightly trailing over her body absentmindedly. 'The manager is long gone. I am at a loss as to who this could be. We have done no harm to any of the villagers, caused no offence to anyone. They all came to our wedding, for God's sake.'

She rested her head against his shoulder. 'That means nothing. They could be a wolf in sheep's clothing.'

'Mr Claymore who farms the property on our north border said he had been running his cows on this land when the manager scarpered, but he happily withdrew them when we arrived to take over Grange Lea. The man has been most agreeable whenever I have met him. I do not believe it can be someone we know.'

'Then who?'

Max sighed again. 'I honestly do not know. But one thing is certain, we cannot keep losing livestock such as we are. My money will only stretch so far until we bring the harvest in and sell it, which is still two months away.'

'I have some of the money Mussy left me. I didn't spend it all on the wedding clothes. It's yours to do with as you see fit.'

'No, darling.' He kissed her. 'Keep your money to buy the things you need.'

'I don't need anything, Max.' She kissed him back, aching for him. 'Just you.'

They made love tenderly, quietly, taking their time to explore, to kiss inches of skin, to reaffirm their love and to bring the other joy and fulfilment.

Afterwards, Caroline lay sated in his arms, but she sensed his restlessness. The small carriage clock on the mantel showed twenty minutes to eleven o'clock. She leaned away from him with a soft smile. 'Go. You want to be outside with Jacob and Dickie and you need to be.'

'I cannot rest, my love.' He cupped her cheek. 'As much as being in your arms is my one desire most of my waking hours, tonight my unsettled mind is driving me mad.'

'Of course. I understand. Go, and if I can't sleep, I'll get up and bring you all some supper.'

He kissed her goodnight. 'Stay in bed. Try to sleep, one of us should.'

'Be careful.'

Max winked as he closed the door, and she nestled down into the pillows and blankets. The random killings of their livestock had thrown a cloud over their happiness. She hated to think someone held a grudge against them. What had they done? Both she and Max had gone out of their way to make friends with the villagers and local farmers. No one had any reason to hate them so much.

Tomorrow she would go visit both South and North Carlton and talk to every person she saw. She'd knock on every door and speak to the wives. As a woman, she might be able to find the answers from other women. Max couldn't suffer another blow to the livestock. Whoever had a vendetta against them would be found out and if Constable Wells couldn't bring them to justice, Caroline would.

* * *

Pinning on her hat, Trixie looked in the small square mirror hanging on a hook in the scullery. 'You understand what to do, don't you, Rosanna?' She called over her shoulder into the kitchen where Rosanna was slicing the last of the ham.

'Yes, Miss Wilkes. Luncheon of cold meats and salads for the dining room and left over rabbit and potato pie for us lot,' she replied tartly.

'Don't rely on Annie to do most of it, either. I'll be asking her,' she warned. 'I won't be long.' Trixie collected her leather purse that held some money for purchases, though most of what she ordered today would be put on account at various shops, the butcher, greengrocer and general grocer.

She went out into the yard, spying Elsie and Bertha in the

garden identifying and drawing flowers. A task Caroline had set them. 'Girls,' Trixie called to them. 'I'm away into town.'

'Can we come?' Bertha asked, obviously bored with her project.

'No. If you don't want to do your lesson, you can always weed the vegetable garden or clean out the hen boxes.' Trixie shrugged. 'It's up to you.'

'You're no fun!' Bertha scowled and returned her attention back to the rose she was drawing.

Snorting humorously at her little sister, Trixie crossed the yard to the barn, hoping Jacob would be ready to take her into Lincoln. The cart wasn't harnessed to a horse, and she frowned. 'Jacob?' she called.

From a large door at the back of the barn, Thomas emerged, carrying a saddle. 'Good morning, Miss Wilkes.'

'Oh, good morning.' She blushed, awkward in his presence. Her chest tightened as he stared at her. 'I was looking for Jacob. He's meant to be taking me into Lincoln this morning.'

'He is not here.' Thomas hung the saddle on the wooden bar in the tack room and came back out to her. 'He accompanied Caroline to South Carlton.'

'He's forgotten about taking me.' She took a step back. 'I'll find Dickie.'

'Dickie is in the north field, watching over the cows. He has just relieved me from my watch.'

'You're watching the herd during the day as well as night?'

'My brother is taking no chances until the villain is caught.'

'Right, yes, of course.' She turned to go back to the house, needing to be away from him, from his handsome face, those blue eyes that seemed to look into her soul. She gathered her thoughts, forcing him from her mind.

Food. She had to plan what meal she could make for tonight when the food supply was so low after feeding so many people for the wedding. There was a brace of pheasants hanging in the cellar, but they'd need to be plucked and gutted, a chore she hated. There was enough rice to make a rice pudding.

'Miss Wilkes, Trixie…' Thomas took a step towards her. 'I can drive you into Lincoln.'

'Oh no, no need.' The very idea thrilled and scared her. To be in a cart alone with Thomas? She shook her head, that wouldn't be wise. She backed away. 'I'll go later.'

'Miss Wilkes, please. You need to order produce, and I can take you. It makes perfect sense.' He paused. 'Max and Caroline have enough to worry about without wondering why there is limited food in the house.'

Guilt rose, overriding her own concerns. She couldn't cause them more anxious moments. 'Yes, you are right. They have enough to concern themselves with, the lack of food doesn't need to add to it,' she murmured, feeling backed into a corner.

'I will bring one of the horses in from the field and hitch them up to the gig.' Thomas took a rope down from a hook.

'Not the cart?' The gig was small. They'd be nearly touching on the seat. Her mouth went dry.

'Do we need such a large vehicle as the cart? Are we bringing back supplies or will they be delivered?'

She felt foolish. All goods were delivered to Grange Lea, everyone knew that. 'Er… delivered, but there might be some things I can take straight away.' Why did she act like a half-wit in his presence?

'There is a shelf under the seat. We will manage I am certain. Give me ten minutes.' He left the barn and entered the field behind where the plough horses grazed.

Trixie paced the yard, again her heart and mind at war. Why hadn't Jacob remembered to take her! Angry at being forced into Thomas's presence, she blamed Jacob. All this was his fault!

She had done her best to not be in Thomas's presence since they left York, not since the day he learned of her past and he showed his scornful reaction of it. She knew what he thought of her. Rightfully, she was beneath him, not of his class. She'd told him so to his face when he'd asked her to marry him. The moment he found out about her, his love had turned to disdain, as she knew it would. So, from that day onwards she'd remained at a distance, sealing her heart away from any pain he could cause her.

Through the open barn doors, she watched Thomas guide one of the horses into the barn and back it in between the gig's shafts. Why was he offering to do this? He'd made it clear that he thought less of her. They'd barely been civil to each other since York.

Thomas worked quickly and soon the transport was ready. He smiled as he offered his hand to help her up onto the seat. 'Your chariot, my lady.'

Pulse racing at his touch, Trixie frowned. She had no idea what a chariot was, and her anger grew. She was an uneducated dolt in his company. This was another example why her foolish heart needed to calm down. It was one more reason why she needed to stay clear of Thomas.

If Jacob had been here, she'd never have to sit next to Thomas, her skirt touching his leg. She shivered and kept her face turned from Thomas. Lincoln wasn't far away. She could do this.

'Do you have any thoughts on who would wish to harm Max's animals?' Thomas asked as they drove along the drive.

She groaned inwardly, not wanting to talk to him. 'No.'

'I reason it is a neighbour who perhaps wanted to buy the place, or at least run their livestock on the fields while Grange Lea remained empty.'

She didn't comment.

Thomas steered the horse out of the drive and onto the dusty Ermine Street towards Lincoln. The sun shone from a clear blue sky. The dirt road held some traffic, a farm cart and a carriage passed them. On either side of the wide road, hawthorn hedges lined the ditches and beyond them, crops of barley and wheat grew green and healthy out of the dark soil. Swallows swooped, looking for insects, while a kestrel hovered above, waiting to seize an unsuspecting field mouse or shrew for its prey.

It was a beautiful day. Warm, sunny, only it was lost on Trixie as she held onto the small seat rail so she wouldn't be jerked closer to Thomas whenever they bumped over a rut in the road.

'How are you liking living at Grange Lea?' Thomas asked, giving her a sideways glance.

'Fine.'

'Just fine?'

'Don't think you have to talk to me, Mr Cavendish,' Trixie snapped, irritated that he was trying to be friendly. She understood his true feelings.

'You once called me Thomas,' he said softly.

'I once did a lot of things I regret.' She turned more away from him on the seat.

'I, too, regret many things,' he murmured.

Trixie didn't want to hear them, but she guessed it was him kissing her, asking her to marry him. The slow plodding of the big horse annoyed her further.

'Trixie, can we—'

'Can't we go any faster?' She cut him off. She wanted this journey to be over with as quickly as possible.

'Is there a hurry?'

'Yes! I've got a lot I need to be getting on with.'

'Indeed, the full responsibility of the kitchen. You have gained excellent cooking skills, Trixie.'

'Thank you,' she said begrudgingly.

'Each meal I am impressed with what you serve in the dining room. I eat the food liking that it was prepared and cooked by your own hands.'

She spun to glare at him. What the hell did he mean? 'I cook for Caroline and Mr Cavendish, you just happen to be sitting at the same table.'

He stared straight ahead but grinned at her waspish reply.

She hated him. They didn't speak again until they reached the bustling centre of town. Thomas halted the horse and gig at the bottom of Main Street. Trixie scrambled down before he had a chance to help her.

'Do you want me to come with you?' he asked.

'There's no need.' She adjusted her skirts, not looking at him. 'I'll be as quick as I can.'

'Take your time. I shall wait for you here.'

She desperately wanted to tell him to go away, and she'd rather walk back than be in his company again, but that would be childish, and he wouldn't agree to it. She strode away, lips tight with annoyance.

Trixie first visited the butcher to order the meat cuts of beef, pork, veal and mutton. Crossing the road, she visited the grocers to order the dry produce such as rice, tea, coffee, sugar and flour. Next, the fishmonger and finally the greengrocer, where she ordered fruit and vegetables to supplement what they grew in the kitchen garden.

Finally, unable to prolong returning to Thomas, she walked back to the gig.

He watched her approach, a thoughtful expression on his face. Again, he handed her up into the gig. Trixie murmured an inaudible word of thanks.

'Did you achieve everything you wanted to do?' Thomas asked, concentrating on guiding the horse through the other vehicles and out of the centre of town.

'I did.'

'Was there anywhere else you wished to go?'

'No.' She gazed at the passing buildings, the cathedral rising high on the hill, the quaint houses lining the road as the horse strained to pull them up the steep incline.

Soon they were away from the noise of people and industry and up on the flat land high above the town below. The sound of birds tweeting and the odd bellow of a cow joined that of the horse's hoofs and gig's wheels pounding on the hard dirt road. The sun was directly overhead, beating down on them.

'I am immensely sorry, Trixie,' Thomas said suddenly.

She barely looked at him. 'For what?'

'For everything that I said and did.' He adjusted the reins in his fingers. 'Last year, I behaved like a cad.'

'Which time was that?'

'I deserved that.' He sucked in a deep breath and let it out slowly. 'Mainly when I found out about your past. I should have behaved better.'

'You reacted as most people do of your class.' She shrugged. '*My class*, the working class, understands the need to do what I did. Women of the night only do it because they have no choice, it's not something anyone ever wants to do because they enjoy it. I had to care for our Elsie and Bertha, put a roof over their heads and food in their bellies. *My* class knows that, *yours* think only the worst.'

'And I am sorry for it.'

She tossed her head. 'It is what it is.'

'I have thought long and hard about the situation for many months. I have had the sense to finally grow up, reflect.'

'It makes no difference now.' She really didn't want to talk to him about it.

'I was hurt.' He shook his head slightly. 'I loved you and felt betrayed.'

'Betrayed?'

'You did not tell me the truth.'

'What did it matter? We were never going to be married, Thomas!' She raised her hands up in confusion. 'Only *you* thought we had a future. I didn't. I could tell we'd never be together.'

'I still wish you had told me.'

'I didn't sense it was important. I was working on the farm, living with Caroline. My life was different. I wasn't living in the slums and being a prostitute anymore. I'd changed. Caroline had given me a new life. I never expected to fall in love with someone like you!'

He stared at her, his blue eyes full of pain. 'You did love me then?'

She couldn't look away. 'Yes…'

'And I loved you, but I ruined everything.'

Impulsively, she grasped his hand. 'We never would have married, Thomas.'

He brought her hand up to kiss it. 'We might, if I had handled the situation better.'

'No.' Emotion was thick in her throat, her body aching for him. Trixie pulled her hand away. 'I'm not good enough to be your wife. I'd have looked foolish trying to be like you, to rise to your station, to pretend to be like the women of your social circle.'

'I do not have a social circle,' he scoffed.

'You grasp what I mean. I can read and write enough to get by, but I'm not an educated lady with fancy dresses and a lady's maid to set my hair and attend to my every need.'

'My brother didn't marry a lady and look how happy he and Caroline are!'

'It's not the same and you know it. Caroline was educated, brought up in a convent orphanage. Her family were respectable. I was from the wrong part of York, poor, living in the slums by the river. You would have been ashamed of me.'

'Never!'

'It's true. You showed me that with your reaction when you found out about my past.' She looked miserably at him. 'None of it matters now. You'll be soon living in Cumbria, and you'll meet other people, another woman who will make you think differently about me…'

'I doubt it.'

'We've got to forget what happened between us. Go our separate ways without regrets.'

'Forge a new life…' he murmured.

She nodded, thoughtful of Jacob and what he offered.

They rode in silence until they reached the gates of Grange Lea.

'Do you forgive me?' he whispered, not looking at her.

'I do.' She blinked away unshed tears, her heart hurting.

No more was said. What more could they say?

CHAPTER TEN

*A*djusting her skirts, Caroline sat opposite Mrs Fleetwood. Beyond the office door were muted voices of children singing a hymn.

'We're teaching the older children a new hymn for church service on Sunday,' Mrs Fleetwood told her. 'We aren't a school, but we like to instruct the good words of the Bible.'

'Any education is of value,' Caroline commented. 'Is Rachel well?'

'She is.' Mrs Fleetwood shuffled some papers. 'We have had a development about her, actually.'

Caroline stiffened. 'Oh?'

'A couple have come forward wishing to adopt a small baby. They have visited twice now, taking particular interest in Rachel. The husband is a solicitor. They are from Boston.'

'Boston?' Caroline had never heard of the place.

'It's about thirty miles southeast of Lincoln. A nice little town near the coast.'

'So far away?'

'They did not want to find a child closer to their home as

sometimes it can cause problems when other people, neighbours and friends, can identify the child.'

'I see.'

The other woman smiled widely. 'The couple have been married for ten years and seem unable to have children. The wife is desperate for a child. They seem very nice.'

For some reason, Caroline wasn't as happy as she expected to be. 'They want to take Rachel?' She'd never see the baby again.

'They do.' Mrs Fleetwood rose from her chair. 'They are here now. May I show them in for you to meet them?'

Taken aback, Caroline could only nod. She stood also and faced the door as the matron opened it and ushered in a couple a little older than Caroline.

'Mrs Cavendish, this is Mr Julian Rycroft and his wife, Lena Rycroft.'

Shaking hands with them, Caroline could find no fault at first glance. They wore finely tailored clothes of excellent quality in the latest fashions. Mr Rycroft had kind brown eyes and a thick beard.

Lena Rycroft was petite with grey eyes that shone with unshed tears, and she kept hold of Caroline's hand longer than was necessary. 'Mrs Cavendish, I am so pleased to meet with you. Mrs Fleetwood has spoken of you greatly in regards to your care of the baby's wellbeing. We understand that you call every week to visit the baby, to hold Rachel.'

Caroline sat once more. 'Rachel is an innocent. She deserves to be loved like any other child born into this world.'

'I completely agree,' Mrs Rycroft gushed.

Mr Rycroft cleared his throat where he stood behind his seated wife, one hand on her shoulder. 'The mother is your maid, Mrs Fleetwood told us, and the father her former employer?'

Looking over at him, Caroline nodded. 'That's correct. Jeannie is my housemaid. She's young, sixteen, but a hard worker and a good person.'

'The father?'

'I have little knowledge of him but a name and what he did to Jeannie,' Caroline said stiffly. 'I have it on two accounts what type of man he was, Mr Rycroft. Jeannie is a decent girl and not to blame in any of this.'

'No, no of course not,' Lena Rycroft put in quickly.

Mr Rycroft patted his wife's shoulder as if to settle her. 'I simply wanted to be acquainted with the baby's parentage.'

'You are not taking home either Jeannie or the man who attacked her, Mr Rycroft.' Caroline's stare was direct. 'You are taking home a tiny innocent baby who needs to be loved and cared for and treated as a member of your family. If you cannot love her unconditionally, then there's no point in your taking her home.'

Before he could reply, the door opened, and a maid brought in Rachel. Mrs Fleetwood gestured to the girl to pass the baby to Mrs Rycroft.

Caroline watched the couple as Mrs Rycroft reverently held the baby to her chest, her eyes welling with tears. Mr Rycroft smiled tenderly down at them, again his hand moving on his wife's shoulder but this time in a caress. His dark eyes softened with love when Lena gazed up at him.

Caroline knew in an instant that man would do anything to make his wife happy.

'Look at her, Julian,' Mrs Rycroft murmured. 'I swear she's grown since we saw her last week.'

'I think she has,' he answered, carefully touching Rachel's cheek. 'Look at those eyes, Lena.'

'She is beautiful,' Lena said in awe. 'More beautiful each time we visit.'

Caroline swallowed the lump in her throat. She glanced at Mrs Fleetwood who nodded slightly as if to say this couple are perfect.

Lena Rycroft looked at Caroline. 'We will love her unconditionally, I promise you that. I've wanted a baby for so long, but it never happened for us and the disappointment over the years has been a bitter blow. Rachel will want for nothing. As her mother I will give her all that I have.'

'I believe that,' Caroline said, knowing it would be the truth. Like herself, Lena Rycroft had been denied a baby from her own womb. If things had been different, if Jeannie hadn't detested the sight of the baby, Caroline would have brought Rachel up herself. But it was better this way. Rachel would be given a new life by people who wanted her.

Mr Rycroft straightened. 'We will cherish this child. Rachel will bring us both much happiness, I'm certain of it.' He grinned at his wife. 'Though I sense she may become one of the most spoilt children in all of England.'

'Can we take her home to Boston?' Lena asked Caroline.

'Yes. Rachel will be very lucky having you both as her parents.'

Lena visibly relaxed. 'Would you like to hold her one last time?' She held out the baby and Caroline took Rachel in her arms.

'Goodbye little one. Be happy,' she whispered into the sweet face, finding it harder to let go than she expected.

'As a mark of respect to you, we will keep her name Rachel,' Lena said. 'It's a pretty name.'

'That's very kind of you.' Caroline kissed the baby's forehead and reluctantly gave her back to her new mother. 'I wish you luck and good fortune.' She hesitated. 'Would you be willing to write to me every so often? Just to inform me how Rachel is faring?'

'Absolutely.' Lena smiled warmly.

'Thank you. Mrs Fleetwood has my details. Good luck. Goodbye.' She turned to Mrs Fleetwood. 'Thank you.' Without waiting another moment, Caroline nodded to them all and left the office, brushing away the tears that fell.

Outside, she waited for Max to return to collect her. He'd

driven them in the gig and after dropping her off at the orphanage, he'd gone to speak with Constable Wells.

A dove cooed unseen in one of the trees in the grounds of the orphanage, but the sound of wheels and hoofbeats on the gravel drowned out the bird as Max came through the gates towards her. She didn't wait for him to assist her onto the seat but instead gathered her skirts in one hand and pulled herself up.

'Am I terribly late?' Max asked full of concern.

'No.'

'Caro?' He took her hand. 'What is it?'

'Rachel is going to a new family, in Boston.' She tried to smile about it but failed miserably.

'That is good news?' he asked hesitantly.

'Yes. Yes, it is.'

'Darling?'

'I'm fine. Take me home, please.' She glanced over her shoulder. 'I shan't ever be coming back here.'

Max drove the gig towards home and once away from the town and on the long straight Ermine Street, he took her hand again and held it tightly. 'You have done the right thing.'

And she did know she'd done the right thing. The Rycroft couple seemed a lovely pair and Rachel was terribly lucky to have gone to them. Yet, the loss, however small, was keenly suffered. No more would she have her weekly visits and hold the baby, admire her growing little body.

'You must not take on the burden of Rachel's welfare, my darling,' he said as if reading her mind. 'She has been chosen by that couple to become a member of their family. No one takes that decision lightly, so I imagine she will be most treasured by them.'

'You're right.' She glanced at Max's profile and her heart ached even more. To be unable to give him a child made her unworthy of his love.

He leaned over and kissed her. 'You have given that child

every chance for a nice life. You are a good woman, Caroline Cavendish. Do not ever doubt that.'

She leaned against his shoulder, grateful for his kindness, his support. 'What did Constable Wells have to say?'

'Nothing much at all.' Max snorted. 'No leads. No suspects. Nothing.'

'What will you do?'

'Continue to patrol the farm every night.'

'You're all becoming exhausted by doing that.'

'What alternative do we have? The night I stop patrolling will be the night we are attacked again. I cannot afford to lose any more stock.'

'Then you should let Trixie and me take our turns.'

'That is not an option, my love. I will not be responsible for you getting hurt.'

'Trixie and I will stay together. If we take the dawn patrol, it'll allow you, Jacob and Dickie to get a couple of hours sleep. Please, Max, let us do our bit.'

'I shall think about it.'

'It makes sense, especially once Thomas leaves for Cumbria. You'll be a man down then.'

'Thomas must leave soon or risk losing his new position. I do not want to be the reason for that to happen.'

Caroline frowned, pondering about Thomas, and Trixie, they'd gone from hardly speaking or wanting to be in the same room as each other, to being together at random times. Caroline had often entered the kitchen to find Thomas hovering about the table, chatting, or finding them both in the vegetable garden. It made Caroline uneasy. She had thought Trixie and Thomas were staying clear of each other. She knew Jacob had seen it as well and his mood had become irritable, and who could blame him?

With that still on her mind, Caroline was pleased to find Trixie alone in the kitchen when they arrived home. 'Where is everyone?'

Trixie basted a leg of pork. 'Rosanna is soaking clothes in the laundry shed. Jeannie is filling the lamps with oil in the cellar. Our Elsie and Bertha are in the barn with Annie learning how to melt candle stubs and remould them. Do you want a cup of tea?'

'In a minute. First, I wanted to ask you about Thomas.'

'Thomas? I don't know where he is. Packing maybe?' Trixie glanced at her before placing the roasting tin back in the oven.

'That's not what I mean and you know it.'

'What about him?'

'You're spending a lot of time together.'

'Are we?' Trixie's cheeks were red either from the oven or the mention of Thomas.

'Be careful.'

Trixie shrugged. 'We've decided to be friends, that's all.'

'Just friends?'

'What more can we be?' Trixie stirred a sauce in the pot on the range.

'I don't want you to get hurt.'

'I won't because nowt will happen between us. He'll be living in Cumbria and that will be that.'

'And Jacob?'

Hanging her head, Trixie sighed. 'He's unhappy with me.'

'I can imagine.' Caroline stepped beside her dear friend, seeing her misery. 'He's jealous, Trix.'

'What can I do?' Trixie whispered.

Caroline gently squeezed Trixie's arm. 'You need to let one of them go. Unfortunately, you can't have them both.'

Trixie huffed. 'Sometimes I wish I didn't like either of them. My life would be a lot simpler.'

'A simple life? Us?' Caroline laughed mockingly. 'Is that even possible?'

Grinning, Trixie consulted her cookbook lying open on the table. 'It'd be nice though, wouldn't it?'

Annie and the girls came in carrying baskets of newly made

candles and the chatter turned to the candle-making process which Bertha enjoyed learning.

'I don't like the hot wax,' Elsie said. 'I burnt my finger.' She held up a red-tipped finger.

'Because you didn't listen to me,' Annie said with a scowl. 'How can you learn to do something properly if you don't listen to instructions?'

'I don't want to make candles again,' Elsie huffed. 'Can I go and read my new book?'

Trixie waved her away. 'Go on, but later I want you helping in the vegetable garden.'

Caroline stayed in the kitchen for a while longer, talking to Annie, but when Jeannie came up from the cellar, she beckoned the maid to come with her to the morning room.

'Am I in trouble, madam?' Jeanie asked, closing the door behind her.

'No, not at all,' Caroline reassured her. 'I have something to tell you.'

Jeannie's shoulders bowed.

'Nothing bad,' Caroline hurriedly assured her. 'In fact, it's good news. Rachel has been taken by a nice couple.'

Jeannie's head shot up. 'Taken?'

'Yes. The couple, Mr and Mrs Rycroft, come from Boston, some thirty miles from here. I've met them.'

Jeannie seemed to sag in front of her.

Caroline went to her. 'Are you well?'

'Relieved, madam. Thirty miles is a good distance away.'

Caroline frowned in confusion. 'Well, yes.'

'It means I'll not have to see her, ever!'

Taken aback by the outburst, Caroline stepped away. 'You feel so strongly about the baby?'

Jeannie stared at the carpet rug. 'Yes, madam.'

'Don't you care what happens to her?'

'No, madam.'

Shocked that the girl could be so heartless, Caroline was lost for words. 'Very well. There is nothing more to say then.'

'Thank you, madam.'

'You may go.'

Jeannie gave her a frightened look. 'I'm not getting dismissed from the house, am I?'

'No, of course not. I'm just surprised by your lack of concern, Jeannie. I thought better of you.'

'In my mind, madam, that baby and *him* doesn't exist. It's better for me to think that way.' The girl looked pained.

Caroline nodded, used to seeing the haunted expression in the maid's eyes. 'I understand. Well, it's over now, Jeannie. We won't mention any of it again.'

'Thank you.' The maid scuttled out.

Caroline stepped to the window and stared out of it. It was amazing to think that Jeannie had easily given away a baby she never wanted, and yet, both Lena Rycroft and Caroline were unable to conceive something they desired most in the world.

CHAPTER ELEVEN

*I*n the stillness of pre-dawn, Trixie stood on the edge of the field closest to the house and scanned the muted forms of the cattle herd. A golden glow from the lantern threw shadows of her and Princess, Max's dog, across the grass.

By the gate, Caroline waited for her. Prince and Duke stood by Caroline's skirts, calm and uninterested in the gloomy surroundings. They and Princess had been on patrol every night with a human for weeks and were used to the routine. It had been an uneventful night.

'Anything?' Caroline called.

'All quiet,' Trixie replied, walking towards her, her skirts swishing the dry grass. The days had remained warm, rainless and uneventful for the last two weeks. She didn't mind going on the dawn patrol with Caroline. It'd become special, precious hours for them to talk quietly about so many things that during their busy days they never got to speak of. For a couple of hours, she and Caroline were together, just the two of them like they used to be, and she had missed that time alone with her friend.

A pink streak appeared in the distance slowly defusing the

midnight-blue sky to pale orange. Trixie yawned. 'Sun's coming up.'

'It'll be another warm day I think.' Caroline unlatched the gate and opened it for Trixie. Once the other side, she secured the latch, checking it twice.

'We could do with some rain.' Trixie turned down the wick of her lantern distinguishing the flame. 'Our Elsie and Bertha are tired of watering the vegetables.'

'I've never known a July as hot as this one has been.'

'And we barely got any decent rain in June.'

They fell into step along the drive, heading for the house. They'd walked the surrounding fields for a couple of hours after relieving Max around four o'clock.

'What are your thoughts about Thomas leaving today?' Caroline asked her.

'He's stayed longer than I thought he would,' Trixie answered.

'That's not what I asked.' Caroline sniffed.

She grinned. 'I know.'

'Well?'

Sighing, Trixie adjusted the handle of the lantern in her hand. 'I honestly think it's for the better if he goes. We've cleared the air between us. We're friends again, which is better than awkwardly trying to avoid each other constantly. Happen we can get on with our lives now.'

'Does yours include Jacob? I've noticed how he's not staying in the kitchen much at mealtimes lately.'

She scanned the field, her thoughts hard to define where Jacob was concerned. 'He's been eating more in his cottage.'

'Because Thomas is likely to be found in the kitchen more than not?'

Trixie didn't answer. Thomas's visits to the kitchen gave her moments of lightness as he made her, and whoever else was in the kitchen, laugh with his jokes and funny stories. He brightened her day with his handsome smiles and lingering looks. The pull of attraction was constantly there, flickering between them. However, she wasn't stupid and knew he wasn't the man for her, despite the ache in her body for his touch.

The rooster crowed suddenly, shattering the quietness.

'It's good that Thomas is accompanying Annie on the train as far as Doncaster,' Caroline broke the silence between them. 'Then she is only on her own on the train from Doncaster to York.'

'I hope she sells her cottage quickly and is back with us soon.'

'Me, too.' Caroline stopped at the next gate that led to the holding yards behind the outbuildings. 'I'll go and start the milking. The new dairy maid should be here this afternoon. If she's suitable, we'll have to get another bedroom in the attic sorted for her. I'll ask Jeannie to make a start on it after breakfast.'

'Right, yes...' Trixie became distracted, noticing Rosanna, along with Annie, coming out of the house and crossing the yard. Rosanna carried a small jug. 'Is Rosanna helping you with the milking?'

'I didn't tell her to. Annie is helping me this morning.'

They parted in the yard and Trixie paused, watching as Rosanna disappeared between the barns. Intrigued, she wondered where the girl was going once Annie disappeared into the milking shed behind the dairy.

Following the maid, Trixie watched Rosanna continue past the other outbuildings until she reached the path leading to Jacob's cottage.

'Morning, Miss Wilkes.' Dickie greeted Trixie as he came out of the stable block.

'Morning, Dickie. Is Jacob with you?'

'No, he's not made an appearance yet, miss.' Dickie yawned and scratched his head under his hat. 'The night patrols are making it difficult to get out of bed on a morning.'

Interested in what Rosanna was doing, she walked on, taking the path to the cottage. The door was open, and she heard voices inside, then Rosanna's coy giggle.

Suddenly incensed, Trixie marched into the small cottage and found Rosanna and Jacob standing in the middle of the room, Jacob buttoning up his shirt, his dark-brown hair uncombed. 'What is God's name are you doing in here, Rosanna?' Trixie barked at the girl.

Without any look of remorse, the younger maid smiled. 'Bringing Jacob a jug of milk.' She held the jug higher as if to prove her point. 'He's been having his morning cup of tea in here, so I thought to bring him some milk.'

'I didn't ask,' Jacob hurriedly put in, tucking his shirt into his trousers. 'I'm capable of coming to the kitchen to get a drop of milk.'

'I'm saving you the bother. I could bring you your breakfast, as well, if you prefer eating your meals in your own home,' Rosanna added saucily.

'Get back to the kitchen!' Trixie demanded.

Rosanna spun to her. 'Why are you so angry? It's only a jug of milk.'

'You have your own duties to preform, and none of those include coming out to Jacob's cottage!'

'Trix…' Jacob held up his hand. 'She was only being kind.'

'Kind?' Trixie spat. 'That girl doesn't do anything unless she's told to and then it's usually under sufferance. But she's come to your cottage unbidden and you're not even dressed properly!' She turned to Rosanna. 'Were you hoping to catch him in bed? Maybe hoping he'd offer for you to join him?'

'Trixie!' Jacob's eyes widened in surprise.

Rosanna gave a nonchalant shrug. 'If he offered…'

'Get out!' She pointed to the door.

'Are you upset because he might want me now and not you?' Rosanna said calmly.

Trixie wanted to throttle the girl. 'He doesn't want you. He asked *me* to marry him and that's what we're going to do, get married,' Trixie snapped the words out.

'We are?' Jacob's eyebrows nearly rose to his hairline.

'Yes. We are.' Trixie glanced at him, angrily. 'Unless you have changed your mind and prefer this one?' She gestured to Rosanna.

'Of course not. I love you.'

The words softened her rage slightly. 'Then that's settled.'

'I'm off back to the kitchen!' Rosanna stomped out of the cottage.

Jacob stepped closer to Trixie and took hold of her arms. 'Do you mean it?'

'About getting married? Yes.' She nodded, and hoped to a God she didn't believe in that she meant it.

He kissed her properly for the first time. A loving, thoughtful kiss that she happily returned.

'We'll see the reverend on Sunday after church service and call for the banns?' Jacob whispered against her lips.

'That's a good idea.'

'There's no point in waiting, is there?'

'None at all.' She smiled.

'You've made me so happy, Trix.'

'I'm glad.' She touched his cheek and gazed into his gentle eyes, knowing he'd never hurt her, never let her down. 'You'd best see about getting an extra room built for a bedroom for the girls.'

'I'll talk to Mr Cavendish this morning.' He grinned and kissed her again. 'I can't believe it.'

'Our Elsie and Bertha will be made up about it.' At least she knew that for certain. Her sisters loved Jacob.

'We'll be a proper family, Trix. All living in here, our home with good jobs and great friends. Our luck has definitely changed since living in the slums of the Water Lanes.'

'It has for sure.'

Jacob reached for his hat but changed his mind and took her

in his arms again for a long kiss. 'I'll never get used to being able to kiss you now whenever I want.'

She playfully slapped him away. 'I've work to do and so do you.'

'We'll talk later though? Make plans?'

She stopped by the door. 'We will.'

'Don't be too harsh on Rosanna. The girl just wants a better life, that's all.'

Trixie tilted her head with a huff. 'She's got a good position in a decent house. She should be thankful if she knows what's good for her.'

Walking back past the outbuildings, she wondered what possessed her to blurt out they were getting married. She hadn't thought about the prospect of marrying Jacob in the last few days. It had always been something she'd pushed to the back of her mind, probably because Thomas was always in the kitchen recently, taking up her thoughts.

Yet, seeing Rosanna eyeing up Jacob as he put on his shirt had triggered something in her brain that had never been there before. A primal ownership, to fight for what she considered hers. When had that happened? When had she believed Jacob was her man?

She turned off the path and entered the milking stalls where Caroline and Annie were both milking a cow each, their heads leaning against the cows' flank, their hands moving in perfect rhythm squirting the milk into tin pails.

'This bucket is nearly full if you need it,' Caroline told her.

'Aye, I'll take it with me, but I came in to tell you both something.'

'Oh aye?' Annie murmured, her cheek against the cow's hide.

'Jacob and me are getting married.'

Both Caroline and Annie sat up straight and stared at her.

'We're going to see the reverend on Sunday to call the banns,' she finished in one breath.

'Nay, that's wonderful, lass, and about time,' Annie joked. 'I'm thrilled for you both, I am that.'

'We all are,' Caroline added, standing up to give her a hug and then the bucket of milk. 'We'll celebrate tonight. It'll be lovely to raise a glass to something as special as you and Jacob becoming betrothed.'

'We need some good cheer,' Annie added. 'Shame I won't be here to celebrate with you on the day, as I'll be back in Melliton then, but I'll be there in spirit.'

'Speaking of which, I'll make up a hamper for you for the train.' Trixie took the bucket of milk with her as she headed back to the kitchen.

Rosanna was subdued and worked without speaking, helping Trixie with whatever needed doing without be asked first. It gave Trixie some satisfaction that she'd finally put the maid in her place. Trixie hummed while she cooked breakfast for the household.

After breakfast had been served in the dining room and the staff had eaten their own and left the kitchen to go about their chores, Trixie took a moment to sit and savour her cup of tea.

Everyone had been told the news, and the cheers rang out, her sisters especially had been so happy they cried. They'd been too excited for their lessons and so Caroline took them with her and Jeannie up to the attic to prepare another bedroom for the milking maid that Max had hired on one of his trips into Lincoln.

She was about to start making up the hamper for Annie when the door opened from the corridor and Thomas came down the step.

His wan smile told her more than any words. 'Forgive me, I am disturbing you.'

She stood. 'No, I'm finished. I've got to get on, anyway.' She took her cup and saucer into the scullery and when she returned, he was still standing by the door.

'Max and I are going for a short ride, I am saying goodbye to some of the neighbouring farms, who have been most welcoming to me.'

'Well, you've a couple of hours before your train leaves.'

'Yes, it is the two o'clock train.'

She knew when the train was leaving, but she also knew he was stalling in saying something else. She wiped down the table. 'I'm preparing a food basket for Annie, but she'll share it with you, no doubt.'

'Have you made the right decision, Trixie?' he whispered, his expression sad.

She understood him, he meant Jacob. 'Yes, I have.'

Thomas nodded. 'Then going to Cumbria is the best thing I can do.'

'It is. We need to go back to being Mr Thomas and Miss Wilkes to each other.' She had to make a stand for all their sakes.

He nodded. 'Anyway, Max is waiting. I had best go.'

They stared at each other for a long moment. Then he turned on his heel and strode from the kitchen.

Trixie went into the larder and pressed her hands against her eyes to stop the tears from falling.

SITTING ASTRIDE QUEENIE, Max waited for Thomas to shake the hand of Mr Cuthbert, a sheep farmer on the other side of Ermine Street, who had been a good neighbour to Max since he took over Grange Lea. Princess sniffed the long grass at the edge of the ditch.

They were in George Cuthbert's upper field close to the road where they'd found him inspecting his drainage. For half an hour they'd chatted and had been invited back to the man's farmhouse, but Thomas wanted to say farewell to some other neighbours and so they said their goodbyes.

'Will my wife and I be seeing you and Mrs Cavendish next Tuesday for dinner, Max?' Cuthbert asked.

'You will, George. Caroline has replied to Mrs Ball and sent Dickie over with the note this morning.'

'Excellent.' He waved them on their way.

Thomas riding alongside Max, patted his horse's neck. 'I will miss riding this fellow.'

Max watched Princess race ahead, having picked up on some scent. 'I am hoping that Caroline will learn to ride him.'

'Yes, you should encourage that.'

'I hope she agrees,' Max murmured. 'I would enjoy going on rides with her over the county. Show her more of the countryside.'

'Caroline said she is keen for you to teach her to drive the gig,' Thomas told him.

'She did mention it to me the other night. It would give her more independence and lessen the need for her to walk everywhere.' Max studied his fields as they rode along the dirt road to the next neighbouring farm. 'It has been so dry, The crops need rain.'

'It will pour when you are ready to harvest and then you will be cursing it.' Thomas laughed.

'Ideally, I wish it to rain this week and then dry out ready for harvesting.'

'You might as well wish for the moon while you are at it, Brother,' Thomas mocked.

'I wish for a lot of things,' Max mused.

'Such as?'

'Not having to reply to Aunt Lucille's letter. I have been putting it off for weeks.'

Thomas grunted and his horse shook its head making the bridle rattle. 'No doubt Wayland rarely sent her many missives in the last few years, but you can bet a Queen's ransom that after the fight, he sent multiple communications complaining about you.'

'With great embellishments added for dramatic effect most likely.' It infuriated him that Wayland had written to Aunt Lucille about their altercation last year. Wayland had been in the wrong.

'Leaving out all the important pieces of information such as the cad that he really is,' Thomas added.

'Undoubtedly.'

Thomas rested his hand on his thigh. 'So, what did our aunt have to say?'

'Mainly about her disappointment in me. I should have behaved better. After all, she did give me all this.' He waved his arm out to encompass the fields of Grange Lea they rode past.

'You need to reply, Max, and tell her everything with brutal honesty.'

'Would Aunt believe me? Wayland got to her first and set the seeds of plausibility that I am not the man she trusts me to be.'

'You must try.'

'But to write in words all that Wayland has done, especially to Caroline... I cannot bring myself to do it.' Max adjusted the reins in his fingers, conflicted about what to write to his aunt, a woman he greatly admired, but who, in the end, will always take her son's side.

'Max!' Thomas's sudden warning tone had Max turning in the saddle to where his brother pointed into the small corpse of ash trees at the corner of a field close to the road.

For a moment Max couldn't see what Thomas pointed at. 'What?' He looked for Princess and saw she had her head in a hedge. 'What is it?'

'Over there!' Thomas pointed to the trees ahead. 'In the shade. I think I can see a man.'

The sound of a wounded cow bellowing turned them in their saddles. In the far field, where the wood grew thicker, another man was piercing a pitchfork into the side of one of the cows.

In horror, Max watched as the cow's legs buckled and it fell, joining other cows already lying in the grass.

'Stop!' Max spurred Queenie into a canter, sending up clouds of dust on the road.

The man raced into the trees.

The woodland covered several acres of the furthest field on his property boundary. He and Thomas reined in at the edge of the trees and dismounted quickly.

'Be careful,' Thomas warned. 'They are armed.'

Jumping the ditch in one angry leap, Max crept into the shaded grove with Thomas right behind him. It took a second or two for his eyes to adjust to the dimness from the thick canopy above. He saw nothing unusual. The grass didn't grow well in the shade and leaves carpeted the ground from the previous winter, cushioning their footsteps. A pheasant hen half flew, half ran out from behind a tree, making them jerk.

Max paused, his blood racing with rage. How dare someone kill his beasts! Ahead he could make out a pile of branches, looking around he noticed lower branches had been sawn from some of the trees.

'Beggars?' Thomas whispered.

'Let us find out.' Max crept closer, Princess on alert beside him. He noticed a small fire, and a blackened tin pot beside it and other utensils as well as empty gin bottles. The pile of branches were a shelter of sorts.

'Can I help you, fellas?' A man spoke from behind them and Max and Thomas spun to face the newcomer. He held a blood-covered axe.

Max studied him. He was certain he had seen that face before. 'You are killing my animals!' Max glared at the man, furious, wanting to beat him to a pulp before dragging him to the police station.

'Says who?' the man taunted.

Princess growled deep in her chest.

'We saw you!' Thomas flung at the scoundrel.

Movement behind them revealed the other man with the pitchfork. Max took a step backwards so he could see them both clearly but the man with the axe advanced, forcing Thomas to step closer to Max and Princess began to bark.

'Now, men.' Thomas held up his hands. 'There is no need for anyone to get hurt. You have been caught. Take your punishment like men.'

'Are you mad? We ain't going nowhere,' the axeman sneered with a chuckle.

'You are responsible for the killing of my animals.' Max wished he had a weapon. The man with the pitchfork looked familiar. Who was he? Princess growled again and Max clicked his fingers to bring her to heel.

The axeman cackled a harsh sound from a mouth full of crooked teeth. 'Do you think we'd confess to that?' He took a step towards Max, his small eyes steely. 'We might not be as clever as you but we're not that stupid. You've got no proof we did anything to your animals.'

Fighting his anger that was making him feel murderous, Max clenched his fist. 'Maybe a night in a cell might make you a bit more talkative?' Max glanced at Thomas. 'Ride to Lincoln and find the constable.'

The axeman snorted with derision. 'You think you alone can keep us both here while he rides away?'

Max approached him, aching to punch the man to the ground. 'Let us find out, shall we?' He gestured to Princess to come around and the dog sprang to the other side of the men ready to pounce.

'You've got balls, I'll give you that.' The axeman grinned, swishing the axe through the air. 'This could be interesting. I've been getting a bit bored butchering animals lately, so this will be amusing.'

'Max,' Thomas murmured in warning.

Max turned to see the man closest to the shelter grab a knife from by the fire. Then it came to him. His name. 'Herman Grover,' Max said. 'You came to the house looking for work some weeks back.'

Grover sniggered. 'I weren't looking for work.'

'You were scoping the farm...' It dawned on Max. 'To do what... steal?' Max's rage elevated up another notch.

'Destroy.' Grover shrugged as though he didn't actually care one way or another.

A cold chill shivered over Max's skin. 'Why? What do you want?'

'All of it,' the axeman commented.

Puzzled, Max looked from one to the other. 'You want Grange Lea?'

Thomas laughed. 'Are you both from the madhouse? You just cannot take another man's home.'

'He did.' Grover pointed to Max.

Max's eyebrows rose in surprise. 'What are you talking about?' Were the two of them insane? 'Grange Lea is legally mine.'

Slapping the knife on his hand, Grover shook his head. His left eye twitched. '*We* don't want the place, no. We just had orders to cause some strife.'

'Who ordered you?'

'You don't need to know that.' Grover flipped the knife in his hand. 'All you have to do is leave, sell up cheaply.'

'I am not selling.'

'Then we'll continue to kill your animals,' the axeman commented as though it meant nothing more than stomping on weeds.

Grover grunted. 'If we don't get paid soon, I'll be doing nowt!'

'Shut your mouth!' the axeman exploded.

'I'll say what I like!' Grover turned on him. 'We've being doing what we were asked, but we've not been paid fully.' He spun back to Max. 'Apparently, we've not finished the job because you're not talking to agents about selling.'

'No, I will never sell.' Max was adamant.

'And we're short on money and I'm sick of living rough.'

'We've got nowt. Not a penny between us.' Axeman glared at Max.

'Am I meant to feel sorry for you?' Max scoffed.

'Either you give us some money, and I mean a *lot* of money, to disappear, or we'll continue to kill more of your animals, maybe do some damage to the barns, set the house on fire… That sort of thing. Our instructions were clear. Do whatever it takes! I fancy a bit of fire, don't you, Grover?' He chuckled. 'And there are some pretty ladies living there that I wouldn't mind having a rumble with… Your new wife is rather impressive.'

White hot anger burst through Max. He lunged for the man, but Thomas grabbed him and held him back. Princess barked madly. 'You touch my wife, and I will kill you.' Breathing hard, Max glared at them both. He would kill them with his bare hands.

'Come, Max. We shall ride to Lincoln and bring Wells back here,' Thomas edged him away.

Axeman chuckled. 'And we'll be long gone by then, but we'll be back.'

Grover stood his ground confidently. 'The police are a waste of time, anyway. When they did come before, they didn't look in here. We were standing right on this spot, and they rode past several times, and never once thought to come in here and have a look about.'

'Bastards,' Max swore under his breath, and the slur was directed at the two criminals before him and Constable Wells. 'Who sent you to kill my animals?'

'The man who it all rightfully belongs to.'

'It belongs to *me*,' Max shouted, his anger rising again like a red mist.

'Who is this other man who has reason to think he is the rightful owner?' Thomas scoffed. 'What kind of man is he to send two degenerates to do his dirty work?'

Axeman grimaced and held the axe above his head. 'Speak like that again and I'll cut your tongue out.'

'Try it,' Thomas taunted, advancing.

Max grabbed Thomas's arm and stopped him. They had no weapons to defend themselves. As much as he wanted to grasp both men around the throat and squeeze the life from them, he had to be clever. They were armed and would win in a fight. 'Who is paying you?'

'We're not at liberty to say,' Grover tittered.

'You want money?' Thomas offered. 'Tell us the name and we will pay you to flee.'

A cunning glint entered the axeman's eyes. 'Five guineas.'

Max scoffed at the suggestion. 'I shan't pay you a penny. Give me the man's name and I will let you live the remainder of your days as free men, or otherwise, I will have you both hunted down for the rest of your miserable lives.'

'We've been here for weeks, and you've not found us,' Grover taunted. 'We're not going to live in fear of you finding us.'

'*A name!*' Max roared. Princess shot forward and bit axeman's ankle. He yelled in pain, but Princess backed away again before he brought his axe down on her head.

Grover grew wary, crouching as though ready to strike. 'It's someone closer to you than you think, Cavendish.'

'Shut up, Grover!' axeman yelled, rubbing his ankle. 'We're not to say who it is.'

'What does it matter? We ain't getting paid,' Grover fumed. '*He's* not content with what's happened so far.'

'*Who?*' Max tried to control his frustration. 'Who ordered you to torment me? Let me deal with them.'

Axeman sniggered. 'Not likely.'

Thomas swore. 'This is getting us nowhere.' He pointed to Grover. 'We have your name. We can identify your faces. I say we tell the police and let them deal with this. No doubt you will receive a long stretch in prison for what you have done.'

In a flash of a moment, the axeman lunged for Thomas. Max turned to warn him off his brother, only Thomas was quicker and grappled with his attacker, the axe close to his throat.

Max sprung to intervene and help Thomas, but Princess got in the way. She was crazy with fear and the need to protect Max. She jumped up and tore at the axeman's arm. He yelled in pain and spun around and with one swipe he brought the axe down on Princess. She yelped and staggered away.

'No!' Enraged, Max leapt for the man, wanting to kill him. Abruptly a sharp pain shot through his lower back. A burning heat seared through him above his buttocks. Confused, he reached behind him and his fingers came away with spots of blood on them. He took a step, half-turning towards Grover who came at him again. Another stab of the knife entered his side. He arched backwards as a jolt of agony ripped through his body. He twisted around to face Grover who held the bloody knife.

Max's brain was slow to register he'd been stabbed. Yet, the pain was nothing like he'd experienced before, icy but also hot, stinging. 'Thomas…'

Max stumbled, put a hand out to steady himself, but touched nothing solid, only air. His knees buckled. He toppled forward and landed face first into the ground.

'Max!' Thomas fell to his knees beside him and pulled him up by the shoulders, causing the pain to ricochet around Max's body like he was in a vice of torture.

He cried out. His vision blurring.

'Jesus Christ! What have you done, Grover!' The axeman peered down at Max. 'You've bloody killed him, man! I'll not swing for this!'

Max frowned, trying to focus on the man. Was he dying? He heard whimpering. Princess! He had to tell the constable, protect Caroline. Oh God, Caroline, his love. He couldn't leave her...

Pain filled his mind, squashing all other thoughts. He closed his eyes and accepted the darkness.

CHAPTER TWELVE

Smiling at the woman seated on the chair in the morning room, Caroline sat behind her small desk, folding her hands on her lap. The sun warmed the room, brightening the yellow painted walls. 'Welcome to Grange Lea, Miss?'

'Baldwin, Nessie Baldwin, and I'm a widow.' Nessie Baldwin nodded nervously. Plump and small, Nessie was dressed in brown serviceable clothes. Her brown hair was tied up under her straw hat and scuffed boots poked out from beneath her worn skirts.

'I'm Mrs Caroline Cavendish. My husband owns Grange Lea. Do you have a reference?'

'I do, madam.' Nessie searched in her carpet bag that sat on her knee and produced a folded bit of paper. 'It's from my previous master, Mr Foley from Low Bottom Farm near Branston. I worked for him for eighteen years, since I was just a girl twelve summers. Me mam was a dairymaid as well, and me father worked the land for Mr Foley. They've both gone now, and my husband joined them in the graveyard nine months ago along with our daughter. Fever took them all.'

'That's tragic, Mrs Baldwin.' Caroline was sorry for the woman. To lose so much.

Nessie bowed her head.

'And why did you leave Mr Foley's establishment?' Caroline scanned the letter, which read of a pleasing, hard worker of honest and cheerful disposition.

'Old Mr Foley is selling up, moving to Lincoln to live with his daughter and her husband. The new owners, well, they spoke of changing things, doing away with the dairy herd. I didn't like the wife much and thought it might be time to leave and start afresh somewhere else. I've no family to speak of now. Nothing to tie me to one place. My three sisters have all married and moved away.'

'And did you perform all the duties within the dairy?' Caroline handed the letter back to Nessie.

'I did, madam. Milking with soft hands, caring for the cows. I can spot udder mastitis with one look. Separating the cream at the right moment is another of my specialities. I churn butter and mould the pats. I can even design patterns on the top. I have a deft hand at making the best cheese you've ever tasted. Different types of cheese, too. Shall I list them?' She held up her fingers, ready to count.

'No, that won't be necessary right now.' Caroline smiled.

'My cheeses have won first prize at many a fair.' Nessie nodded proudly. 'I'm a stickler for cleanliness. My dairy was cleaner than Mr Foley's house and that's no lie.'

'All that sounds wonderful. This is a live-in position. You'd have a bedroom in the attic next to our kitchen maid and parlour maid, Rosanna and Jeannie.'

'Fine by me, madam. My husband and me shared a loft in my parents' cottage. Never had a room of my own before.'

'When could you start, Mrs Baldwin?'

'Please call me, Nessie, madam, if you don't mind, and I can start today.'

'Excellent.' Caroline told her the wage and what her days off were.

'I don't need any days off, madam. I've no one to visit or anywhere to go.'

Caroline stood. 'Well, you have them to do with what you wish, even if it's to walk into Lincoln to look about. Come, I will show you the dairy shed and the herd.' Caroline led the way out of the room. 'All the cows have names and distinct personalities.'

'In my experience, madam, most milkers do. They can be right sweet or right little... performers.' Nessie followed her out.

'They are my special concern on the farm, but I do need help. After marrying my husband, my time is taken up by other things.' Caroline liked Nessie already. She seemed easy to get along with and had a warmth to her that Caroline immediately found genuine.

'You've a lovely home to manage,' Nessie said, staring around as they trod down the corridor towards the kitchen. 'I can understand that you've a lot on, madam. Be rest assured I'll treat the milkers very well, they will become my friends. You'll not find fault with the way I do things. I promise you that.'

'That's very reassuring, Nessie. Now, this is Miss Trixie Wilkes, and Mrs Annie Aspall.' Caroline introduced her once they were in the kitchen. 'Miss Wilkes and Mrs Aspall are my family. Miss Wilkes is also the cook and in charge of the kitchen.' Caroline waited for Trixie, Annie and Nessie to have a little chat, and more introductions were made when Rosanna came up from the cellar.

'Leave your bag here, Nessie,' Caroline instructed before they headed outside.

In the yard, Jacob and Dickie were harnessing one of the horses to the small carriage in preparation for Thomas and Annie's trip to the train station. Again, Caroline made the introductions.

'I hope you like it here,' said Jacob, checking that the carriage's axel was greased well. 'We're a good bunch of people.'

'It seems nice so far.' Nessie nodded, gazing about the yard and outbuildings. Chickens pecked about and Prince and Duke lay panting in the sun. Butterflies fluttered over the vegetable garden and birds twittered in the trees.

A sudden shout shattered the peacefulness.

As one they all turned towards the drive. Caroline's heart jolted as Thomas galloped up the drive, yelling for them, waving his hands.

A tingle of fear ran over her skin, and she knew, deep in her heart, she knew something terrible had happened that would change her world yet again.

Thomas skidded his horse to a stop in a shower of pebbles. 'Fetch a doctor! We need the cart. Help me! Max is hurt!'

Words flew on the air.

Stabbed, in the woods, Princess, ruffians, police, doctor, get the cart, quickly, wounded badly, hurry...

So many words.

Caroline stood still, frozen to the spot. Her mind refused to accept anything Thomas said. Max hurt? She refused to acknowledge it.

In a daze, she watched them all surge into action, talking, panicking, then she was being shaken by Thomas. He had dried blood on his hands. Max's blood. His handsome face was twisted in fear.

He let her go, and she still didn't move. Didn't want to, couldn't. To move would mean engaging in what was happening, and she refused to do that. She'd lost a husband once before because of a silly accident. Hugh had stepped on a rusty nail. A young man in his twenties. Dead. They'd been married for only two years. There was no way she'd go through that again.

No. Not again.

Trixie's anguished face floated before her. 'Dearest, come inside.'

'No,' Caroline whispered, afraid to move a muscle.

'Caro, please. Come inside.'

A knot of despair filled Caroline's chest, making it hard to breathe. 'I will *not* go through this again.'

'Madam, take my arm.' Nessie had hold of her, calm and reassuring. 'Miss Wilkes, you go in and make the room ready to receive... the master, is it?'

'Aye. Aye, I will. We'll need hot water, to strip the bed.' Trixie dashed away, yelling for Annie, Rosanna, Jeannie, Elsie and Bertha.

'Now then, madam, let us go and see our girls, shall we?' Nessie gently led Caroline between the barns. They passed the dairy shed and kept going until they stood at the gate leading to the home field where the milking cows and their calves grazed contentedly.

Caroline saw and heard nothing. Felt nothing.

She stood for a long-time next to Nessie. Her mind blank.

Eventually, Trixie came alongside them and placed her arm around Caroline's waist. 'We've got him comfortable.'

It took an enormous effort for Caroline to look at her. 'He's alive?'

'Aye.'

But for how long, she wanted to know, but didn't say it. With Hugh she'd sat by his bed for days watching him suffer, watching the poison from the rusty nail to seep through his body and steal him away from her.

Was that her fate again? To watch another man she loved die a slow and agonising death?

'You can do this, Caro,' Trixie whispered. 'He needs you.'

She swayed slightly, head spinning.

'Madam, how about a strong cup of tea?' Nessie said.

Caroline stared at Trixie, forcing her numbed mind to work. 'Send for Matthew. We need Matthew.'

'As soon as Dickie comes back with the doctor, I'll send him on the first train to Doncaster. He'll be quicker than sending a note.' Trixie took her hand firmly. 'Come on now. Your husband needs you.'

The walk from the field to the house seemed a mile.

When Caroline stepped into her bedroom, the sanctuary where she and Max made love and whispered sweet words to each other, she faltered.

Max lay on his stomach in their bed, his face turned towards the door, eyes closed. His face was as pale as the sheet beneath him. He was stripped to his trousers. Dark blood smeared across back and side created an ugly pattern. Rosanna pressed two blood-soaked bandages on him and the sight of the girl touching Max's bare skin spurred Caroline into action.

'Change those bandages!' Caroline snapped, rushing forward. 'We need to keep the wound clean.' A bowl stood beside the bed on a chair, the water had turned pink from use. 'We need fresh water.'

'Jeannie's gone for more, madam.' Rosanna folded clean bandages.

Caroline took them from her and applied them to the two stab wounds, which trickled blood, but thankfully weren't gushing. 'Keep the pressure on these bandages, Rosanna, while I wash him.'

Caroline kept busy, not thinking, just doing. She washed Max's upper body with the jugs of warm water Jeannie continued to bring up. Strips of bandages were rolled and placed on the bedside table in readiness.

'Where's Mr Thomas?' Caroline passed the dirty water bowl to Jeannie.

'He's gone to fetch the police, I think, madam.'

'And the others?'

'Dickie hasn't returned yet with a doctor and Jacob has gone to collect... collect Princess...'

'Princess?' Caroline frowned. 'Where has she gone?'

'She was killed in the fight.' Jeannie's voice broke.

A wave of utter despair washed over Caroline. Princess. Oh no. She was such a beautiful dog and Max adored her. She glanced at Max, hoping he hadn't heard. He hadn't so much as twitched since she'd been in the room. The only way she knew he was alive was the slight rise and fall of his body as he breathed, but even that was shallow.

It was late afternoon before the doctor arrived. The man looked harassed, tired and spoke in clipped tones. He stitched the stab wounds in a hurry, poured alcohol on the affected areas and bound Max up with clean strips of linen.

'Leave him on his stomach.' The doctor washed the blood off his hands in another bowl of warm water. 'Change the dressings when you see the blood seep through. Keep him calm. If he wakes, give him some laudanum.'

'*If* he wakes?' Caroline glared at him.

'Your husband has been stabbed, Mrs Cavendish.' The doctor snorted. 'The knife has gone deep. Who knows what damage it has done inside? There may be internal bleeding. The amount of blood he's lost I doubt he'll make the morning. If he does survive the night, he'll likely develop a fever, and possibly gangrene from the wound. God knows what was on that knife. Anyway, Mr Cavendish's prospect isn't one for optimism. You'd better prepare yourself for the worst outcome. I'll return tomorrow.'

Furious at the doctor's lack of empathy and his dismissive concern over Max, Caroline advanced on him, her lips bared back in a snarl. 'Get out! How dare you come into my home and tend to my husband as though he was nothing more than a piece of meat!'

'I'm being realistic, madam.' The doctor picked up his bag. 'I will send you my bill.'

Thomas walked in as the doctor walked out. 'Caroline?'

'Where were you?' she shouted. 'You have been needed here!'

'I was reporting this to the police.'

'Your brother needed you. I needed you!' She spun away from him, back to the bed, to Max who looked dead.

She knelt down, studying the rise and fall of his breathing and sagged in relief when she saw his back rise slightly.

'I am sorry I was not here, Caro.' Thomas moved to the other side of the bed. 'Informing the constable was a priority. Those reprobates cannot get away with what they have done. I am not a doctor, so I am no use to Max at the moment.'

'Nor am I, but I'm here, washing away his blood!' She hung her head. 'Forgive me. You were only doing what you thought was right.'

Thomas came back to her and held her against him, but she couldn't cry. She was too angry to cry, and too afraid.

'What did the constable say?' she asked.

'Constable Wells is going to report this to his superiors and make it an urgent investigation. He will call in the morning with an update, but they are spreading the word about Grover and the other man. Wells has been made to look a fool for not catching them before, and that has hurt his reputation and that of the Lincoln station. They will want to rectify that.'

'Let's hope they will do a better job this time of finding the scum.' She sighed and gazed down at Max, distraught that he was so close to death. 'I can't lose him, Thomas,' she whispered.

'I will help you nurse him back to strength,' Thomas vowed. 'My brother will survive this.'

'Tell me what happened.' She sat on the chair, feeling exhausted already.

'We came upon two men in the far boundary field, near the wood. They were stabbing the cows in the shade thrown by the trees. I think they have killed at least four.'

'In broad daylight?' she asked in surprise.

'They were obviously confident of not being seen. Us patrolling at night, must have forced them to do their deadly work during the day. They had the wood to hide in if anyone rode by. But I just happened to see one just as he stabbed a pitchfork into one of the cows. When Max shouted, he ran into the woods. We dismounted and went in to confront them.'

'You should've got help not confronted them on your own unarmed.'

'Max was in a rage. I could not have stopped him.'

She accepted that. Her husband was no one for backing away from a situation.

'Those men were the ones who have been killing the animals.'

'But why?'

'They were ordered to do it. Paid.'

'Paid?' Shocked widened her eyes.

'Someone wants Max off the property. Apparently, they do not consider Grange Lea is rightfully his. These fellows were to cause enough damage for Max to want to leave Grange Lea. Sell it for a small amount just to be rid of it.'

'A property dispute? Someone believes Max isn't the rightful owner? Why not go through the courts?'

'Good question. This way is likely cheaper and easier.' Thomas ran his hand through his hair. 'Talking to Wells, I sense whoever it is, wants Max to just give up and move elsewhere.'

'They don't know Max very well then, do they?' She gazed lovingly at her husband, wishing he'd wake up.

'One of the criminals said the person paying them to do all this was someone closer to Max than we think.'

'Close to Max?' A chill quivered over her. 'It's someone local? Someone known to us personally?'

'Seems that way.' Thomas paced the room. 'I have been going over it repeatedly, but I cannot think of anyone who would want to do this to Max.'

Suddenly a name came to her. A vision of a smarmy face full of evil. Caroline closed her eyes and groaned.

'What?' Thomas came to her.

'We do know who would do this to Max, to us. *Wayland.*'

'No.' Thomas gasped. 'No.' He shook his head. 'Wayland would not stoop so low as to have Max killed.'

'Wouldn't he?'

Thomas paled. 'The stabbing... That was a spur-of-the-moment thing. They did not expect us to find them in the woods. Their instructions were to drive Max off the property, not kill him.'

Caroline wondered if she'd faint. 'Wayland has paid those men to cause as much damage and disruption as possible. Who else could it be?'

'He wants Max to give up on the place.' Thomas rubbed his hand over his face. 'To walk away, sell cheaply and start again somewhere else.'

'Would it end there though?' Caroline implored Thomas. 'Who's to say Wayland wouldn't find us again and start the tormenting once more?'

Thomas was quiet for a moment. 'I expect Wayland wants Grange Lea because our aunt gave it to Max. Wayland considers this place is rightfully his as her son.' He gave a snort. 'That makes perfect sense. Wayland wants revenge on Max for the beating and for having this estate.'

'But Wayland has the abbey estate and the village at Melliton, and so many other places he inherited from his father. Why would he need or want Grange Lea?'

'Because Max has it.'

She nodded numbly.

'Wayland wants Max to pay for what he did to him. The humiliation of the beating, but more importantly he knows Max is happy with *you*... He will want to destroy what you two share, and you must appreciate more than anyone that our cousin always gets what he wants.'

She shivered, knowing all too well how Wayland takes what he wants, just as he'd taken her body without consent. 'We have to stop him, Thomas.'

'Agreed. Max will kill him when he finds out.'

'We have to make sure we're right about this first before Max becomes aware of it.'

A dead light came into Thomas's eyes. 'Once Max is awake, I shall travel to London and find my cousin. I will get the facts before a word is spoken to Max about it.'

She sighed deeply, feeling helpless. 'Wayland can wait. Max is our concern now.' She grasped her beloved husband's hand and held it firmly. 'Stay strong, my love, I beg you.'

CHAPTER THIRTEEN

*I*t was in the early hours of the morning when Caroline heard the sound of a carriage on the drive. She rose from the chair by the bed and moved the curtains aside to see the carriage pass the house and disappear into the yard. She glanced at Thomas who slept in another chair, his head resting on his hand. The clock showed a quarter past two.

Quietly she opened the door and stepped out onto the landing. Muted voices drifted up and a moment later Trixie was coming up holding a lantern with Matthew following behind, carrying his black medical bag.

'Caro.' Matthew embraced her. 'I came as quickly as I could.'

'I wasn't expecting you so soon.'

'From what Dickie told me, it sounded like I had no time to waste. How is he?'

'Hot.'

Matthew grimaced and entered the room.

'Will you not go to bed for a little while at least?' Trixie asked her.

'No, I couldn't sleep.'

'You'll need your strength for tomorrow.'

'Max needs me.'

'He needs Matthew and Matthew will take care of him now.' Trixie gave her a knowing look. 'Get some rest, please.'

'I will, soon. You go to bed.' Caroline kissed her cheek and returned to the bedroom.

Thomas woke and stretched with a wince as his neck cracked.

'Matthew is here now. Get some proper sleep,' she encouraged him.

Turning from the patient, Matthew gave them both a stern stare. 'I don't need either of you and would prefer it if you both went to bed so you're fresh tomorrow to help me.'

'*This* is my bed.' Caroline smiled sadly.

'You must have my room, Caro,' Thomas instantly offered.

'Don't be silly. I'll not sleep for a minute.' She touched his arm in thanks.

Matthew opened his bag. 'Well, if you're not going to sleep, you can go down and make me a cup of tea and something to eat. My last meal was this morning, and I'm famished. I said no to Trixie making me something, as I knew she was exhausted. But if you're staying up, Caro, then you can be useful.' Matthew waved her to the door. His tone was kind but forceful. At that moment he was the doctor not the friend. 'Thomas, stay a moment if you please? I might need assistance turning Max over.'

Caroline stepped forward. 'I can help.'

'No.' Matthew didn't look at her. 'Food, please, Caro.'

Downstairs in the kitchen, she stirred up the fire and put the kettle on to boil. Cutting ham and cheese, she also sliced bread and buttered it, putting it all on a plate for Matthew. Keeping busy was the key.

As she reached up to take a cup and saucer down from a shelf on the dresser, she wobbled slightly. For a second the room spun. She gripped the edge of the dresser and breathed deeply. She realised she'd not eaten since breakfast, either. Was it any wonder she was feeling light-headed? She had to look after herself and keep her strength up to nurse Max to health.

Sitting down at the table, she nibbled some cheese, savouring the creamy taste. While the tea mashed in the pot, Caroline ate a slice of bread and butter and then more cheese. Down in the cellar, she found milk in a jug sitting on a cold marble slab. She drank a cup of that before she finished setting the tray for Matthew.

Her hunger sated, she carried the tray upstairs and into her bedroom.

'I've sent Thomas to bed.' Matthew rolled his shirt sleeves down.

Pouring him a cup of tea, Caroline glanced at Max and was surprised to see some colour in his cheeks. 'What's your opinion of him?'

Matthew took the plate of food from her. 'The stitches are roughly done, possibly to stem the bleeding. Max will support some ugly scars.'

'But will he live?' she dared to asked.

'I'm not a fortune teller, Caro,' he said softly. 'Max has a fever, which is to be expected. I see bruising, though that could be from the fight, not internal bleeding. I'll have to watch for signs.'

'What are the signs?'

'Swelling, tightness of the abdomen, vomiting blood, clammy skin. So far there has been none of those signs. But he'll need to be watched constantly in the next few days. If the wounds turn nasty, we'll have to watch for sepsis as well. The next few hours will be critical.' Matthew touched her shoulder in sympathy. 'I wish I had better news.'

'What can we do?'

'Keep the wounds clean, try to get some water down his throat, keep him comfortable and hope to God he has the strength of will to fight any infection and come through the other side of this.'

'Max won't give up,' she said determinedly.

Matthew smiled. 'That is what I'm counting on.'

Caroline aided Matthew in nursing Max for the rest of the night. They changed his dressings, wiped the sweat from his hot body as the fever took hold. Matthew managed to get some of the opium poppy syrup into Max's mouth to settle him when he became restless.

Dawn lightened the sky outside when Max groaned and opened his eyes. He'd not been awake since he was brought into the house the day before.

Sitting by the bed, Caroline jerked off the chair. 'Max!'

Matthew woke from a doze and bent over him, checking his forehead with the back of his hand. 'You're back with us, my friend.'

Max grimaced and groaned again as he moved.

'Stay still,' Matthew warned. 'You've stitches that aren't the best.'

'Hot…' Max murmured, trying to sit up.

'Lie down.' Matthew held him down on the bed. 'Come on, old chap, don't be a bad patient. Just rest.'

Caroline wrung out a cloth in cool water and placed it on Max's forehead. 'Shh,' she soothed.

'Caro…'

'Yes, my darling, I'm here.'

'Princess…'

'No, talking now.' Matthew spooned some water in to Max's mouth and followed it with some laudanum. 'Sleep some more, my friend. It'll do you good.'

Thankfully, Max slipped back into slumber.

Matthew let out a long breath. 'He made it through the night, Caro.'

'Yes.' Tears filled her eyes. 'He wouldn't leave me.'

'Strange that he mentioned Princess.'

Caroline swallowed back emotion. 'She died. Killed in the fight trying to protect her master.'

'Blast. What a tragedy.'

'She was a lovely dog. This will upset him greatly.'

'We can't tell him. Not until he's well.' Matthew was adamant. 'Tell the others. There's to be no mention of anything that could set his recovery back.'

'Absolutely.'

Matthew became the professional doctor again. 'Now, while he's asleep, let's get those dressings changed. I want to give the wounds another good clean and check those stitches. We'll change the sheets, as well.'

Matching his mood, Caroline fetched fresh sheets from the linen cupboard on the landing.

Trixie came out of her bedroom, yawning, but dressed and ready to start the new day. 'Morning. How is Max?'

'He's woken. Survived the night.' Caroline clung to the cupboard shelf for a moment. *He had survived the night!*

'That's good news. You and Matthew must be exhausted.'

'We are.' She couldn't lie.

'I'll have Rosanna bring you up a breakfast tray each, and I'll not mince my words if any food returns to me, understand? You're no good to Max if you don't eat.'

Caroline nodded with a smile.

'And later,' Trixie waved her finger in Caroline's face, 'you will lie down and rest properly for a few hours in my bed.'

'I'll try.'

Trixie raised her eyebrows. 'Well, if you don't, I'll let Annie have a stern word with you and see how you like that!' Trixie hugged Caroline roughly and then marched down the staircase.

Thomas watched over Max while Matthew and Caroline ate breakfast and then washed and changed. Matthew napped for an hour in Thomas's bed.

'Caro, Constable Wells is downstairs,' Thomas told her coming into the bedroom mid-morning.

Max was stirring, his face flushed from fever. The sheets were wet again with sweat.

'Can you deal with Wells?' Caroline didn't want to leave Max.

'Yes, of course.' Thomas left her, passing Annie in the doorway.

'Now then, lass, how's he faring?' Annie stood behind Caroline's shoulder and handed her another cool cloth.

Caroline sponged Max's face. 'He's burning up again.'

'Aye, happen he will for a few days.' Annie opened the window. 'Fresh air is needed in this room. It'll be another hot one today and the last thing Mr Cavendish needs is this room being like a furnace.'

The scent of the roses in the garden below drifted through the lace curtains on a gentle breeze. 'He won't catch a chill?'

Annie snorted. 'A chill, in this heat? He'll thank you for the breeze on his skin, trust me.' She settled on the chair Matthew had occupied all night. 'I want to discuss something with you, before I mention it to Trixie.'

'Oh?' Caroline said distractedly.

'I'm going to return home and pack my things. I've been thinking it over and I'm going to rent my cottage for the time being and sell it at a later date when things have calmed down here. I'm quite content to have a cot in the attics until we can sell my cottage and build another one next to Jacob.'

'Yes, that makes sense.'

'I was thinking of taking Elsie and Bertha back to Melliton with me while I pack up. They will be a help to me more there than being under everyone's feet here. You'll all have enough to worry about without me and the girls getting in the way. Less for Trixie to cook for as well.'

'Are you sure? The girls can be exhausting.'

Annie grinned. 'Aye, but they're good girls and I'll keep them busy, never fear on that.'

'When will you leave?'

'As soon as I've spoken to Trixie, and we've packed our few bits. Can you spare Jacob or Dickie to take us to the train station?'

'Of course.' Caroline stood and hugged the older woman. 'Don't stay away too long. I'll miss you.'

Annie cupped Caroline's cheek fondly. 'Nay, lass, you've enough to be getting on with here. Stay strong.' The old woman paused. 'If owt goes wrong...' She glanced down at Max. 'Send word. We'll be back on the next train.'

Later, Caroline dragged herself away from Max's bedside to say farewell to Annie, Elsie and Bertha. The girls were so excited to be going on a train again, and to revisit their old village and see the other children they thought they'd never see again.

Caroline stood in the yard with Trixie and waved them goodbye as Jacob drove them in the cart to Lincoln train station. She'd given Annie a purse of money for the girl's food during their stay and reminded Elsie and Bertha to write every couple of days and be on their best behaviour.

'I hope they aren't too much for Annie to handle,' Trixie said worriedly.

'Annie can handle those girls better than we do.'

Trixie smiled. 'True.'

'It'll be quiet around here without them,' Caroline commented sadly.

'Yes, but they'll enjoy being with Annie more than being here with such sadness in the house.' Trixie gave a final wave and turned back to the house. 'Our Bertha has cried on and off about Princess since yesterday, and our Elsie wasn't much better.'

'How am I to tell Max about her?'

'I don't envy you that conversation at all.' In the kitchen,

Trixie checked the bread, proving on the shelf near the fire. 'I've never been without the girls before. It's going to be interesting not having them with me for the next couple of weeks.'

Rosanna, standing at the table chopping carrots, looked at Trixie. 'Less food for us to cook though.'

'Don't imagine it'll be an excuse to not work as hard,' Trixie reprimanded. 'Without our Elsie and Bertha around, you and Jeannie will have to cover their jobs.'

Rosanna pouted. 'That Nessie is here now. She can help out.'

'She is a dairymaid, Rosanna,' Caroline snapped. 'Her days are busy in the dairy shed.'

'What, she's in there all day, every day? What is she doing after she's milked, separated and churned?'

Caroline's mouth tightened in anger at Rosanna. She looked at Trixie in frustration. 'I can't deal with her right now,' she told Trixie. 'You speak to her before I lose my temper.' She stormed from the kitchen.

She heard Trixie's raised voice through the thick door from the corridor. Passing Max's study, Caroline hesitated and then went in. Was there correspondence that needed dealing with? Were there bills to be paid? She studied some of the correspondence on Max's desk, nothing of much interest, mainly from other local farmers discussing breeding stock and sale prices. There was a small box in a bottom drawer of the desk which held money for wages and to pay for sundries.

In another drawer she found a half-written letter to his aunt.

DEAREST AUNT LUCILLE,

Please forgive me for what I have done to Wayland and for causing you anguish and concern. You must understand my reasoning for what I did to Wayland. He has behaved as no gentleman should.

. . .

CAROLINE FROWNED. Max was writing to his aunt to explain the confrontation with Wayland. She assumed he had done that a long time ago. Had he been putting it off all this time?

Impulsively, she searched through the desk again and found a folded letter in an envelope that bore his aunt's Indian address. She pulled the thin papers out and read them, wanting to know exactly what his aunt had written.

DEAR MAXWELL,

An alarming report reached me today from Wayland. He writes that he has been convalescing from a terrible beating. A beating that YOU gave him. How is this possible?

You would appreciate my shock and my concern to read such news. Could this be true? Pray tell me it is not!

Wayland writes that the attack upon his person was unprovoked and unwarranted and that you fled the abbey in disgrace!

I must strongly communicate my displeasure, my anger and my great disappointment that you, of all people, would do this to my son.

I trusted you to guide him, to be his teacher in all things, for I held you in such high esteem, but you have failed me. That you would be so brutal to your own cousin astonishes me.

After all I have done for you since your parents died, I am betrayed in this way!

I fully understand that Wayland can be difficult at times, and a law unto himself when he chooses. However, I never expected you would ever take matters into your own hands.

I require a full report on the events leading up to your attack on my son. I want the whole truth on your side of the shocking incident. Spare me no details.

I have sent this letter to Grange Lea, since that is where you said you now lived in your letter to me at Christmas, a letter which made no mention of the circumstances leading to your departure from the abbey.

Why would you keep something so monumental from me? I have so many questions, Maxwell.

I beg you to answer me promptly with an explanation.

Yours sincerely,

Aunt Lucinda.

CAROLINE SLAPPED THE PAGES DOWN. How dare the woman! To place all the guilt on Max when Wayland was at fault! Disappointed that Max hadn't shown her his aunt's letter when it first arrived, she tapped her nails on the desk in thought. He'd been carrying this guilt for months. He loved his aunt and to have hurt her would be causing him such anguish. He didn't deserve any of that!

Grabbing a piece of paper, Caroline picked up Max's pen and opened the ink pot. She wrote quickly and from the heart, trying to keep her emotions in check and her anger out of the words completely. It was a difficult task, but she believed she'd succeeded when she read the letter once she'd completed it. Max was in no state to defend himself, but as his wife she could and would tell his aunt the truth even if it meant sharing the shameful details of what she endured at Wayland's hands.

Jeannie passed by the open door on her way to the kitchen.

'Jeannie.' Caroline wrote the address on the envelope. 'Will you give this envelope to Dickie and ask him to go into Lincoln and post it straight away, please?'

'Yes, madam.' The maid hesitated.

'Yes?'

'Madam, it's my half day off. I'd be happy to walk into Lincoln and post this for you to save Dickie from leaving his duties at this terrible time.'

Caroline smiled with gratitude. 'You are a good girl, Jeannie. Thank you.' She rose and gave the maid some money from the tin. 'I've never sent a letter to India before so I'm not sure of the price of it, but that amount is plenty and should cover it.'

'I'll bring back the change, madam.'

'Treat yourself to a drink and something to eat while in town.'

'I couldn't, madam.' Jeannie took the envelope.

'I insist. You are doing this for me. Enjoy your afternoon off.'

'I wasn't going to go anywhere. If you or Miss Wilkes needed my help, I'd have been happy to stay and work.'

'You deserve some time to yourself, Jeannie. You've earned your afternoon off, please take it even if it means strolling around Lincoln or sitting by the river in the sunshine.'

Jeannie nodded and gave as close to a smile than she'd shown in many months.

Caroline hurried back upstairs to Max. She'd been gone longer than she expected and, if she had doubts about what she'd just done by writing to Lucille, then she quickly pushed them away. If Wayland was behind those two men causing damage to the farm, for Max's stabbing, then his mother needed to know about it. Lucille needed to be informed of everything!

She sat beside Max and took his hand while Matthew left the room for a break. She stared down at his handsome face that was flushed with fever. 'Wake up, Max, my darling, please.'

He lay still, not responding to her voice.

'My love, I need you to stay with me,' she pleaded.

Thomas entered the room, closing the door behind him.

She sighed heavily. 'Any news?'

'Constable Wells has gone to Wayland's London townhouse to question him, if he is there, of course. If not, Wells will travel to all his homes to speak to him.'

'They are making speaking to Wayland a priority?'

'Yes. Wells considers himself a fool for not taking this case seriously in the first place. He wants to redeem his reputation. Also, they have sent out warrant notices for Grover and his accomplice for if Max dies… it becomes a murder investigation.'

Caroline shuddered at the words. 'So, now we wait.'

'Something I am not accomplished at doing.' Thomas stepped closer to the bed. 'How is he faring?'

She glanced back at Max. 'No change. He's fighting the fever. He has to win that battle before he can heal.'

'He is a fighter, Caroline. Do not doubt him.'

CHAPTER FOURTEEN

Trixie glanced around Jacob's cottage. Lamps lit the room to a soft golden glow now the sun had set. The one-roomed cottage was sparsely furnished. A table and two chairs near the cooking fire, shelves above the double bed set against one wall and a set of drawers. Jacob had few personal items, and the cottage seemed a little dreary.

'It's not very big,' Jacob said tentatively. 'Max said before that I could add a bedroom on the back for the girls. I'm going to start digging out the foundations for the bedroom next week. I want to get them done before we start harvesting. Dickie is going to help me on an evening.'

Trixie glanced at the bed she'd be sharing once they were married and quickly looked away again. After years of suffering her old profession, she wasn't a prude, and she wondered why now she couldn't contemplate sleeping with Jacob.

She watched him hang a coat on a hook on the back of the door. He was a good-looking man, decent, kind. Why wasn't she in rapturous delight to be marrying him?

'Trix?'

She blinked, coming back to the present. 'Sorry?'

'I said do you wish for me to paint inside? It could do with a coat of whitewash, but I could buy a coloured paint if you'd prefer?'

'Whitewash is fine.' She spun to the door. 'I'd best get back to the kitchen. Caro might need me.'

He stood by the door and gave her a gentle smile. 'I'm excited to speak to the reverend about the banns.'

'Not yet, Jacob,' she spoke sharply. 'Not until Max has recovered. We can't think about any of that until Max is out of danger. Caro needs us.'

'I know.' He kissed her cheek, but she knew he wanted more.

Purposely, she placed her hands on either side of his face and kissed him properly.

As though that was all he'd been waiting for, Jacob gathered her in close, kissing her back with a rising passion that surprised her. She found she liked it, and the relief flowed through her. She did desire him, after all.

Feeling more confident about marrying him, Trixie pulled away with a smile. 'Good night.'

'See you in the morning.' Jacob grinned.

Walking back to the house, Trixie gave herself a talking to. She'd been anxious since announcing her and Jacob were to be married. She thought that was what she wanted but since that day, she'd been plagued by uncertainty. She was concerned she'd been too hasty, reacting to Rosanna's flirtations. Jacob was her friend, someone she'd known all her life. To suddenly imagine him as a husband was difficult to overcome. However, the kiss had changed things, made her easier in mind and spirit that they could be together and it would be no hardship.

Entering the kitchen from the scullery, she checked the fires were banked down for the night. Everyone had gone to bed, except Caroline and Matthew who were staying with Max during the night as they had done for the last five days since the stabbing.

She lowered the wick of one lamp and left it on the table for the night in case Caroline came down to make some tea in the early hours.

Taking another lamp, she went into the corridor and climbed the servants' staircase to the floor above. She never used the main staircase if she could help it, for she was a member of staff. True, she was Caroline's best friend, but she was still a member of staff and the servant staircase is the one she used. She felt the same about sleeping in one of the main bedrooms, which made her uncomfortable. Sleeping in the attic would be more fitting, but Caroline wouldn't hear of it. She'd never become used to sleeping on the same level as the main bedrooms, but soon it wouldn't matter for she'd be in the cottage, and so would the girls, leaving the main bedrooms to Max and Caroline and their guests when they stayed.

On the landing, she faltered as Thomas come out of Max's bedroom. They both stared at each other. Then she saw his distraught expression. He'd been crying and her heart somersaulted, dreading the news. 'What's happened?'

'Max has taken a turn for the worse,' he whispered brokenly.

Trixie rushed to him and hovered by his side. 'What does Matthew say?'

'The fever has him in its grip and not letting go. He's failing fast.' Tears flowed over Thomas's eyelashes. 'I cannot...'

'I should go to Caroline.'

'She is washing Max to cool him down. They have stripped him naked to cool his body, and she refuses my help.' Thomas rubbed his face with both hands and took a shuddering breath. 'I cannot lose my brother. He is all I have...'

'You won't!' Trixie vowed. 'We must be positive.'

Thomas's face crumbled again. 'For days I have been confident he will make it, but tonight...'

Abruptly, Trixie pulled him into her bedroom and shut the door. 'You can't give up and Caroline can't see you like this. She has to stay strong for Max and we have to stay strong for her. Cry if you must but don't let Caroline see you.'

'I am sorry.' He wiped the tears from his face again and straightened.

Her heart twisted at his sorrow and pain. She embraced him, holding him tight as he cried on her shoulder. Despite their height difference, she deemed herself to be the stronger of the two at that moment. 'Cry with me, but don't let Caro see your tears, not yet.'

She held him closer, caressing his back, giving him the support he needed.

'Trix...' He raised his head, his face inches from hers. 'God, Trix.'

When his mouth pressed against hers, she melted, as she'd done before at his touch. The simmering fire ignited between them, familiar and achingly real. Denied for so long, they lost all reason as their lips sought for more intimacy and their hands gripped tightly to the other, seeking, yearning, finding. The passion between them was hot, definite and explosive.

They tore at each other's clothes, desperate with need to caress the other's skin, to kiss, to touch, to explore, to take.

Trixie arched her neck as Thomas kissed her throat, his hands bringing her alive in ways she'd never experienced despite her history with men. She welcomed Thomas onto her bed, into her body in one swift movement that blew all rational thoughts from her mind. For two years she'd wanted this man, ached for him, loved him. She'd tried to hide it, to fight it, to ignore him, her feelings, this desire that burned through her like wildfire.

When it was over, Thomas withdrew from her and rolled onto his side, panting.

The cool air whispered over her skin where seconds before it'd been warm. The slow realisation of what she'd done stole into her brain, sweeping away the delicious sensations of moments ago. The madness ebbed away, allowing sanity to prevail once more.

Thomas's hand caressed her stomach. 'That was everything I imagined it to be.'

She couldn't speak. What had she done?

'Look at me, Trixie,' he demanded softly.

She turned her head. Her eyes locked with his.

'I have loved you for two years, and you have loved me. None of what we did was wrong.'

'It was wrong in every way.' A sense of remorse filled her, erasing the lovely experience they just shared.

She hurried from the bed and wrapped her dressing gown around her naked body. 'I'm marrying Jacob.' She didn't know why she said it out loud to him. Was it to remind him or herself?

'You don't have to.'

She frowned. 'What do you mean?'

'You can live in my house in Oxford. I can visit you throughout the year when I can.'

'From Cumbria?' An icy chill crept over her skin.

'Yes. Thankfully, they are keeping the position for me. I wrote and explained my delayed departure because of Max…' His eyes misted again, and he sat up. 'I should go back to him.'

She took a step forward, needing clarification. 'When you say I could live in your house, what do you mean?'

Thomas dressed quickly. 'You and the girls can live there.'

'As your wife?' She remained perfectly still, bracing herself for the answer she already knew was coming.

'Er…' Thomas tucked in his shirt and couldn't meet her eyes.

'As your mistress?'

'No!' He looked aghast at the idea.

'Then what?'

'We would work something out.' He pulled on his boots. 'I love you, Trixie. You are like a magnet, I can't keep away. No, that's not what I mean.' He shook his head, and his overlong hair fell forward over his forehead. 'I mean, I cannot live without you.'

'Or *with* me in Cumbria.' She watched him closely, her heart shrivelling.

His blue eyes softened. 'I do not have the answers just yet, but I will. I need to contemplate everything, my future.' He came to her and kissed her.

This time there was no rising passion simply an acceptance of something that was done. She felt cold.

Was Thomas out of her system for good? She hoped so for her own sanity, but she was also both sad and relieved.

When he had gone, she sat on the edge of the bed. Mixed emotions played in her head and her heart over Thomas. She couldn't blame him for any of it. For two years he'd been under her skin, making her crazy with desire and breaking her heart in equal measure. What happened tonight was inevitable, really.

Still, she was sorry she'd done it because now she'd have to tell Jacob and hurt him. He didn't deserve that, but nor could she keep it a secret from him.

She sighed deeply. Footsteps outside on the landing made her get up and open the door a crack to see if she was needed. Matthew, looking dishevelled, walked past and threw her a tired smile.

'How is Max?' she asked.

'The evening has been rough for him, and honestly I thought we might lose him, but in the last hour he's settled, and his temperature has lowered.'

'That's good. Would you like some tea?'

Matthew shook his head. 'Caroline will be making pots of it through the night, I shouldn't wonder. You get some sleep as I might need you tomorrow. I want Caroline to rest, she's exhausted. If she doesn't sleep soon, I will have another patient to deal with. Between us we must convince her to rest.'

'Of course. I'm at your service. Rosanna can run the kitchen, and I'll help you.'

'Thank you.'

Trixie closed the door and donned her nightgown. The house was eerily quiet. Climbing into bed, she thought of Elsie and Bertha. She hoped they were behaving for Annie and being helpful. She missed her sisters. The house didn't seem the same without their chatter and giggles.

She gazed at the pillow where Thomas's head had laid. She touched it lightly. If she'd been born anywhere but the slums, she could have been his wife. Then she snorted at her own foolish mind. Living in the slums had given her the chance to find Caroline, and it had given her Jacob, both of whom she never wanted to be without.

* * *

CAROLINE'S EYES were gritty like someone had thrown sand in them. She'd stayed awake all night, sending Matthew and Thomas to bed not long after midnight, promising Matthew she'd fetch him if Max grew worse. Her lovely friend had barely slept more than an hour since his arrival and was swaying with tiredness.

In the hours that followed, she continuously bathed Max as he tossed and twisted with fever. His hot skin dried the damp cloths fast and so she was constantly soaking them and sponging him down. He rambled and murmured words she didn't catch, he spoke in half sentences and moaned. He'd been fighting the fever all day, and she knew Matthew feared he would be taken before midnight, but Max was stronger than they gave him credit for, and she begged and pleaded with him to stay with her, to never leave her. She didn't know if her words reached him in his fevered state, but he settled a little with another dose of laudanum. She kept washing him, kept talking to him, kept praying.

Before dawn she changed his sheets by rolling him to each side, which took so much of her flagging strength, but she didn't want to wait for Matthew. Max had sweated out the fever and his damp sheets needed replacing.

Once he was in clean sheets, Max seemed to fall into a deeper sleep.

As the sun rose, she turned out the lamps and opened the heavy damask curtains to let in the light. It surprised her to see low grey clouds of rain on the horizon. Every day for a week she'd opened the curtains to a glorious blue and cloudless sky. She hoped it would rain for a couple of days to nourish the crops and grass and to refill the water butts and the spring-fed well.

At the washstand, she poured water into the basin and washed her face to wake herself up. Refreshed, she went into the dressing room and changed her clothes, selecting clean undergarments and a front-buttoning corset in cream silk and cream silk stockings that Max had bought for her for their wedding. Over the undergarments, she donned a pale-pink linen bodice with white lace on the sleeves and a matching skirt, another one of Max's gifts, and an outfit she'd not worn much because she wore her sensible house clothes mostly, which were in the colours of dark blues and greens, tans and browns. However, today she needed to wear something light-coloured and something Max would like to see her wear.

After combing and pinning her hair up with combs, she returned to the bedroom. She gasped. Max was staring at the window. Her heart flipped. 'Darling!' She hurried to his side and took his hand.

'I... I thought you... to be... downstairs...' he croaked, his voice raspy, his lips dry.

'Here, you must drink.' She held the cup for him for he was as weak as a newborn kitten. 'Drink it all.'

'Prefer…tea…' His smile was fleeting.

'I'll get you as much tea as you can drink,' she joked, kissing him lightly on his cracked lips. 'How do you feel?'

'Tired,' he whispered.

'You're ill, you're bound to be tired, my love.'

His blue eyes weren't as brilliant as they normally were, and his skin held a flush to it that was unnatural. Tears burned behind her eyes at the shadow of the strong man he used to be.

'Matthew will be so happy to hear you've woken.'

'Matthew?' He seemed confused.

'He's here. I sent for him.'

'Closer.' Max lifted his hand, and she leaned closer to him so he could rest it against her cheek. She held his hand in place, feeling the heat from his skin. 'I… shan't… leave… you…'

Tears pricked her eyes again. 'You had better not.'

'Caro?'

'Yes, darling?' She smiled, blinking away the threatening tears.

'Love… you…' His eyes closed and his hand fell limp.

Caroline froze, staring at him. No. He's not gone! 'Max!' she yelled. 'Max!'

His eyes flickered.

She sat unblinking, watching his chest rise and fall. 'Max!'

The door opened and Matthew strode in. He frowned at her stillness. 'Caroline?'

'He woke up.' She kept her eyes on Max's chest. 'Then he… I thought he'd *gone!*' she blurted out, her voice high.

Matthew calmly but efficiently examined Max. A few moments later his shoulders relaxed. 'Max is sleeping. His pulse is good.'

'Sleeping.' She nodded, feeling light-headed. 'He said he loved me and then he went floppy, and I thought… I thought…' Her chest tightened. The shock of him dying, at least she thought he had, made her dizzy and sick.

'It would have shocked you.' Matthew patted her arm. 'He will come in and out of sleep now while his body recovers. He's much cooler to touch now. His breathing is rhythmic and steady, see?'

She couldn't see. She couldn't see or hear as the bedroom spun around her and then all was black.

When she woke, she was in Trixie's bed. Matthew, Trixie and Jeannie were hovering about the bed, whispering.

'Here she is. Back with us.' Matthew beamed, coming to her side.

Her body was heavy with tiredness. 'What happened?'

'You fainted.' Matthew checked the pulse on her wrist.

Trixie took her other hand, her expression fierce. 'You gave us all a fright and I'll not have it, do you hear? Poor Matthew had to holler for someone to help him, luckily, I was coming out of my room. Matthew has enough to deal with looking after Max and you not eating or sleeping is a problem we don't need.'

'I'm sorry.' She was embarrassed to have caused a fuss.

Trixie's tone softened only a bit. 'You frightened us.'

'I'm sorry,' she repeated.

Trixie grew fierce again. 'Right, well, I'm telling you now, no more sleepless nights. I bet you've not slept more than two hours in a week, have you?'

'I—'

'No need to answer for I know!' Trixie fumed. 'You getting ill helps no one, does it?'

'No, I—'

'Max is doing better this morning so you're going to sleep and rest all day, and not leave this bed. Do you understand?'

'Trix, no—'

'Oh, it's not up for discussion! Is it, Matthew?' Trixie glanced at Matthew. 'We've decided, haven't we?' She turned back to Caroline. 'You don't leave this bed. Now, I'm going to make you some scrambled eggs, bacon and toast and a pot of tea. Don't you dare leave a crumb on the plate, will you? And take just one foot from that bed and you'll have me to answer to!' She stormed from the bedroom taking Jeannie with her.

'Lord, she can be terrifying for someone so small.' Matthew grinned. 'I wouldn't argue with her.'

'I don't have the energy even if I wanted to,' Caroline replied.

Becoming the doctor once more, Matthew grew serious. 'You must rest, please. Max has turned a corner, I believe, for the better. His wounds look less inflamed. I'm going to try and get him eating something later, and once food is in his body, he should start to recover his strength, but if he finds out you're unwell, that will set him back as he'll be too worried about that to take care of himself, understand?'

'Yes.'

'Good. I have Thomas and Trixie to help me. You're not needed. You've done enough. You've pulled Max through a dangerous situation but now you need to look after yourself. We'll keep you updated on Max's condition. Jeannie will do all your bidding if you need anything. Promise me, you'll stay in bed all day?' Matthew gave her a questioning stare.

'I promise you.' It would be a difficult promise to keep for being at Max's side was all she wanted to do, but she didn't want anyone worrying, especially Max and having a setback on his own recovery.

She nestled back against the pillows as rain pelted against the window, turning the morning a dull grey. She was dreadfully tired and hungry now Trixie had mentioned scrambled eggs for they were her favourite.

Closing her eyes, she waited for the breakfast tray, but when she opened them again, it was dark outside and a lamp lit the room.

Trixie rose from a chair. 'Right, now perhaps you'll have something to eat?'

'Max?'

'He's fine. He's had beef broth. He's doing well and Matthew is happy with him.' Trixie smoothed the bedcovers. 'He's sleeping now so I'll get you something to eat. You can see him in the morning.'

'In the morning?' Caroline argued.

Trixie glared at her. 'Yes, *in the morning.*'

'I feel better. I can get up.'

'Oh, no you won't.' At the door, Trixie gave her a warning look. 'Stay in bed. I'll bring you some food.'

'You're very bossy.' Caroline tutted, but then smiled. In truth she was as hungry as a fox in a hen house.

CHAPTER FIFTEEN

*W*ithin two days, Max showed signs of recovering from the fever and his wounds. His appetite began to return as did the normal colour of his skin. Although still weak and he had long bouts of sleep, when awake he wanted to sit up and be involved in conversation with whoever entered the bedroom. His wounds were healing, looked less inflamed and Matthew was confident that Max was out of danger.

Relieved that he seemed to be over the worst, Caroline sat beside the bed and passed him the newspaper and also his mail that had arrived that morning. 'Matthew leaves on the two o'clock train this afternoon. He says he's not needed here anymore.'

'Indeed, I am much better. We cannot keep him from his responsibilities in Doncaster.'

'I will miss him.' She picked up her darning out of her sewing basket. Sitting beside Max for days had given her the chance to finish a lot of darning and sewing that she usually didn't have time for.

'As will I. He is a good friend.' Max flipped through his post.

'Jacob is taking him into Lincoln.'

Max put his letters to one side. 'I need to speak with Jacob about the crops. The rain has fully stopped?'

She nodded. 'We had a good day's worth of rain two days ago. The sun is out once again, but there's a wind.'

'Good, that will help dry out the wheat and barley. I need to inspect the fields.'

'You are not leaving this bed.' She glared at him. 'You might consider yourself to be improved, but you are not strong enough to be walking the fields. I'll have Jacob bring in samples of the wheat heads for you to inspect, or Thomas can.'

'This is a busy period, my love. We need to start harvesting soon.'

She raised her eyebrows at him. 'And we will do that while you rest and get your strength back.'

A look of frustration crossed his handsome face. 'Where is Thomas?'

Caroline smoothed out her skirts. 'Likely out on the estate somewhere,' she lied.

If Thomas wasn't sitting in with Max, he was usually in some tavern in Lincoln. He often came home smelling of ale and pipe smoke. She didn't comprehend what was going on with him, but something certainly was. Thomas had become withdrawn and sour in the last few days. He no longer laughed and jested as was his way. He never stayed in anyone's company for long and reso- lutely avoided the kitchen. Something had happened between him and Trixie, their truce had failed and the tension between them, on the odd occasion they were ever in the same room together, was palpable.

Thomas had hinted of leaving today with Matthew, but no decision had been firmly made as far as she knew. But Max didn't need to know any of that.

Max took her hand. 'I want to speak with Thomas and Jacob. They need to be ready for the harvest.'

'Darling, I've told you, we can deal with the harvest. Jacob has the names of the men and their families you've hired from the local villages, and he spoke to them yesterday to prepare them for starting next week. Besides, I've brought in a harvest myself, don't forget.'

'As my wife I would rather you were not toiling in the fields.'

'If that's where I'm needed then that's where I'll be,' she reminded him. 'Bringing in the harvest is more important than me being the lady of the manor.'

Max chuckled. 'You *are* the lady of the manor!'

'And one who wants to see that the harvest is completed.' She leaned over and kissed him. 'No more arguments.'

'I never win anyway.' He huffed. 'I am eager to get out of this bed though.'

'Perhaps tomorrow you can sit on a chair by the window?'

'Or venture downstairs?' he asked hopefully. 'I could sit outside for an hour. Princess must be missing me.'

Caroline's heart sank. She glanced away, gathering her thoughts.

'She is dead, is she not?' Max abruptly stated.

She straightened her shoulders and faced him. 'Yes. I'm so sorry. She died in the fight.'

Max nodded. 'I knew it. Thomas refuses to mention Princess when we have talked of what happened and you and Matthew have changed the subject whenever I have mentioned her.'

'Forgive me.' She gripped his hand. 'I didn't want to tell you while you were so ill.'

He nodded. 'She was a good dog.'

'She was. Prince and Duke still look for her, I'm sure. Dickie buried her under one of the apple trees, the first tree nearest to the barn.' She'd been unable to watch Dickie preform the task. She knew it would break Max's heart when he found out.

'Thomas told me yesterday that Constable Wells is still investigating Grover and the other fellow. I shan't rest until they have been brought to justice, or until I learn who paid them.'

Before she could reply, Matthew knocked on the open door and entered with a smile.

Caroline was relieved to see him. She didn't want to discuss Grover and the possible link to Wayland with Max just yet, not until they were certain he was behind it.

Matthew, dressed in his best suit, carried his hat. 'I thought to sit with you until I must take my leave.'

'Are you all packed?' Caroline asked.

'I am.'

'I'll have Jeannie take your portmanteau and medical bag downstairs.' Caroline rose from the chair. 'I'll have a tea tray sent up for you both.'

Caroline found Jeannie in the linen cupboard under the servant's staircase and asked her to take down the doctor's luggage.

Once downstairs she found Trixie alone in the kitchen. 'Where's Rosanna?'

'Out in the garden, picking tomatoes and other salads.' Trixie dressed a leg of pork ready for the oven.

'We're having salad for luncheon?'

'Aye, is that a problem?' Trixie snapped.

Taken aback, Caroline frowned. 'No, it's just that we had fish written down for today's midday meal.'

'We'll we're having cold chicken and salads, plus strawberries and cream afterwards. Unless that's not good enough for you?'

'Hey, what's wrong?' Caroline took a step closer, frowning. 'Why are you angry at me?'

'I'm not angry at you.' Trixie puffed her dark hair out of her eyes. 'Rosanna was driving me mad. I wanted her out of my sight for five minutes, so I sent her out to collect the things to use for a cold meal.'

'Why was she driving you mad?'

'Because it's Rosanna, and she only has to look at me sometimes and I want to slap her.' Trixie salted the leg of pork.

'You've been off for the last couple of days.' Caroline added tea leaves into the teapot. 'Care to tell me what's troubling you?'

'There's nowt wrong.'

'Is there too much for you to do? You've been so busy since I spent a day in bed.'

'I'm fine. I like to be busy.' Trixie put the pork in the oven.

'Then what is it?'

'I'm just missing our Elsie and Bertha, that's all.'

'You're a terrible liar, Trixie Wilkes.' Caroline shook her head and mashed the tea. She set out the tray with cups and saucers, a pot of milk and a bowl of sugar cubes.

'There are lemon curd tartlets in the larder,' Trixie suggested.

They worked in silence for a while until Jeannie came in and took the tray up to the bedroom.

When Rosanna came in with a full basket of produce, Caroline told her to mind the kitchen and grabbing Trixie's elbow propelled her outside and around to the front garden where she knew they'd not be disturbed.

'Caro, what are you doing? I've got to get back,' Trixie protested as Caroline pushed her down onto a stone bench by the rose garden.

'You're taking a minute or two.'

'I'm fine.'

'So, you keep saying, but I don't believe you, just like you don't believe me when I say those words.' She gave her a raised eyebrow questioningly. 'Out with it now please and don't insult me by lying and saying there's nothing wrong.'

Suddenly, Trixie burst into tears and that shocked Caroline more than anything because Trixie wasn't one for tears. She hugged her friend to her and let her cry.

Eventually, Trixie straightened and fished for a handkerchief from her apron pocket. 'I'm fine.'

'Say that *one* more time, I dare you,' Caroline warned. 'What's happened?'

'I did a terrible thing.' Trixie wiped her eyes.

Surprised, Caroline scowled. 'What terrible thing? In the kitchen? With the food?'

'No. Nowt like that, and I'd tell you about something like that straight away.'

'What then?'

Trixie sniffed. 'With Thomas. Me and Thomas…'

Realisation dawned and Caroline took a second or two to calm her amazement and shock. 'Oh.'

'Yes. Oh.' Trixie blew her nose. 'I'm such a fool.'

'When did this happen?'

Trixie stared down at the grass. 'When Max was in high fever. I was going to bed and Thomas was very upset, thinking Max was going to die. I only wanted to give him comfort, to help him through it.'

'But one thing led to something else entirely?'

Trixie whipped her head around. 'I didn't plan it!'

'No, maybe you didn't, but you recognise the attraction that is between you two, that has always been between you both. You and Thomas are like Max and me. Like moths to flames.'

'Only you waited for marriage,' Trixie murmured gloomily.

'Did you consider that was easy for Max or for me? Sleeping down the hall from each other for months without giving into our desires?'

'I held Thomas at bay for *two years*,' Trixie defended.

'Then why ruin it now?' Caroline sensed the anguish seeping from Trixie. 'Will he marry you?'

'I don't think so, no.' Tears spilled over Trixie's lashes once more. 'He'd have said something about that by now. Instead, he's avoiding me.'

'He's avoiding everyone.' She tutted. 'He's let not only himself down but everyone else who thinks highly of him. Max keeps asking for him.' She gazed over the gardens and the fields beyond. The crops were high and ripened, ready to be harvested.

'Max wants Thomas to stay longer and help with the harvest. Thomas's employer has written to him and said they'll keep his position for him until Max is ready for him to leave, which is very considerate of them.'

'And I want Thomas gone,' Trixie said quietly.

'Do you really? Honestly now, what is it that you want more than anything? Is it Thomas or is it Jacob?'

'I definitely don't want Thomas,' Trixie said with steadfast certainty. 'He's shown his true colours to me. He wants me but doesn't want to marry me, and even if he asked, I'd say no.'

'Are you sure about that?'

'Absolutely. I've always understood the divide between us because of our different classes, but it's more than that. Thomas is ashamed of his feelings towards me, I see that now. He desires me but wishes he didn't. I'm the forbidden fruit.'

'Regrettably, I agree with you.' Caroline wrapped her arm around Trixie's shoulder. 'You need to talk to Thomas.'

'He mentioned me living in his Oxford townhouse and he would visit me every now and then from Cumbria.'

'He said what!' Caroline stared at her. 'Like some mistress?'

'Aye.'

'What did you say?'

'Well, when I said the word, mistress, Thomas denied that's what I'd be.' Trixie huffed. 'Of course, that's exactly what I'd be.'

'I'll be having words with him. How dare he treat you this way?'

'Leave it. There's no point you getting involved. He's your brother-in-law, and hopefully, he'll be gone soon.'

The last thing Caroline wanted to do was upset Max, and her having words with Thomas would do that. 'I won't confront him. You need to find out where you stand.'

'I've realised that Thomas is not important to me, not as much as I thought. Oh, I care for him, I can't deny that, but... Oh, I don't know. It's all so confusing.'

'And Jacob?' Caroline asked gently.

'Dear Jacob. I will confess to him.'

'And then what?'

'That's up to Jacob, isn't it?'

'No, it isn't.' Caroline twisted on the bench to look at her properly. 'It's what *you* want that's important, Trix. Whether it be Thomas, Jacob, or remain a spinster, it's your decision.'

'I honestly don't know what I want.'

'Then don't make any decisions, not yet. Be thankful that you have choices, most women don't. You have a roof over your head and a good wage and people who care about you. You don't need a man unless you want one.'

'Of course, I'm thankful. I haven't forgotten where I came from.' Trixie let out a long breath. 'Only, once I've confessed to Jacob, I don't think he'll want to marry me anymore, and I've found out too late how sad that makes me.'

'We can't be certain of his rejection.'

'I've betrayed him.' Trixie bit her lip as more tears fell. 'He might leave Grange Lea.'

Caroline rubbed her forehead in torment. That was the last thing she wanted. She needed Jacob more than ever now with Max's injuries. 'What a mess.'

'I'm sorry.' Trixie wiped her eyes again. 'You don't need to deal with all this.'

'You're my family.' Caroline bumped her shoulder against Trixie's. 'Being in some form of mess is typical for us, isn't it?' she joked to lighten the mood.

'Life's definitely not boring.'

Caroline laughed. 'Come on.' She stood and dragged Trixie up beside her. 'We'll get through it, we always do.'

Inside the house, Caroline smiled at Matthew as he came down the main staircase.

'Max is asleep,' he told her. 'I bored him with my conversation on the medical conference I'm attending soon.'

'He wouldn't be bored with that.' Her smile wavered. 'He is well enough for you to return to Doncaster?'

'He is, I assure you.'

'Good. You'll have luncheon with us before you leave?'

'I won't, if you don't mind. I've letters to post, and I thought to visit a few of the shops in Lincoln before boarding the train. I can walk into town if Jacob is too busy to drive me.'

'Nonsense, you're not walking four miles carrying your luggage.'

They collected his belongings and after he'd said goodbye to Trixie and the maids, they walked out into the yard to where Jacob was harnessing the gig.

'I will never be able to thank you enough for what you've done,' Caroline said to Matthew.

'You're my very good friends. Naturally, I would want to help you whenever I can.'

'You dropped everything to come straight away. I'll never forget that.'

'You'd do the same for me.' He smiled bashfully. 'I think of you as family. You've replaced the one I lost.'

'And you've always a home here with us if you're ever in need.'

Matthew shuffled his feet a little. 'Actually, I was pondering the notion of opening my own offices in Lincoln.'

'Leaving Doncaster?'

'Yes. There's nothing in Doncaster to keep me there. I was talking to Max about it earlier. I can practise anywhere. I'm not tied to the hospital or to my offices in Doncaster.'

'How wonderful that would be to have you so close.'

'Well, it's something I'll seriously consider then, if you trust it's a good idea?'

'I do. Write and tell me what you decide.' Caroline embraced him as Jacob led the horse and gig closer.

'I will and you must keep me updated with Max's progress. If anything happens and you're worried, send Dickie for me.' He held her tightly for a moment. 'Until next time, dear Caro.'

'Take care, Matthew, and thank you again.'

She stood in the yard and watched the gig until he was gone from sight down the drive.

Thomas came out of one of the barns, unshaven and looking worse for wear.

'There you are.' She smiled forcibly. 'Max wants to talk to you about the harvest starting next week.' When Thomas walked closer, she noticed his bloodshot eyes and the smell of alcohol on him. Suddenly, the sight of him whipped up her temper. 'Look at the state of you. When did you last wash or take a bath?'

'Forgive me, I…' He shrugged.

'This is not good enough, Thomas. Whatever has happened between you and Trixie has to be pushed aside for a little longer. Max needs you.'

His blue eyes widened. 'You know about us?'

'Yes, and I'm disappointed in you both, but I'll not go into that now. Get upstairs and clean yourself up and then go sit with Max.'

'I cannot sit with him, Caroline. He keeps going on about the fight, about Grover and what are the police doing. I do not have the answers.'

'Then go out and find the answers!' she snapped.

'I need to leave, Caro. Go to Cumbria. My position is waiting for me, and I cannot stay here another day. Max is well enough for me to go now, as Matthew has done.'

She clenched her fists. 'And what of Wayland?'

'We don't know for certain if Wayland is involved. Let the police do their duty.'

'Max is unable to leave his bed without help. The police are incompetent.' She waved him away. 'Oh, just go. You're of no use to me or Max in this state, anyway. I shall see to everything myself. I will talk to Constable Wells. I will bring in the harvest and I will care for your brother and run this estate. Go to Cumbria, Thomas, and start again. Don't come back for a long while, I beg you.'

He bowed his head in shame. 'I have dishonoured myself in your eyes.'

'You have, yes, and Trixie as well.'

He mumbled an apology and stumbled into the house.

Frustrated, Caroline walked to the dairy, a place she always found peace and quiet.

Nessie was churning butter, but stopped as Caroline walked in.

Caroline grabbed a clean apron hanging on a hook. 'What needs doing, Nessie?'

'The cream needs separating from this morning's milking, madam. I was going to do that next.'

'I'll make a start.' Caroline hesitated. 'I've not had the chance to thank you for your kindness on the day that my husband was stabbed. You stood by me when I couldn't function...'

'Shock does that to people, madam.'

'I'll not forget your kindness,' Caroline said sincerely.

'Kindness is free, madam.'

'Are you happy here, so far?'

'That I am, madam. Coming here, away from my own sad memories has given me something else to focus on. The memories are still there, mind, but I'm not surrounded by the place that reminds me of what I've lost. If you understand my meaning.'

'I do, Nessie, very much.'

'I have this dairy to myself with no one to bother me. I do my work, I eat good food and sleep in a comfortable bed. Not many a folk can say that, and I'll not take what I've got for granted.'

Caroline nodded and stood at the large stone sink to wash her hands. For a moment she envied Nessie's simple life. She'd experienced it so briefly when married to Hugh. Then she thought of all that she'd gained since his death and chastised herself for her foolish feelings. She was lucky, terribly lucky to have all that she had.

Yet, a sense of unease flittered like a trapped bird at the back of her mind, and she couldn't shake it.

CHAPTER SIXTEEN

rixie knocked on the door of Jacob's cottage with a shaking hand. It was late, and she hoped he wasn't in bed. She gripped the lantern handle tighter, forcing herself to remain at the door and not flee back to the house, to her bedroom and safety, keeping the secret hidden from Jacob so as not to hurt him.

A moment later, Jacob opened the door, his dark hair array and tucking his shirt into his trousers. 'What's happened?'

'Nowt!' she said quickly to put him at ease. 'Nowt at all.' He looked rakishly handsome, and she wondered briefly why she'd only just become aware of how attractive he was.

'What time is it?' he squinted.

'Past ten o'clock I think.'

'Am I wanted to patrol? Dickie was meant to be doing it until midnight.'

'I'm not here about that.'

'Oh right. Come in then.' He rubbed the sleep from his eyes and stepped aside.

Once in the cottage, Trixie's knees wobbled. She really didn't want to do this, to speak of something that would cause him pain, or to see him look at her in a different way.

Jacob lit some candles. He sent her a loving smile as he did so, which only made her feel worse and she nearly bolted.

'Can I be cheeky enough to ask for a kiss?' He grinned, pushing his fingers through his brown hair.

She placed the lantern down and ran to him with a sob in her throat. She held him tightly and searched for his mouth, eager to give him whatever he wanted, not realising until that moment that she needed his embrace as well.

'I can't wait until we're married,' he whispered against her mouth.

His words yanked her away, and she twisted her hands together. 'There's something I need to tell you.'

He reached for her, but she moved backwards. 'Jacob.'

'You look upset, Trix.' He frowned. 'What is it?'

She took a moment to gather her thoughts and then squared her shoulders. She had to tell him. 'I shared a bed with Thomas.'

Jacob's eyes widened and then he sagged in front of her. 'I shouldn't be surprised, should I?' he said dully. 'I knew it would happen.'

'I didn't plan for it. I... We... Thomas was upset, assuming Max was about to die.'

'And you thought to comfort him.' It was a statement not a question.

'Yes, innocently at first, I promise you that. Then, well, things happened.'

'And he wasn't enough of a gentleman to stop it.'

'No, but then nor did I...' she admitted.

Jacob bent over the table and rested his hands on it. 'No wonder he's not been able to look me in the eye recently. He took what was mine. But then, were you ever really mine?'

'Yes! Yes, I'm yours, Jacob.'

'It doesn't seem that way to me. I was living in a dream,

thinking I'd finally have the woman I loved. I should've known better. People like me don't get what they want against a man like Cavendish. I'm a poor man and he's rich. The rich always win.'

'It has nothing to do with money and you know it.'

'No? If he'd been a poor fellow, would you have looked twice at him?' he scoffed. 'I don't think so. He's a gentleman's son. Handsome and educated and he desired you.'

'You make me sound like I was after his money. I never was!' she defended hotly.

'A blind man could see it's all about desire, has been since you two met. I could see it. Everyone could see it.'

'We tried to fight it. For two years I've tried to keep him at bay.'

'Until you couldn't.'

She bit her lip to stem the rising tears. 'I could have lied and not told you, but that would be wrong.'

'What is wrong is that you let him touch you in the first place. You didn't fight hard enough, Trixie. We are betrothed!' he said heatedly. 'Or does that mean nothing to you?'

'Of course it means something to me. I love you.'

Jacob winced and moved away. 'Only, you love him, too.'

'I will agree with you that I thought I did love him, but I don't.'

He turned to her, a quizzical look in his eyes. 'You don't love him? But you still shared a bed?'

'After we shared a bed that's when I realised I didn't love him.'

'Right, so once *we've* shared a bed you might feel that same way about me? Thought you loved me, but you don't really,' he said sarcastically.

'No, that's not right.' How was she making this worse?

'Isn't it?'

'Of course, not!'

'How will you know?'

'Jacob, please, listen to me. I made a mistake.' She wasn't explaining it very well. Her mind whirled but her spirit that had been beaten down so many times came to the fore and she refused for another second to be a simpering fool. 'Yes, I did wrong. I betrayed you. I accept all of that. But actually, what I did needed to happen.'

'*Had* to happen?' he asked incredulously.

'Listen to me, please, because me being with Thomas, made me realise that he wasn't the one for me. It was as though I'd got rid of the fascination I had about him, that yearning for him which has plagued me since the moment I met him. It's gone. All of that madness has gone. Do you understand what I'm saying?'

'You lanced the boil?' he mocked.

'Something like that, yes.' She held her hands up in anguish. 'Thomas was like a poison in my veins. I had to get him out. I'm not explaining this well, but that's the best I can do.'

'Oh, trust me, you're doing a marvellous job.' Jacob crossed his arms. 'The woman I love rutted with another man and isn't sorry for it.' He stared into the candle flame. 'I understood your past. I spent years watching you walk away from the Water Lanes and go into York to give your body to gentlemen for coin. We were poor, desperately poor. You had no choice, needed the money and it paid well. You earned money to keep your sisters and yourself alive. I didn't like your profession and wished I could have helped you more, but I had my own problems. I was just a young labourer often out of work myself, trying to earn a few shillings doing whatever I could to support my sister and her children. I loved you from the shadows, never revealing my thoughts to anyone. Now I wish I had, back then, back in those filthy slums. Maybe then you might have looked at me as someone other than your friend.'

'I'm sorry, I am, for hurting you. I'd never want to do that on purpose. But I'm not sorry for doing something which has now released me from the ache I carried with me.'

'Oh, so as long as you're content now, that's all that matters?'

'That's not what I meant.'

'Was he everything you expected? Did you enjoy it? Was it everything you imagined it to be? You had sex for fun and not to earn coin. That must have felt different?'

Trixie grimaced at his choice of words. She shook her head. 'I won't speak of it.'

'No? Not to me, the man you're meant to be marrying?' He laughed a chilling sound.

'I didn't want to lie to you. You deserved the truth.'

'I deserved loyalty, Trixie, the same as I have always given you.'

She bowed her head in disgrace.

'What do you want me to do with this truth? Call Cavendish out for a duel?'

'Don't be ridiculous!' she snapped.

'Then what? Shake his hand? Or tell you I forgive you?' His gaze never wavered. 'Right now, I can't say that I can.'

'And I don't blame you.' She swallowed a lump in her throat. 'What I've done to you is unforgiveable.'

'Is Cavendish wanting to take you away to Cumbria now?'

'No.' Her humiliation was complete. Thomas had been avoiding her. At that moment she hated Thomas and herself.

'He's tossed you aside now he's achieved what he wanted?'

'We both tossed each other aside,' she defended hotly. 'I told you, it needed to happen, and it did and now it's all over.'

'But for how long? Until the next time he comes to stay?'

'No!' She was adamant about that. 'There will never be a next time. Thomas and I are done!'

'I've heard those words before, Trixie.' Jacob's face crumbled a little, but he pulled himself together. 'You can leave now.'

'You won't go, will you? You won't leave Grange Lea?'

'At this moment I really don't have any idea about what I should do.' His shoulders slumped.

'I'm so sorry, Jacob. I never meant to hurt you. I hope you

stay. This is your home now.' She meant every word. In fact, the notion of him going away floored her.

He turned his back on her. 'Close the door on your way out.'

Trixie nodded even though he couldn't see her, and collecting the lantern, left the cottage.

* * *

A SHOUT WOKE CAROLINE. She rolled over and her hand touched Max's arm. He didn't stir. Had she imagined the noise?

She'd started sleeping in their bed again now Max was recovering, and he'd insisted, saying he would sleep better if she was beside him getting a proper rest as well. She hadn't argued for she still suffered the effects of sleeping in a chair for over a week, and then sharing Trixie's bed.

Closing her eyes, she settled again, her hand on Max's arm, careful not to disturb him. The sound came again. What was it?

Inching out of bed, she stepped to the window and pulled back the curtains. To the right of the drive, yellow lights flickered. Was it Dickie or Jacob patrolling? She peered closer and gasped. A shiver of fear trickled over her skin. Men were running about with lighted torches. They were burning the crops!

'No!' she yelled.

Max jumped in bed and winced. 'Caroline?'

'They're burning the fields!' She grabbed her dressing gown and raced from the bedroom. 'Thomas! Thomas!' She ran into his room but found it empty. She dashed down the staircase, nearly tripping on her dressing gown hem.

Thomas came out of the drawing room, holding a brandy glass. 'Caroline?'

'They're setting fire to the crops. Hurry!' She rushed to the front door and unlocked it.

'Christ!' Thomas ran past her and outside into the night.

The smell of burning filled Caroline's nose. She ran after

Thomas, seeing Jacob and Dickie running down the drive. Prince and Duke were running alongside them but sensing their mistress, they came straight to her, ready to protect her.

'Caroline!'

She turned to see Trixie coming out of the house and running towards her. 'Get the others! Fill buckets of water,' she yelled at her.

Smoke clouded over the wheat heads like a rolling mist. Caroline squinted in the dim light at the figures ahead. Men were shouting. Someone was on horseback, circling the other men, giving orders. Prince barked and Duke growled deep in his chest.

The closer Caroline came to the mayhem, the angrier she became. How dare they destroy everything Max had created? The harvesting of this field was to begin in the morning.

Jacob was whacking at the flames with his jacket. Dickie had broken off a tree branch and was doing the same. However, the flames nearest to them was nothing compared to the long line of fire stretching right across the field. The rogues were continuing down the field lighting more spot fires.

Caroline hurried to where Thomas was running after the man on horseback. She screamed at Jacob and Dickie to help. Prince and Duke sprinted ahead. 'Prince! Duke! Come behind!'

The night sky glowed orange and yellow as the flames crackled and leapt, feasting on the dry wheat crop. There was no stopping the blaze as it ripped through the acres at lightning speed.

Thomas was shouting, swearing. He grabbed one of the men, but the scoundrel twisted on Thomas, brandishing the flaming torch in Thomas's face.

Jacob and Dickie overtook Caroline, and they joined in the fighting, each knocking a man to the ground. Prince leapt at one man, tearing into his arm while Duke took the leg of the man fighting Jacob.

Caroline picked up a dropped torch and raced forward to

where Thomas was trying to drag the rider off the horse at the edge of the field.

She waved the torch in front of the horse, and it reared back on its hind legs. The rider tried to keep in the saddle, but on the second rear, he lost his grip and landed with a grunt on the ground. Thomas dived on top of him and punched him in the face. The rider's hat fell off, but he wore a black handkerchief over his face. Thomas pulled the handkerchief down and they wrestled.

'You bastard!' Thomas yelled, full of rage. He grabbed the man by the coat and hauled him up, but the rider was taller and stronger. The rider spun Thomas around in a headlock and suddenly put a revolver to his temple.

Caroline froze.

Wayland.

'Not so cocksure now, are we, cousin?' Wayland drawled. His eyes triumphant. 'Do you like my new piece of fun?' He waggled the revolver against Thomas's head. 'It is American, a colt. Very fine. I had it sent to me from New York.'

'Don't do anything foolish, cousin,' Thomas muttered.

'Keep still or I will put a bullet through your brain,' Wayland counselled.

The three of them didn't move. Time had stopped.

'Please, Wayland, let Thomas go,' Caroline begged.

'Shut your pretty mouth,' Wayland cautioned. 'I would rather shoot you than Thomas, but I shan't hesitate to kill you both.'

Caroline was sure her heart would burst from her chest. Then she heard Max calling her name. How had he managed to get down the stairs in his weak state?

Prince and Duke came running to her and dropped at her feet, panting, but on alert, their eyes never leaving Wayland. Prince whimpered in eagerness to attack Wayland and Duke growled.

'Do not try to run,' Wayland warned her. 'If those dogs come at me, I will shoot them and then you.'

Standing perfectly still, even though her knees felt weak enough to make her topple over at any moment, Caroline silently begged for Max to stay at the top of the field with the others. That he was even out of bed in his condition, frightened her nearly senseless.

'Let me go, Wayland,' Thomas demanded.

Wayland tapped the end of the revolver on Thomas's temple. 'You are in no position to order me about, dear cousin.'

'Put the gun down, please,' she pleaded to the man she hated most in the world. Duke took a step, but she clicked her fingers to stop him.

Wayland glared at the dog. 'Not yet. Let us wait for Max, shall we?'

'He's injured. You won't touch him,' Caroline said fiercely. She would protect her husband with every ounce of her strength.

'Yes, I am aware. Shame Grover did not finish the job properly.' Wayland's stare never left hers. 'That is my fault for sending a fool to do a complicated job.'

'You have gone too far this time, Wayland,' Thomas murmured.

'Shut up.' Wayland tightened his hold on Thomas's throat making him gargle. Thomas's eyes bulged.

'Leave him!' Caroline stepped forward, the dogs with her.

'Stay where you are!' Wayland adjusted his grip on the revolver.

'Caroline!' Jacob was the first to reach them. His lip was bleeding and his shirt torn. On seeing Wayland, he stopped and turned to run back to Max.

'Not so fast!' Wayland advised.

Jacob remained where he stood.

Max hobbled into the flickering light of the torch Caroline

still held. He nodded as if to himself. 'I did wonder if it was you behind all of this.'

'And you wondered correctly.' Wayland grinned. 'Now, since we are all here,' he joked. 'Shall we begin?'

'Begin what?' Max spoke quietly, held himself stiffly. Blood soaked through his nightshirt from his stab wounds. Caroline sensed his rage.

'Stating my terms,' Wayland said joyfully.

Caroline speculated if he was mad.

'What would they be?' Max lifted an eyebrow as though it didn't bother him in the slightest that his brother had a gun to his head.

'This place, Grange Lea. You are to sign it over to me. It is mine by right. It belongs to my mother.'

'Aunt Lucille gave it to me.' A muscle clenched in Max's jaw.

'Mother had no right to do that. It is part of my inheritance when she dies.'

'Do you not have enough?'

Flames crackled closer to them as the fire spread down the field. The roar of the blaze grew louder.

'A gentleman can never have enough,' Wayland boasted, raising his voice. 'Now. Let me be clear. When the sun rises, we will travel into Lincoln and meet with your solicitor to have the deeds transferred into my name.'

Max folded his arms. 'And if I decide not to do that?'

Wayland grinned evilly. 'Then I will continue to wreak havoc in your life.'

'I will take my chances on that then.' Max gave him a nod of dismissal. 'Good night, Wayland.'

'Do not dare to mock me!' Wayland snarled. 'I will have Grange Lea, and I will destroy *you*.'

'*Why?*' Max shouted. 'You have more wealth and properties than you know what to do with. Why do you need my home?'

'Because you have it,' Wayland replied airily. 'And because you beat me so viciously that I nearly died.'

'I doubt that,' Max scoffed.

'I have suffered from headaches ever since that day. I was in bed for a week. You broke my nose, some of my ribs, knocked out a tooth and left me with severe pains in my head that have me bedridden whenever they occur.'

Max shrugged. 'Well, perhaps that is fate, cousin, for raping Caroline, and God knows who else in your life you have brutishly harmed. You have paid me back by destroying my stock and nearly having me killed.'

'You believe we are even now?' Wayland laughed like someone demented. 'Oh no. We are not even. I have seen the letters you have written to family friends and acquaintances. You have driven people away from me. Do you think I would allow that to happen and not punish you in return?'

'I merely warned some friends of your behaviour.'

'What did you write to my mother? Whatever it was she will not believe a word of it. *I am her son.*'

Caroline flinched. For she had sent a letter to Lucille and told her exactly what Wayland had done, not Max.

Max sighed in frustration. 'What do you plan to do, Wayland? I will never sign Grange Lea over to you.'

'Then I shall simply take everything else you have.' Wayland abruptly pointed the revolver at Caroline. 'Starting with her.'

'No!' Max shouted.

The revolver blasted.

Caroline screamed. Max knocked her to the ground. The revolver blasted again. Caroline couldn't see anything for Max laid on top of her, burying her under him, protecting her with his body.

Another shot ricocheted around the field.

Was Wayland killing them all?

She couldn't breathe. Had she been shot? Why couldn't she feel any pain?

The revolver blasted again.

Someone was screaming. Trixie? Oh, dear God!

Yelling and cries filled the air.

She could smell blood. She squirmed and pushed at Max who limply rolled off her.

'Max!' She gasped, seeing the blood seeping through his shirt. 'Max! No!' Fear took her breath away. Had Max been shot and not her?

'Caroline!' Trixie fell to her knees beside her. 'Are you hurt?'

'I don't know! No... The bullet missed me. Max! Is he dead?' Her chest constricted in horror. She pulled Max into her arms, crying. She couldn't lose him. 'Trixie, help me.'

Suddenly, Trixie stood, a hand over mouth, staring.

Caroline followed her gaze. Jacob stood holding the revolver. At his feet were two bodies. Wayland's eyes were open in death. Blood seeped from the wound in his neck. Next to him lay Thomas. His waistcoat was ruby when it should have been silver.

Dazed, Caroline gazed down at Max. The blood on his shirt came from his stab wounds which had reopened, but he was breathing. Alive. His eyes flickered, and he groaned. 'Stay still,' she told him.

'Caroline.' He winced as he moved. 'Are you hurt?'

'No.' She checked him over. 'The bullet missed you, but you've opened up your stitches. You must have passed out from the pain as you knocked us to the ground.'

Max grunted, his face full of agony. 'I will survive.' He turned his head and saw his brother. 'Thomas!'

'Wait, Max.' She wanted to shield him from the sight of Thomas bleeding to death.

'Get help!' Max yelled, crawling to his brother across the grass. 'Thomas!'

Caroline helped Max to Thomas's side.

Max cradled Thomas's head on his knees. 'Lie still, my brother. A doctor will soon be here.'

Thomas's eyes rolled in his head. 'Max.'

'Hold still, Thomas. Save your strength.'

'Trixie…' A trickle of blood ran out of the corner of Thomas's mouth.

Max yelled for Trixie, but she was already standing behind him.

Slowly she came around the other side of Thomas and knelt down. 'I'm here.' She took his hand.

'So sorry.'

'Don't talk now,' she crooned, tears running down her cheeks.

'Always loved you…' Thomas made a gurgling sound in his throat and then his eyes closed, and his body sagged.

'Thomas!' Max shook him. 'God, no!'

Trixie bowed her head with a sob.

Caroline put her arms around Max to comfort him as he held his dead brother.

They stayed that way for some time.

'I had no choice…' Jacob kept repeating to no one. 'Wayland had shot at Caro, and then at Thomas… I thought he would shoot us all…'

'It was self-defence. I saw it all happen as I ran down,' Dickie was saying to him. 'If you hadn't grabbed the gun, that fella would have killed someone else, I swear my life on it.'

'I'll hang for this.' Jacob swayed.

Caroline raised her head from Max's shoulder and saw the anguish in Jacob's face. Carefully, she rose to her feet.

Nessie came to Caroline. 'Let me help you, madam.'

Stunned by what had happened, Caroline needed to take control of the situation. 'Dickie. Go to Lincoln. Fetch the constable.'

'Now?'

'Yes, lad, now. Be quick about it.' She walked over to Jacob, the revolver hanging from his hand. He gazed at her with torment in his eyes. 'You did a good thing, Jacob,' she soothed. 'Wayland would have killed us all if he had the chance.'

'I'll swing from a rope, Caro,' he whispered in shock.

'No. I won't let that happen to you.' Carefully she took the revolver from his hand and dropped it to the ground. 'Sit down for a moment.' She gently pushed him down to the grass at the edge of the charred field. 'Take some deep breaths.'

Beyond them the fire reached the end of the field, stopped by a water ditch. Flames sparked and flickered in certain areas. The smell of burnt wheat and smoke grew stronger now she focused on it, but the fire remained contained within the field boundaries and she was thankful no wind could cause the flames to jump the ditches and devour the next crop.

In the distance a pale pink streak fringed the horizon. She sighed heavily, her heart broken for Max, for Thomas.

'Madam?' Nessie came to her. Behind her stood Rosanna and Jeannie, their nightgowns blackened with soot from fighting the fire.

'Rosanna, go and make some strong tea with plenty of sugar. Jeannie fetch some blankets.' Caroline rubbed her forehead. She was so very tired.

'I'll start the milking, madam, so I can be finished for when the police arrive and want to ask me questions.'

'Questions?' Caroline frazzled mind didn't understand.

'The constable will want to know what occurred here and we'll all be asked questions.'

'Yes, of course.'

Nessie lightly touched, Caroline's arm. 'Jacob shot Wayland in self-defence. He saved lives. That is what the constable needs to hear.'

Caroline stared at her and realised she spoke the truth. Jacob had saved them by wrestling to get the gun away from Wayland.

She glanced at where Jacob sat on the ground, head bowed, his hands hanging between his drawn knees. 'Yes, he saved us. Jacob is good at doing that.'

CHAPTER SEVENTEEN

*M*ax sat in the drawing room that was full of people. The pain from his opened stab wounds throbbed throughout his body and he felt the need to vomit but by sheer will he managed to avoid doing that in front of everyone. He'd argued with Caroline, who insisted he went to bed, but he needed to be downstairs and be a part of what was happening.

All who lived at Grange Lea had to stay in the drawing room while Constable Wells and his superior officer, Robinson, conducted their investigation. No one spoke unless addressed by a policeman. They all stood or sat about the room in silence until it was their turn to be questioned.

Max held a cup of tea that Caroline had forced on him, but he couldn't drink it. He watched her now, his beautiful wife, her face set like granite as she kept her emotions in check and made sure everyone had tea to drink, or brandy if preferred. Every so often she would look at him, checking to see if he was coping with his pain. He loved her more than life. Wayland could have killed her. How the bullet had missed them both he'll never know, but that they had come so close to being dead chilled him to the marrow.

Instead of their deaths, Thomas had paid the final toll.

Upstairs lay the body of his dear brother. They very idea of that made his head spin.

Thomas.

His funny, kind and loving brother was no more. Never again would they share an evening of talking, drinking, and discussing ideas. Never again would they ride together and debate over farming techniques. Never again would his brother make him laugh or sigh at his antics.

Max blinked away the sting of tears. Now wasn't the moment to give into his grief. That would come later when he was alone.

He'd listened to Jacob and Dickie give their versions of events, as well as Trixie and the three maids, who'd all witnessed the scene. Yet he still couldn't fathom it. Wayland had killed Thomas.

'Mr Cavendish.' Robinson and Wells came to stand before him.

'I am afraid I cannot rise,' Max told them. 'My wife will give me a tongue lashing if I try to move from this chair.'

'No, please, stay seated.' Robinson took the chair opposite him.

Wells glanced worriedly across at Caroline. 'I've already been on the receiving end of your wife's… displeasure once this morning. I don't care to repeat it.'

Max nearly smiled. 'My wife will protect those who she loves with the fierceness of a lioness.'

'Indeed.' Wells scowled.

Robinson coughed behind his hand to draw the attention back to him. All eyes turned to him. Robinson nodded to Wells and flipped through his notebook. 'We have questioned everyone who was in the field this morning. They all say the same thing.' He read from his notebook. 'This morning at dawn, in the lower field of Grange Lea, Lord Wayland Stockton-Lee held Mr Thomas Cavendish in a strangle hold while brandishing a revolver. His lordship had aimed his weapon at Mrs Caroline Cavendish and fired to kill her. Fortunately, you, Mr Maxwell

Cavendish, knocked her out of the way and the bullet missed. Your brother, Mr Thomas Cavendish, now unrestrained by his lordship's hold, then lunged for the weapon. His lordship fired and shot Thomas Cavendish, causing his death. His lordship then aimed the revolver back at Mrs Cavendish and yourself, but Mr Jacob Adams fought with his lordship and in the process the revolver fired, and his lordship was fatally wounded.' Robinson looked up from his notes to Max. 'My colleague and I regard the death of Lord Stockton-Lee as a misadventure.'

There was a collective gasp in the room.

'Misadventure?' Max repeated.

'Death by misadventure, that's correct,' Wells said unwaveringly. 'His lordship brought this awful business upon himself.'

Max had fully expected them to arrest Jacob for murder. He glanced at Jacob who looked as white as a sheet. Trixie held his arm and Max wondered if it was to keep the man from falling in shock.

Robinson closed his notebook. 'Our report to the Justice of the Peace, Mr Cornellius Smedge, in Lincoln will state that Lord Stockton-Lee committed murder on your brother with intent to commit murder on Mrs Cavendish and yourself. The revolver firing as Mr Adams fought to wrestle it from him was the cause of his lordship's death. Mr Adams, in our minds, is innocent. I would think Mr Smedge will say the same with our report findings and the witness statements. I expect Mr Smedge to dismiss the case from going to court.' Robinson lowered his voice. 'Mr Smedge is also my brother-in-law.' His slight nod told Max all he needed to know.

Max sighed in relief. 'Jacob saved my wife, and us all. He does not deserve to be tried in court.'

'He won't be,' Robinson stated with confidence. 'My findings are the gun was fired by his lordship's own hand in the struggle. He shot himself.'

'Indeed. Mr Adams is a hero,' Wells added.

Robinson sniffed with disdain at Wells before giving Max his attention again. 'My aim is to keep this whole incident quiet. My constables have not covered themselves in glory throughout this event. They should have done a better investigation when you first brought the matter to us. I apologise sincerely for that. They should have acted quicker, more thoroughly and had a result long before now. Instead, I'm ashamed to say they were lax in their judgement about how serious this affair was. I have no wish to broadcast this to the public and show the weakness of my team.'

Wells shuffled his feet, heat suffusing his whiskery face.

'My cousin was a lord. His death will draw attention.' Max hated the thought of what the newspapers would make of it all.

'Yes, that's true, but we will do our very best to keep the news of the incident from spreading. I have friends at the *Lincolnshire Chronicle* and will tell them that his lordship died from a shooting accident and no more. We will also find Grover and his accomplice and get their confessions with regard to his lordship paying them to cause criminal damage to your livestock and farm, as well as confessing to your stabbing.'

'How do you plan to get them to confess, should you find them?' Max asked, not convinced of their success to find Grover.

'We have our ways, Mr Cavendish. Murder has been committed by Lord Stockton-Lee. Those men are his accomplices and in his pay. Such a serious matter as this must be given every resource at hand to complete the investigation.' Robinson rose and tucked his notebook in the breast pocket of his jacket. 'Did your cousin have a next of kin?'

'My aunt. She lives in India. My cousin's solicitors are in London. I have the details.'

'No need for them right now. I'll send a constable to you this afternoon to get the details. Oh, and the body? Burial?'

Max flinched. 'I will see to the burial.'

'Would you care for me to call in at an undertaker's office on my way back to the station and ask them to call on you? They can take your cousin to the morgue if you wish it? Your brother as well.'

'I would appreciate that very much. Though my brother will stay here.'

Robinson stood and held out his hand to Max. 'We shall take our leave now but will keep you updated on our progress.'

Max shook his hand. 'Thank you. I appreciate that you have dealt with this morning's incident with speed and consideration.'

'I'm sorry it came to all this. If we'd done a better job of catching Grover all this might have been prevented.'

'No, it would not, I am afraid to say. My cousin was intent on destroying me. Killing my wife would have been the only thing to give him satisfaction.'

'Your cousin sounds like a man with a disturbed mind.' Robinson nodded and glared at Wells. 'If my men had done their duties to the best of their abilities… Let us just say, things may have turned out differently.'

Max gave no reply to that. Clearly Wells and the other constables hadn't taken this matter seriously until it was too late. If they had done more, found Grover, got him to reveal Wayland's involvement maybe, just maybe, Thomas might still be alive.

Constable Wells stood in front of Max. 'My condolences, Mr Cavendish.'

Max reluctantly shook his hand. 'Perhaps next time you will be more exhaustive in your duties when someone asks for help?'

'Yes, sir.' Wells couldn't meet his eyes.

When they'd left, Max sagged against the back of the chair, his wounds throbbed like hell. He managed a smile as Caroline came to him. He held her hand as she stood beside his chair. They faced the others, who were all still in a state of shock. 'Now the police are gone, let me say how much I appreciate what you have all done for me, for us,' Max told them, looking at each person. 'We are safe now.'

'Is it true I won't be charged?' Jacob asked, his face pale.

'I believe you will not be charged, Jacob. Misadventure will be reported and likely the case will be dismissed by the Justice of the Peace. My cousin shot himself is what the police report will say. We have all given witness statements to that fact.'

Jacob's legs gave out from under him and Trixie and Dickie rushed to hold him up.

'Help him to his cottage, Trixie,' Max suggested. 'Take care of him.'

The other staff followed them out, leaving Max alone with Caroline.

Tears sparkled in her green eyes as she knelt beside him. 'I'm so relieved. I thought they would charge him with murder.'

'The police have not done well in this instance. Robinson wants the matter ended and kept quiet. The less noise made about his men and their incompetence the better, I suspect.'

'I don't care about his men or their reputations. If they had acted sooner Thomas would still be alive.'

He caressed her cheek, wiping away a fallen tear. 'Thomas paid the price of Wayland's vindictive mind.'

'We have all paid the price in one way or another, but Thomas... Thomas didn't deserve to die because of that evil swine.'

'No.' Max's chest swelled with grief. 'I cannot believe he is gone.'

'I'm so sorry, my love. I am responsible. If Wayland and I had never crossed words back in Melliton...'

'No. None of this is your fault. My cousin was malicious, selfish and a cad of the highest order. He brought all of this upon us. I am grateful he is dead. I just wish he had not killed my brother.' Hot tears burned his eyes. A sob lodged in his throat.

'Oh, my darling.' Caroline held him tightly and he let the emotion out. He cried for his brother, who he had loved and looked out for since the moment Thomas was born.

After a few minutes, he dried his eyes and kissed Caroline gently.

She stared at him with such love in her eyes. 'You mean everything to me. I can't bear to see you suffering.' She kissed him and he wished he could take her to bed and make love to her, but his wounds prevented that. The slightest movement and his body ached severely.

Instead, he kissed her again before resting back in the chair to find a more comfortable position that didn't hurt his injuries. 'The undertakers will arrive this afternoon. We need to select Thomas's best suit.'

'His grey one with the grey and blue embroidered waistcoat and blue cravat. He liked to wear that.' She gripped his hand. 'Will we bury him beside Mussy?' Her voice broke saying Mussy's name.

'Yes. They can keep each other company,' he tried to joke.

She gave him a watery smile. 'Mussy will look after Thomas. They liked each other.'

'Imagine the stories they will be telling one another?' A tear slipped out and ran down his cheek. He brushed it away. 'We must buy more plots next to them, so we are all together.'

She nodded. 'Agreed. Only, I hope it's a long while before they are filled.' She paused. 'Where will you bury Wayland?'

'At Misterton Abbey with his ancestors.'

'He hated the abbey.'

'That is not my problem. Besides, it is rather fitting, really. He took my brother from me. So, I shall lay Wayland to rest in the place he hated most.'

'Don't let anger eat away at you,' she said sadly. 'Wayland will win otherwise.'

He understood her meaning, but he couldn't help experiencing a spark of satisfaction that Wayland would be at the abbey. 'I will write to Reeves at the abbey and inform him to prepare for Wayland's arrival.'

'Will you accompany the body?'

Max took a deep breath. 'No. I should, at least for Aunt Lucille's sake, but I would be a hypocrite. To stand beside Wayland's grave and pay respects? I did not respect him.'

'Then don't go. You have enough to deal with regarding Thomas's funeral.'

'I will organise for Wayland's body to be sent by train to York. Reeves can engage the undertakers from that side.'

'I have something to confess,' Caro said suddenly. 'I found the letter your aunt wrote to you about the fight you had with Wayland. I couldn't let her believe you were not the person she thought you were. So, I wrote to your aunt and told her everything.'

That statement shocked him. He had tried to keep his aunt out of Wayland's sordid business to shield her from hurt, and he wanted to protect Caroline.

'Are you angry with me?'

'No, my darling, only sad that my aunt will learn the ugly truth about her only child, and soon she will receive another letter informing her about his death.'

'None of which was your doing,' she reminded him. 'Wayland was a monster. You could have easily died this morning alongside Thomas.'

'True, and so could have you. At one stage I thought I had lost you,' he murmured, bringing her hand up to kiss it. 'I never want to go through that again.'

'I thought the same when you passed out knocking me to the ground. Are you in a lot of pain?'

'Some.'

She snorted. 'Some? That means a great deal then, doesn't it?'

He couldn't argue with her. He was too exhausted by the pain. His bandages were soaked with blood.

She peered at his shirt. 'You're bleeding again. I need to change the bandages.'

'I think I need new stitches, my sweet.' He grimaced as she helped him to stand. The two stab wounds had stopped bleeding after Caroline had bandaged him tightly when they got back to the house, but he knew they had opened again and would need more stitches. He prayed they wouldn't get infected. He doubted he had the strength to fight another fever.

'I'll send Dickie for Matthew.'

'No, Matthew needs to sort out his affairs in Doncaster. Send for a doctor from Lincoln. I just need a stitch or two and I shall be fine again.' He had to believe that. There was an urgency for him to regain his strength again, and soon. Caroline need him fully fit, so did Grange Lea. He'd lost an entire field, acres of wheat, on top of all his other loses. He had to quickly rebuild his finances to pay his debts before the bank started to send out notices of foreclosure.

CHAPTER EIGHTEEN

On a rainy September day, Caroline and Trixie waited on the station's platform as the train steamed and hissed to a screeching halt. They stretched their necks and stood on tiptoes to see over the heads of waiting people as the doors opened and passengers disembarked.

'Is that them?' Trixie lurched forward, but then stopped. 'No.'

'Oh, they're over there!' Caroline saw Elsie first, stepping off a carriage at the end of the train. 'Trixie, this way.'

'Trixie! Caro!' Elsie ran up the platform with Bertha close behind. They all hugged and laughed.

'You've been gone over a month, and you've both grown an inch for sure,' Trixie said in awe.

'Annie.' Caroline embraced the older woman. 'How are you?'

'Aye, I'm fine, lass.' She patted Caroline's arm. 'Better than you I suspect?'

'It's been a trial for certain,' Caroline admitted. 'Let's get your luggage. It's so busy here today. Jacob stayed with the carriage as they're queued up out on the road.'

Trixie took the girls' hands. 'Give me your luggage ticket,

Annie. The girls and I will get the luggage and find a porter. You go with Caroline to the carriage.'

'How's Mr Cavendish?' Annie asked as they exited the station.

'Recovering. He won't rest, of course.'

'And the funeral went all right?'

'Funerals are funerals, aren't they? Sad. We buried Thomas next to Mussy. It was the last day of sunshine before the rain arrived. It's been stormy weather for a week now.'

They reached the carriage and Jacob climbed down to assist them into it. A few minutes later Trixie and the girls arrived with a porter pulling a trolley with their luggage, which Jacob loaded and tied to the top of the carriage.

'Caro, the girls and me are going to spend a few hours in town,' Trixie said, coming to the open door. 'You don't mind, do you?'

'No, spend some time together. They'll have so much to tell you. I'll send Dickie back for you.'

'No, don't bother, I'll hire a hansom when we're done.' Trixie took the girls hands again, and they wandered off up the street towards the centre of town.

'She's missed them,' Caroline said to Annie as Jacob guided the horse out onto the road.

'Aye, and they missed her, but they were such good girls for me. So helpful. They played with their old friends a lot but always gave me a hand whenever I needed them.'

'Are you sad the cottage has sold and not rented out as you planned?'

'I'm not sad in the slightest. I got a good price for it from a retired teacher who didn't want to live in York anymore. Now, I can pay to have my own little cottage built next to Jacob's, with Mr Cavendish's kind permission. In turn, when I die, I hope Elsie and Bertha can live there when they're older. By then Trixie and Jacob could do with some peace no doubt.'

Caroline twisted in her seat. 'Didn't Trixie write to you and tell you they aren't getting married?'

'What?' Annie looked shocked. 'No, not a word of it. What happened?'

'Trixie and Thomas…' Caroline hoped Annie would get the hint.

'Goodness.' Annie clearly got the hint. 'Well, I never thought she would, not with him. He'd made it plain that she wasn't wife material.'

'It was one time. When Max was very ill, and Thomas was upset.'

'One thing led to another.' Annie nodded.

'She told Jacob.'

'And lost him over it. Silly girl.' Annie sighed. 'I'm sad for her. Jacob is one of the better men I've met in my long life.'

'It's done now. Not that either of them are happy. Trixie has come to realise Jacob is the one she loves.'

'And naturally, Jacob being a man, is pig-headed and won't reconsider in taking her back?' Annie huffed. 'A foolish pair.'

'Exactly.' Caroline grinned. 'It's good to have you home.'

'I feel the same, lass. I missed you all.' Annie's eyes narrowed. 'I'll pull my weight on the farm or around the house. There's no fear of that.'

'Don't worry about any of that.'

'Nonsense. I'm not dead yet. I'll do my bit, help in the kitchen or the laundry, even the dairy if Nessie lets me.'

'Huh, Nessie barely lets *me* in there.' Caroline laughed, and it felt good to laugh again. There'd been so much worry and sadness in recent months that she'd forgotten how to laugh.

When they arrived home, Jacob took Annie's luggage up to the attic bedroom she was to share with Nessie until her cottage was built. He put the girls' bags in their room before joining Max and Dickie out in the fields. Despite the drizzle of rain, the harvested fields, including the burnt acres, needed to be ploughed and fertilised.

Caroline made Annie and herself a cup of tea in the kitchen. Rosanna was in the laundry shed with Jeannie ironing the weekly washing. A task Rosanna complained about, saying she was a kitchen maid, but Caroline refused to consider hiring another maid when Max needed all the money he could get to buy live-stock and seed.

'Are you hungry?' Caroline asked Annie. 'There's some pork pie. Trixie made it yesterday and fresh chutney as well.'

'Oh aye, that'll do nicely.'

Caroline entered the larder to get the pie when an awful smell made her gag. 'Oh!' She retched again.

'What is it, lass?' Annie came in and screwed up her nose. 'Lord above what is that?'

Caroline retched again, her eyes watering. 'The bacon. It's been left on the shelf.'

'Aye.' Annie took the offending meat. 'Why isn't it hanging up in a bag down in the cellar where it's cold?'

Retching again, Caroline took a moment to catch her breath and wipe her wet eyes. 'Rosanna hasn't put it away, the lazy piece!'

'Well, she'll not be getting away with any idleness now I'm back. She needs to smarten her ideas up and no mistake.' Annie took the offending meat into the scullery. 'I'll take it to the midden.'

'No, take it to Rosanna and she can throw it in the midden.' Caroline retched again. The rotten smell stuck in her nose. She was about to retch yet again when Matthew walked through the scullery door.

'Now that's a welcome I don't get every day.' He laughed.

'Matthew!' Surprised, she embraced him happily. 'You never mentioned you were coming in your letter that arrived yesterday.

We were just now at the station ourselves. Annie and the girls have returned from Melliton.'

'Forgive me for not sending word ahead. I wrote that letter to answer your letter telling me about Thomas. I'm so sorry I was away while you were going through such an ordeal. It's been a hectic few weeks.' He gazed at her. 'How are you?'

'Coming to terms with it.'

'And Max?'

'Doing well.'

'But could rest more, yes?' Matthew added.

'Definitely. He's out in the fields every day, or at markets bargaining for stock. He won't sit still for more than a few minutes.' She gently pulled him to the table. 'Sit and I'll fetch you a cup of tea.'

'And is all that ghastly business with Wayland over? No trial?'

'No trial. The verdict was misadventure by the Justice of the Peace, and he never sent the case to court. We are extremely relieved that not one of us had to give statements before a judge. Senior Constable Robinson handled it all.' Caroline poured him a cup of tea.

'You all must have had a shocking time of it.'

'We have, but I fear Jacob is taking it the worst. He is adamant it was his hand that pulled the trigger that killed Wayland. We have no way of knowing for sure, mind. Nothing any of us say gives him comfort.'

'Shall I have a word with him?'

'Would you?'

'Absolutely. He is a good man. Wayland was not.'

'How are you?'

'Firstly, why were you retching?'

'Rotten bacon.'

'Ah.' He grinned. 'Could I be a burden and ask to be put up for a few days?'

'Of course, as if you need to ask. We'd be delighted to have you stay. Tell me your news. Your letter that arrived yesterday was short.'

'That is because I wanted to tell you in person. I've gone into partnership with a physician in Lincoln.'

'That's wonderful!'

'He, Doctor Ingles, has an office surgery on Carline Street, opposite the Lunatic Hospital. Doctor Ingles has a position at the Lunatic Hospital as well as his own private patients, but was searching for another doctor to join him and expand the client book. We met at the medical conference in Leicester last week, which was why I couldn't attend Thomas's funeral. I didn't even learn what had occurred until I returned to Doncaster and opened my mail.'

'I did worry something might have happened to you when we didn't receive a reply about the funeral. I was going to send Dickie, but he was ill in bed with a bad tooth. Then Max remembered you mentioning a medical conference when you were last here. I was pleased when your letter arrived yesterday saying you'd been in Leicester, and you were well.'

'Is Dickie all right now?' Matthew took one of the lemon curd tarts that she offered him.

'Yes, he got Nessie to pull the tooth out with plyers. It was a bloody sight apparently, and Dickie nearly fainted with the pain of the extraction, but the swelling in his cheek has gone down and he is eating again. Anyway, tell me more about Doctor Ingles.'

'Edwin is a lovely chap. Older than me, married with a son living in America. We would meet up each day after the lectures had finished, and, over dinner, we'd talk for hours. Three days later, he offered me the partnership.'

'That's brilliant news!' Caroline grasped his hand across the table. 'I'm so excited for you.'

'So, you're stuck with me now. I'll be a constant visitor.'

'Nothing would make me happier.'

'Will you come with me tomorrow to inspect some rooms? If you're not busy?'

'Absolutely. I was going into town anyway for a dress fitting.' She munched on a tart. 'All Trixie's good food is making my skirts too tight.'

Matthew paused in taking another bite. 'Perhaps you're pregnant.'

She winced. 'I'm barren. I told you that once before.'

'That's what you told me, yes, but it might not be true?'

'I was married for two years to Hugh and no baby.'

'Maybe the fault was with Hugh, not you.'

'And then Wayland's attack... No baby came from it.'

'That's hardly surprising. It was one time and traumatic.' Matthew sipped his tea. 'It's something to think about. When was your last monthly show?'

She blushed. 'I can't talk about that with you.'

'Why ever not? I'm a doctor, your family's doctor. I treated Mussy and Max, and anyone else here who needs me. Why not you? So? Your last monthly show, when was it?'

She had to think very hard and couldn't remember. 'I don't know.'

'Before or after your wedding? Have you had anything since the day you got married which was June, wasn't it?'

'Yes, the first day of June...' She tried to think.

'Are your breasts tender?'

Caroline blinked and blushed even more. 'Matthew!'

'Well, are they?'

They were. Max touched them last night in bed and they'd been a little sore. 'That sometimes happens before my monthly show.'

'And your skirts are tight?'

'Yes.'

'Are you tired during the day and not only at night?'

She nodded. 'But it has been a period of upheaval and strain with everything that's been going on. I worry constantly about Max pushing himself too far.'

'And you just retched at the bacon.'

'But it was rotten.'

'Did Annie retch as well? I saw her carrying it across the yard when I arrived.'

'No, she didn't.'

He tapped his fingers on the table. 'We'll measure your waist and do it again in a month's time if you haven't had a show.'

'I can't be with child,' she whispered. 'I'd resigned myself to the fact I was barren.'

'If you got pregnant on your wedding night, or that week, and it's now early September, that makes you three months gone. Another month and you might experience the sensation of fluttering as the baby starts to move. We'll monitor your symptoms for the next few weeks.'

Her heart seemed to stop beating. It couldn't be true. She refused to believe it. 'We can't tell anyone, not yet, not until we're definitely sure. I won't get Max's hopes up.' She wouldn't get her own hopes up either.

'Understandable. Tomorrow, we shall talk with Doctor Ingles and get his opinion, yes?' Matthew drank the last of his tea as Annie walked in with Jeannie, both carrying freshly ironed clothes.

'Yes,' she whispered to him before smiling at Annie. 'Where have you been? The teapot is no longer hot.'

'I've been helping Rosanna and Jeannie with the ironing,' Annie explained her absence. 'The three of us managed to make a good effort of reducing the ironing pile to a few bits, which Rosanna is finishing off.'

'She'll hate that.' Caroline rolled her eyes. 'The girl reminds me constantly that she's a kitchen maid and nothing more.'

'Rosanna will be whatever you tell her to be!' Annie scowled.

'Sit down and rest.' Caroline added more hot water to the teapot.

'We'll take these upstairs first,' Annie said, heading for the corridor.

Matthew stood and opened the door for them.

Annie smiled her thanks. 'It's good to see you again, Doctor.'

'And you, Annie.' Matthew returned to the table. 'Where is Max? I'll go and make my greetings.'

'He and Jacob were ploughing the stubble in the top field today.'

Matthew's eyes were warm. 'Don't worry about what we've just discussed. One way or another we'll soon find out.'

She couldn't reply, her throat closed at the very idea of being with child. Her dearest wish was to have a baby, and she could not let her imagination run away with her until she knew for certain.

The following morning, Caroline rode in the gig with Matthew into Lincoln. They drove around the imposing walls of the castle and down Union Street, where Matthew pointed out the large, long building of the Lunatic Hospital. At the end of Union Road, the view of the town spread out below was magnificent. Caroline still wasn't used to how elevated the north end of Lincoln was to the low south end.

Matthew halted the horse along Carline Street, and they alighted in front of an elegant house of stone with black painted window frames. A gold plague by the door proclaimed *Edwin Ingles, Physician.*

'He said he'd be home today.' Matthew handed her down from the gig. 'But he is in demand at the hospital, which is just over there. We can't see it from this side.' He pointed opposite to a tall brick wall that dominated the street and hid the hospital from view.

The door opened at Matthew's knock. A plump woman wearing an apron gave them an inquiring stare.

'Doctor Matthew Gibb and Mrs Cavendish. We have an appointment with Doctor Ingles.'

'Yes, he is expecting you, sir. Come in.' The older woman led them down a narrow hall and knocked on a door, before opening it wide and announcing them.

Caroline shook hands with Doctor Ingles and liked him instantly. A man in his sixties, she gathered, with receding white hair and spectacles. He had a warm countenance and a strong grip.

'Matthew, you did not tell me you were bringing a lady with you. I would have asked Winnie to stay at home.' Doctor Ingles smiled at Caroline. 'My wife has instead gone to a church meeting.'

'Forgive me, Edwin. I asked Caroline to accompany for two reasons, one to help me choose a suitable abode to rent and the other to ask your opinion on her possible state of pregnancy.'

Caroline baulked at the words, still disbelieving Matthew. She'd hardly slept last night, tossing and turning, her mind whirling with the possibility of being with child.

In the darkness, with Max sleeping soundly next to her, his arm over her waist, she prayed desperately that underneath his hand their baby lay in her womb in safe comfort, but just as quickly, she dismissed the foolish idea and pushed it from her mind.

'Well, indeed I would be honoured to give my view. Would you permit me to examine you, Mrs Cavendish?'

'Yes,' she murmured, feeling flustered.

'Come into this room, if you please, Mrs Cavendish.' Doctor Ingles gestured towards a door on the other side of the room. 'Afterwards, we'll have a nice cup of tea.'

Doctor Ingles was thorough. He asked questions, manipulated her stomach and asked her to urinate into a cup. 'I will keep some of the urine for a few days,' he told her. 'If it develops a film on top, it usually indicates pregnancy. I will also boil some of the urine and if white streaks appear, that will also confirm pregnancy. I will write to you with my findings in two days. Please, get dressed. I will wait for you in the other room with Matthew.'

When Caroline rejoined the men and sat down, Matthew was smiling. 'Edwin confirms my suspicions.'

She stared at him and then at the other doctor. 'You think I'm with child?'

'I certainly do, Mrs Cavendish.' Doctor Ingles beamed. 'I will still test the urine and inform you of my findings, but all your symptoms and what I could feel would suggest you are with child.'

Caroline felt light-headed. 'How can you be completely sure though?'

Matthew took her hand. 'You said you can't remember having a monthly since your wedding.'

'That's true. I was awake most of the night thinking about it and I don't recall having a show since my wedding in June.'

'Well then, trust us, Caro. We have studied medicine for years, and we know what we are doing,' he joked.

No matter what words Matthew uttered, Caroline couldn't believe in them.

She spent the rest of the day in a daze, only functioning enough to help Matthew choose a set of rooms to rent at the top of a terraced house on Westgate near the castle walls. She cancelled her dress fitting at Matthew's suggestion, for if she was with child then she'd need bigger clothes made soon.

'You're in shock,' Matthew said as they drove home with a cold wind at their backs.

'How could I not be?'

'Try to accept it and be happy.'

'I'll not believe it until there is a baby in my arms.'

Matthew grinned. 'You'll believe it when the little fellow is kicking you in the ribs.'

Tears sprang to her eyes, and she looked out over the fields as they headed towards Grange Lea. She would not think of it. She couldn't, for if it was all false, it would grieve her severely.

CHAPTER NINETEEN

Outside the kitchen window, a storm lashed the countryside. Inside the kitchen, another storm was brewing.

Trixie marched into the scullery and glared at Rosanna. 'Where did you put the sack of potatoes?'

'In the larder.' Rosanna kept her back to Trixie and continued to peel the potatoes in the sink.

Anger fired through her veins. 'They go in the cellar. How many times must I tell you? And where is the jug of cream Nessie brought in?'

'I used it in the pudding.'

'All of it?'

'No, I threw the rest into the slop bucket.'

'You threw it away?' She wanted to throttle the girl.

Rosanna tilted her nose in the air. 'It was on the turn and I'm not taking any chances after being blamed for the bacon last week.'

'You ask *me* first, and I'll check whether it's on the turn. That was fresh this morning.' Trixie glanced at Elsie and Bertha, who were at the table cutting up apples gathered from the orchard and tried to calm down. She took a step closer to Rosanna. 'If you still want this position, then smarten up your ways. I'm tired of you constantly shirking your duties and doing whatever you like.'

'I don't shirk my duties. I work hard.'

'When it suits you. And less answering back as well!'

'Yes, Miss Wilkes,' Rosanna answered sulkily.

Trixie knew Rosanna had been flirting with Jacob again. As soon as the girl found out that Trixie and Jacob weren't getting married, she'd been after him like a bitch on heat. Not that Jacob returned her advances. Since the shooting, Jacob had barely entered the kitchen. He worked on the land and stayed in his cottage, eating meals he cooked himself. Trixie missed his presence, his smile, his eyes that used to look at her with such love.

Annie and Nessie came in from outside, their hair in disarray and clothes drenched.

'My that's a storm and no mistake,' Annie declared, taking off her shawl to hang it on a hook.

'I've fires lit in the laundry shed to dry the clothes, but it'll take days in this weather.' Nessie sighed. Lately, she'd taken over the laundry shed as well as the dairy as autumn slowed down the production of milk from the herd. Nessie divided her hours between the dairy and the laundry sheds with Annie helping her. The two had become good friends.

'What's wrong with you, lass?' Annie asked Trixie.

'Nowt!' But her bottom lip quivered, and she was close to tears.

'Now then, lass.' Troubled, Annie led Trixie out into the corridor. 'What's all this?'

'I'm just tired,' she lied. She knew what was wrong with her and the very notion of it frightened her to death.

'Let me and the girls serve dinner tonight. You take it easy. I've noticed that you've been working yourself to the bone recently, always doing something, never sitting still for more than five minutes. You're nothing but skin and bones. You're not eating enough.'

Annie's concern made the tears flow.

'Nay, lass!' Annie held her tight. 'You're scaring me now.'

Caroline came down the corridor and, seeing Trixie in tears, hurried to her. 'What's happened?'

'Nowt.' Trixie clapped a hand over her mouth to stop a wail.

'Something certainly has. You don't cry so easily.' Caroline peered into her face. 'It is about Thomas dying?'

Trixie couldn't say the words.

'Tell me, please,' Caroline cajoled.

'I can't,' she mumbled. Not wanting to admit the truth out loud.

'Come, the three of us will go into the morning room. We won't be disturbed there.' Caroline took Trixie's hand before she could protest.

Once seated in the yellow room, which didn't look so cheery on a cold blustery day, Trixie wiped her eyes. How was she to break it to them?

'Out with it, please,' Caroline said gently.

'I'm having a baby I think,' Trixie blurted out before breaking down into sobs.

'Goodness.' Annie gasped.

After a moment, Trixie raised her head to Caroline, who'd said nothing. 'Caro, I'm so sorry to bring this to your home.'

'It's your home, too,' Caroline said, her voice tight and a strange look shone in her eyes.

'Is it Jacob's?' Annie asked hopefully.

Trixie shook her head and wished with all her heart it was his. 'Thomas is the father.'

Caroline closed her eyes briefly. 'Are you certain you're with child?'

'I've missed my monthly flow twice and if I smell onions cooking, I gag.' Talking about it helped slightly. However, she was still so scared. She was unmarried and carried a Cavendish in her womb. A Cavendish baby! When her dearest friend wanted nothing more than to carry such a baby. Guilt tormented her day and night.

'You mustn't worry,' Caroline managed to say, though her beautiful face was slightly pale.

'What will Mr Cavendish say?' Trixie dreaded him knowing. 'I will leave if he wishes it.'

'He wouldn't do that to you.' Caroline took a deep breath. 'You carry his brother's child. He will want to provide for it.'

'I'm so sorry, Caro,' Trixie cried. 'You're the last person I'd want to embarrass.'

Abruptly, Caroline stood and paced the room. 'I've something to tell you as well. Something I've been hiding from you all...'

'I can guess.' Annie beamed.

Trixie glanced from one to the other. 'What?'

Caroline gave the slightest glimmer of a smile. 'I'm also with child.'

'No!' Trixie jumped up. 'But you're barren.'

'Not any more she ain't,' Annie jested, chuckling. 'I knew it! Your waist is thicker and you've done nowt but eat pickled eggs as if your life depended on it.'

'I've been examined by Doctor Ingles and Matthew and they both agree that I am. Doctor Ingles tested my urine last week and wrote to me three days ago with his verdict that I am.' Caroline seemed ready to faint.

Trixie dashed to her side. 'Oh, Caro! This is splendid news.'

'I really can't believe it,' Caroline whispered to her. 'I'm petrified something bad will happen though, so I've kept it to myself.'

'Mr Cavendish doesn't know?' Annie asked in surprise.

'No. I didn't want to get his hopes up in case I or the doctors were wrong.'

Trixie kissed her dear friend's cheek. 'I'm so happy for you, truly I am, but I'm ashamed for not seeing that you needed me.

I've been so wrapped up in my own misery for weeks that I've failed to be there for you when you've been dealing with this news alone.'

Caroline hugged her. 'You've had your own problems. You should have come to me sooner.'

'And so should you,' Trixie reprimanded. 'We don't keep things from each other.'

'No.' Caroline gripped her hands. 'I wanted to tell you, to tell you both, to talk to someone about it, but I couldn't make it real.'

'That's understandable.' Annie nodded.

'We've both been in denial,' Trixie murmured. 'But for such different reasons. Your baby is desperately wanted. Mine is not.'

'We'll cope.' Caroline squeezed her hand.

Annie smiled. 'Well, now. This is the situation we find ourselves in and we'll deal with it. We've two babies to look forward to, aren't we a lucky household?'

Trixie's stomach swooped in despair. 'I don't think my baby is going to be welcome news. It'll be a bastard. I'll be shunned.'

'I won't let that happen,' Caroline said fiercely. 'Max won't allow you or your baby to be treated differently.'

'But it will be. A dead man's bastard.'

'You will keep it though?' Caroline asked.

'I've not decided.' How could she decide such a thing when her mind refused to acknowledge it?

'Max won't want the child in an orphanage. He'll want to raise it if you don't.'

'You should tell Jacob,' Annie added, her gaze on Trixie. 'The poor man is hurting enough and if he was to hear your news from someone else...'

Trixie sighed heavily. 'I'm dreading it.'

'You tell Jacob, and I'll tell Max.' Caroline took a deep breath. 'Then we can start to plan.'

Trixie and Annie returned to the kitchen, but the sight of Rosanna laughing with Dickie instead of watching the food that was cooking irritated Trixie, and her anger rose. 'Rosanna! Check the oven.'

'I just did,' the maid retorted.

'Don't I have a name?' Trixie barked.

'I checked the oven, *Miss Wilkes.*'

Trixie clenched her teeth. 'Have you finished the potatoes?'

'Nearly.'

'Then go and do that!'

Anne put her hand on Trixie's back. 'Get some fresh air. I'll deal with that one.'

Despite the wind and the rain, Trixie ran outside and across the yard, nearly getting blown off her feet in the process. She hurried into the large barn and stables, hoping Jacob would be in there but the only movement was the horses in their stalls and some chickens sheltering from the rain.

Covering her head with her shawl, she ran down the path between the outbuildings to his cottage. The wind howled as she knocked on the door.

'Trixie?' Jacob ushered her in as the rain lashed them. 'What are you doing out in this?'

'I needed to speak with you.' She took off her shawl. She hadn't been to his cottage since the day she told him she had lain with Thomas.

'Come by the fire.' He moved away the harness he was mending and cleared a chair for her to sit down.

She glanced about the cottage, noting how clean it was. Everything was tidy, sorted, with a cheery fire and on the rug by the hearth, slept Prince and Duke. 'I didn't realise they were in here with you.'

'They have since the weather started to cool. Caroline said it's fine for them to be with me. In the summer months they were always out on patrol at night but since the… since the…'

'Since the accident with Wayland,' she finished for him, her heart breaking at the anguish he still suffered over that incident.

'*Accident,*' he mocked.

'It *was* an accident, Jacob. The revolver fired in the struggle. It could easily have been you who was shot and killed.'

'Only it wasn't me, was it? A man died by my hands.'

'We aren't certain of that. None of us can be.'

'I am.'

'Stockton-Lee deserved to die,' she said with conviction. 'He would have killed more of us if you hadn't wrestled the gun from him.'

'We'll never know, will we?' he said harshly.

'You blame yourself unnecessarily.'

He faced the fire and threw a short log onto the flames. 'What did you want to speak with me about?'

Returning to the reason why she'd knocked on his door, made her knees weak. She couldn't be a coward. Jacob needed to hear her secret. Yet, she'd be hurting him again. It's all she ever did, hurt him, cause him pain.

'I'm not going to like what you have to say, am I?' Jacob murmured, staring down at the flames licking the wood.

'No.'

'Then don't mention it.'

'I have to before you hear it from others.'

'You carry his child, don't you?'

'Yes,' she answered to his back.

'I wish Wayland had killed me. If he'd killed me and not Thomas, you'd have got your lover and a child.'

'Don't say that.' She swallowed back tears. 'I don't want his child.'

'Will you give it away as Jeannie gave hers away? Will I be driving Caroline to the orphanage on a weekly basis again?'

'I've not decided.'

Jacob half-turned to look over his shoulder at her. 'You won't be allowed to give it away. Max Cavendish will want his brother's child.'

'It's not his decision.'

Jacob snorted in contempt. 'Well, either way, you've helped me make up my mind. I'll be leaving here.'

'No!' Her heart leapt in her chest. 'Don't go!'

'How can I stay and watch your belly grow large with his child?' Jacob's face twisted in agony. 'I can't do it.'

'Please, stay. I'll go away.'

'You're being ridiculous. Caroline would never allow you to move away.' He folded his arms. 'You're like Caroline's sister, and then there are the girls. Mr Cavendish can easily replace me.'

'I want you to stay,' she said brokenly. 'I've no right to ask you to, but I couldn't bear it if you left. I love you, Jacob.'

'Sadly, it's too late. You'd best go. I've packing to do.'

She panicked. 'You can't just leave now.'

'No, but I will by the end of the week. I'll speak with Mr Cavendish in the morning. I won't leave him without help. He'll be able to hire someone within a few days. We're at the cattle market tomorrow. He'll be able to speak to some men about the position.'

'Please, don't go,' she begged.

'Good night, Trixie.' He opened the door for her and reluctantly she trudged out into the rain and didn't care how wet she became.

* * *

CAROLINE BRUSHED her long hair in front of the dressing-table mirror. She'd bathed and washed her hair, drying it before the fire in her bedroom, wearing only her nightgown.

The day had been an emotional one. Learning of Trixie's predicament and telling her and Annie about her own baby.

She touched her stomach and imagined her child, finally allowing herself to think of the baby as something real. Matthew predicted a February birth, and it seemed all a little unreal. A dream.

She was scared, of course. Things could still go wrong between now and the birth, and then the birth itself terrified her witless. However, she'd been given this miracle, and she'd do everything in her power to protect her baby in the womb, and to birth it into the world healthy and safe.

She smiled at Max as he entered, loosening his cravat, as he shut the door.

'I missed your bath,' he said, coming to her.

She raised her eyebrows at him. 'I waited as long as I could, but the water grew cold.'

'Forgive me.' He kissed her. 'I was answering letters.'

'We have many engagements coming up this month,' she said. 'I've written dates down on a piece of paper. I'll give it to you tomorrow. I've left it in my desk.'

He took the brush from her and started to make slow strokes down her hair. 'What delights await us?' he asked sarcastically.

'Don't be like that. Our neighbours are good people.'

'True, but it doesn't mean I wish to dine with them every week.'

'And yet, that is exactly what we should do. I do enjoy the Cuthberts' hospitality. Since your stabbing, we've entertained no families here, nor gone to any events we've been invited to.'

'We've been in mourning.'

'True,' she said quietly. 'But it's been a month since Thomas died. A quiet dinner party with a select few neighbours is suitable. I think it would do you good to mingle with other men.'

'I meet with men all the time at the markets and business meetings in town. I had luncheon with my bank manager today.'

'Yes, and how did that go, because you've not told me? At dinner you let me ramble on about Reverend Trott wanting donations for the church roof, and about Mrs Todd losing her prized rooster.'

'You also told me about Nessie burning my best collar when ironing it.' He grinned.

'Ah, yes, accidents happen. Nessie is still learning the ways of the laundry shed.'

'It's good of her to work in there as well as the dairy.' Max kissed the top of Caroline's head. 'Which reminds me, I have written to a farmer I am acquainted with, in Nettleham, I met him at the market the other day and after I told him about your desire for milking goats, he's offered me three of his youngest kids.'

'That is good news. Soon we shall have goat's milk and cheese.' She smiled at him in the mirror's reflection. 'But what of the bank manager?'

Max grew serious. 'He is willing to extend my loan for another year. Thomas bequeathing everything he owns to me, has softened the bank manager's attitude. Once I can sell Thomas's house in Oxford, we'll be in a better financial state. I can use the money to repay some debts and purchase new stock.'

She spun on the stool to face him. 'I'm so pleased. The strain of paying the loan has taken a toll on you.'

'I would rather be in debt and have my brother alive though.' Max sat on the edge of the bed. 'When I first took out the loan, I fully believed it would not be a struggle to pay back. With the wool sale, and the lambs and calves sold at market, and the crop harvest, I could have easily paid the repayments. Only, none of that was possible when Grover and his friend killed the lambs, the pigs, slaughtered four cows and burnt acres of wheat.'

'But it wasn't your fault. Surely the bank understands that?'

'The bank does not care about who is at fault. They simply want their money.'

She went to him and stood between his legs as he wrapped his arms around her waist. 'You weren't to know Wayland would cause us so much torment and destroy what you were trying to build.'

His hands caressed her back. 'Thomas's death has saved Grange Lea. The sale of his townhouse in Oxford will repay my debt. However, the price he paid was too much,' he said sadly. 'I miss my brother.'

She bent and kissed him lovingly, wishing she could heal his pain. 'I have something to tell you,' she whispered against his mouth.

'I hope it is not about Mrs Todd and her rooster.'

She laughed, feeling wonderful at being able to give him this gift. 'I have spoken with Matthew and Doctor Ingles, the latter has examined me and—'

Max reared away from her in horror. 'You are ill? Tell me you are not!'

'No, darling. I'm perfectly well.'

His blue eyes darkened as his gaze searched her face. 'Why did you need to see a doctor?'

She kissed him again and then held his hand over her stomach. 'We have a child to welcome in February.'

The colour drained from his face. 'A child?'

'Our baby.'

'But you're barren. You told me to never expect a child.'

'I thought I was. I truly believed I was.'

'And Matthew and the other doctor are certain?'

'Yes, very much so. My waist has thickened, my breasts are tender at times, and I've had no monthly bleed since our marriage.'

'Nothing at all...' Max blinked rapidly.

'No.'

'A baby. Our *baby!*'

'Matthew says soon I'll experience the baby moving.'

Max stood and gathered her into his arms. 'My love. My precious darling. I cannot tell you how happy you have made me.' Tears filled his eyes, and he kissed her. 'I love you so much.'

She held him tightly. 'And I love you.'

'I am to be a father,' he murmured against her hair.

'You'll be a wonderful father.' She sat on the bed and faced him. 'There is something else I must tell you.'

'More?' He sat beside her. 'What more could there be? Apart from marrying you, this is the happiest moment of my life.'

'It's about Trixie.'

'Trixie?' He frowned.

'And Thomas.'

The happiness seeped from his face. 'What about them?'

'Trixie is expecting Thomas's baby.'

Max's eyes widened. 'Thomas's baby?' He walked to the window and back again. 'Thomas never said a word to me.'

'He wasn't aware of it. Trixie has only realised recently that she's having his baby.'

'Thomas never knew he was to be a father?'

'No.'

'When did they... I mean I was not aware that they were anything more than friends.' He looked confused.

She touched his chest, knowing it was difficult for him to talk of Thomas. 'It was while you were very ill. A night of weakness for them both.'

'I see. When I was recovering, I thought he was acting oddly. He smelled of drink a lot.'

'Yes. After they were *together*, Trixie realised she'd made a mistake and then Thomas suggested that she live in Oxford as his mistress. Trixie didn't take it well.'

'Hell's teeth!' Max fumed. 'What had he been thinking of suggesting such a thing?'

'Trixie knew she didn't love him as much as she thought she did, and it's with Jacob where her heart belongs.'

'But they called off their wedding.' Clarity brightened his eyes. 'Ah, yes I see why now.'

'Trixie told Jacob the truth about being with Thomas. Tonight, she is telling him that she carries Thomas's child.'

'Blast!' Max ran his fingers through his hair and paced the room. 'We will lose Jacob over this. He will not stay and witness this play out before him. What man could?'

'I agree.' She felt desperately sorry for Jacob and will miss him greatly.

'We cannot blame him if he does leave us.'

She shook her head. 'He must find happiness elsewhere.'

'Thomas's child…' Max pondered. 'What will Trixie do?'

'She hasn't decided, but I hope she keeps the baby. Would you allow it?'

'Of course. The child will be my niece or nephew. I could not see it be given to another family to raise.' He stared at her. 'Am I right?'

She went to him and rested her head against his chest. 'Thank you. I knew you would wish for the child to be raised at Grange Lea.'

'Alongside our own child.' His smile returned. 'We will do right by Thomas and give his child every opportunity as our own.'

As they readied for bed, Caroline wondered what Trixie would have to say about Max's involvement in her child's upbringing, but that was something to be discussed another day.

Max pulled her into his arms. 'I have never looked forward to winter coming in all my life,' he joked. 'For at the end of it, our baby will arrive.'

She nestled into his arms, welcoming his kiss, desire rising. At that moment, she was the happiest she'd ever been in her life.

CHAPTER TWENTY

Three days later, Caroline stood in the doorway of Jacob's cottage watching him pack for his new life in York. Prince and Duke were sitting by her feet. 'Will you go to Sarah's?'

'Yes. I've some money saved and I'm going to persuade my sister to move out of the slum quarters she resides in. Once I can find a job, we'll move somewhere better than Walmgate.'

'I'll miss you.'

'And I'll miss you.' He threw another shirt into his bag. 'You'll write to me? I'm not good with my reading but I'm getting better.' He gestured to the shelf of books, Max had lent him. 'I'll miss the ending of *Moby Dick*. It's taken me all year to read it.'

'Take it. Max won't mind.' She took the book off the shelf and placed it in his bag. 'You need to read how the story ends.'

'Really?' Jacob gave the slightest of smiles, but it soon faded. 'Thank him for me. I'm letting him down, but he said he understood my reasons for going.'

'He does. We both do, but it still is hard to accept. You're like family to me and I'd like for you to see my baby grow into adulthood.'

'You're having a baby?' His face registered surprise.

'Yes. Due February.' She still found it amazing to say.

'I'm so happy for you, Caro. Truly, I am.' He looked sad though.

'Thank you. Max appreciated how hard you worked and how diligently you've taken on your role here. No doubt he's told you all that.'

'He has.' Jacob paused slightly. 'I'll always be your family, Caro, and I'll always be grateful for the trust Mr Cavendish gave me to be a manager when I've had no proper schooling. I'm just a slum boy from York.'

'You've never been just a slum boy from York, Jacob.' She embraced him tightly and then let him go. 'You have your references from us both?'

'I do.' He tapped his jacket's inner pocket. He fastened the bag and placed it beside the other one he'd packed earlier. 'I'm all done.'

'I'll walk with you.' The dogs bounded ahead. 'They are going to miss you as well.'

'They're good dogs,' he said fondly.

'They'll be back sleeping in the scullery again and wonder why they're not by your fireside.'

Jacob paused and looked across the bare fields and outbuildings. 'I never thought I'd leave here. It had become a home.'

'It is your home, Jacob.'

'Not anymore.'

'Can't you find it in your heart to stay,' she implored.

'And watch Trixie be a mother to another man's child? No.'

'I thought you loved her.'

'I do.'

'But not enough.'

He frowned at her. 'I would die for her! Christ on the cross I nearly did die for her two years ago!'

'You're leaving her when you know she loves *you*.'

'I can't stay, Caro!' he snapped.

'Why? Because of your pride?' she scoffed. 'How pathetic.' She kept walking, annoyed now.

'You don't understand.' He fell into step beside her.

'I understand well enough.' She shrugged. 'You're not the man I thought you were.'

'Two months ago, I *killed* a man for you all!' he shouted.

Caroline spun back to him. 'Is that it? You can't stay because of what happened with Wayland?'

'I can't stay for lots of reasons.'

'Oh, Jacob.' She leaned against a fence rail, ignoring the cold breeze whistling over the fields and filtering between the outbuildings. 'We've been through a lot you and me and Trixie. All the troubles we had in York with Victor Dolan, you and Mussy in prison, then moving to Hopewood Farm, and you becoming a farmer as though you were born to it. Mussy teaching you to read, then our coming here. Wayland, the beast, brought more strife to our lives. It's been tough. Yet, through it all we stuck together. Me and Trixie, the girls, you, Mussy, Annie, Max, Thomas and Matthew. We watch out for each other. We are family. We've lost Mussy and Thomas. Do we have to lose you as well?'

He hung his head. 'Do you think, in my heart, I want to go?'

'Then don't leave. Stay. Stick it out and see what happens. Don't run away like a coward. Be the man I know you to be. Brave and strong and someone I admire.'

'I can't face it.' He let out a long breath. 'I wanted Trixie to carry *my* child.'

'And she could once you were married. Raise this baby with her and then in the future have your own children. This baby is an innocent and deserves to be loved like any other baby. Raise him or her as your child, with your values. Let it call you father and sit on your knee and give you unreserved love as children do.'

'You make it sound so easy.'

She tutted. 'No one is saying it'll be easy, Jacob. It'll be difficult, but the rewards may outweigh the hard times. All of us are here for you but most of all Trixie will be your wife, and I thought that was what you wanted above all else?'

'I need to think about.'

'Fine.' She threw her hands up. 'Go to York. Stay with Sarah and consider deeply about what you're giving up. A good job, your own cottage, a loving woman and the future of children and happiness.'

His eyebrows drew together. 'Will Mr Cavendish allow me to go away for a few days to think about it, or has he engaged someone?'

'As you know, he's spoken to some men at the markets. You were there, he wasn't taken with any of them.'

'No. He said they were either stupid or lazy-looking or both.' Jacob snorted.

'Exactly. I'll speak with Max. He'll wait until you write to us with your decision, I'm sure of it.'

'I'm not sure I'll change my mind and come back. Thinking about all this for days has driven me to near madness. I can't take much more.'

'I understand. But take some more time. Another week or so. Time in York might make you see things differently.'

'Aye, all right. I'll not keep you waiting long. Thank you, Caro. I appreciate it.' He nodded, and they walked to the gig where Dickie waited to drive Jacob into Lincoln's train station.

Trixie stood at the back door with the others to see Jacob off. She didn't look well, and Caroline knew she wasn't eating or sleeping properly.

Max had said his farewell to Jacob earlier before going to visit the farmer in Nettleham.

Elsie and Bertha ran to him, crying and hugging his waist, begging him not to go. However, he gently pulled himself away and climbed into the gig. With the goodbyes said, and Rosanna openly weeping, Jacob disappeared down the drive.

Caroline prayed she'd see him return again very soon, but honestly didn't know if she would. Perhaps York, his old hometown, would pull him into her familiar streets and he'd never want to stray from them again.

She clicked her fingers to Prince and Duke. She needed to walk. She'd go into South Carlton and pay a visit to Mrs Todd. She needed the old woman's stories to cheer her.

After knocking on the Todds' door and bidding Prince and Duke to sit outside, Caroline smiled warmly at the old woman.

'Well now, Mrs Cavendish, come in.' Mrs Todd invited her inside her farmhouse on the edge of the South Carlton village. 'The wind is growing colder each day.'

'How are you and Mr Todd?' Caroline asked, feeling the warmth of the fire after her walk across the fields in the cold air.

'As to be expected at our grand age. We get by.' Mrs Todd peered at Caroline. 'Ye look a little different, Mrs Cavendish.'

'Do I?' Caroline glanced down at her brown skirt with black piping, one she'd worn many times.

'Ye've a look of contentment,' mused Mrs Todd, putting the kettle over the heat to boil. 'Anything to tell me?'

'What do you guess?' Caroline smiled.

'That there'll be an addition to Grange Lea next year.'

'February,' Caroline said. She couldn't stop smiling.

'Ah, that's nice.' Mrs Todd gave her approval. 'Ye and Mr Cavendish will be lovely parents. That babe will be most lucky.'

'What a kind thing to say.' Caroline didn't know how she'd be able to mention Trixie's child and decided not to bother. She'd deal with telling that piece of news another day.

'Sit down, sit down.' Mrs Todd waved her to an ancient sofa. 'Did I tell ye that Mrs Makepeace next door scalded herself?'

'No, you didn't.'

'Oh, aye. Silly woman. Spilt a kettle of hot water all down

herself, luckily her skirts took the brunt of it. Tripped over her blessed cat, I tell ye. Why she lets it sleep in the house, I've no idea. Cats should be in the barns, mousing as is their job, not sleeping on her bed like some feline queen.' Mrs Todd tutted.

'We have no need for a cat. The dogs keep the mice down.'

'Aye, but they're not as good as cats, who can get up in the roof.'

'True. I shall speak to Max about getting one.'

'Keep it in the barn and don't feed it, or it'll never catch a mouse,' Mrs Todd warned. 'Let the darn thing fend for itself.'

'I will.'

'And did ye hear old Fred Lockier died? No, ye'd not have heard for it only happened last night.'

'Oh, that is sad.' Caroline made a mental note to tell Max. 'We shall attend his funeral.'

'Aye, it's next week, so the reverend told me this morning when I saw him. Fred had no family left. It'll be just village folk.' Mrs Todd mashed the tea. 'He lived a good life, did Fred, but he'll be missed. It means his cottage is empty and who'll move into it, I ask? Another stranger.'

'Oh dear. You've had a few strangers to deal with in the last year, with all of us at Grange Lea.'

Mrs Todd huffed. 'Nay. I'll not be saying anything about that. All of ye at Grange Lea are good people and keep to yeself, no lording it about the village as most gentry can do, or so I'm told that can happen. Mr Cavendish is a generous man, always willing to help one of the farmers out.'

'Just as you helped us with the harvest.'

'What was left of it,' Mrs Todd huffed. 'Imagine Mr Cavendish's very own cousin causing such harm and destruction.'

'Yes, it's been a trying time.'

Mrs Todd handed Caroline a cup of tea. 'Did ye hear about Flossy Munn from North Carlton?'

'No, I don't think I've made her acquaintance.'

'Nor would ye want to, flighty piece. Skipped off with another woman's husband, I tell ye. No better than she ought to be, that one. It's a regular occurrence, her running off. She'll be back, ye mark my words. Her mam is raising her four kids an' all. Imagine having a daughter like that?'

Caroline settled down with her cup of tea and listened to the old woman's gossip, not that Mrs Todd ever gossiped, or so she said, she was simply passing on important news, like the village's very own town crier.

In this farmhouse, Caroline could, for a little while, forget her responsibilities at Grange Lea and simply relax, knowing nothing was expected from her.

She stayed with Mrs Todd longer than she planned. They visited Mrs Makepeace and Caroline bandaged the poor woman's hand where she'd scalded herself. Then, she and Mrs Todd, along with Mrs Makepeace, walked to the church to change the flowers on the altar, replacing them with the last of the summer roses growing against the stone wall of the church. It was late afternoon when she finally left the village.

When she entered the house, she poured some water into a bowl for Prince and Duke and left them in the scullery. In the kitchen, she found Annie at the range basting chickens, while Rosanna was peeling vegetables.

'Oh good, you're back,' Annie said. 'I've sent Trixie up to bed. She looked dreadful. Our Elsie and Bertha have taken up a cup of tea for her.'

'I'll go up. Is my husband home?'

'Not yet.'

Caroline left the kitchen and made her way up to Trixie's bedroom. Inside, she found Trixie sitting on the edge of the bed. 'Annie tells me, you're not well,' she said, walking around the bed to Trixie. Abruptly, she noticed the bloodstain seeping through Trixie's nightgown. 'Trix!'

'It hurts, Caro,' Trixie whispered through gritted teeth.

'Oh, my Lord.' Caroline bent down beside Trixie. 'The baby?'

'Aye. I've such bad cramps.'

'I'll send Dickie for Matthew.'

'The girls. I've sent them out, asked them to find a book to read to me…' Trixie grimaced. 'I didn't know what else to do.'

'I'll see to the girls. Stay right there!' Caroline ran to the door nearly colliding with the girls. 'Elsie, Bertha, Trixie needs to rest.' She turned them about, not letting them into the bedroom. 'Will you both check the eggs for me, please? And Annie might need some help in the kitchen.'

'Jeannie wanted me to help her fold the linen,' Elsie said as they walked quickly along the landing.

'Good, yes, go and help Jeannie.' She gently pushed Elsie in the direction of the servant staircase. 'Bertha, will you check to see if we have any eggs?' She hurried down to the kitchen where she pulled Annie aside. 'She's losing the baby,' she whispered.

'Dear heaven,' Annie murmured low. 'I knew something wasn't right.'

'We need Matthew.'

'Aye.'

Caroline dashed outside and luckily found Dickie in the barn, refilling the lamps with oil. 'We need Doctor Matthew, Dickie. Take the gig.'

Dickie jumped to his feet. 'What's happened, madam?'

'Miss Wilkes isn't feeling well. Hurry now.' She left the barn and was crossing the yard when Max rode in. She hurried to him.

'Caro?' He quickly dismounted Queenie on seeing her distraught face. 'What is it?'

'Trixie. Dickie is going for Matthew. I think she's losing the baby.'

Max hugged her to him and sighed deeply. 'I hope that is not the case. What can I do?'

'Nothing. There is nothing any of us can do.'

'Right, I will fetch Matthew. Dickie can continue with his

work. I would rather do that than sit around. I shall be as quick as I can.' Max led Queenie into the barn and Caroline returned to the house.

'Here.' Annie held out a tea tray. 'Ginger tea. See that she drinks it.'

'Ginger tea?' Rosanna stated from the other side of the table. 'Has Miss Wilkes got her monthlies and cramping?'

Caroline gave the girl a sharp stare. 'Trixie is not feeling well. That's all you need to understand.' She took the tray from Annie. 'Max is fetching Matthew. I'll stay with her. Can you keep the girls down here?'

'Aye. Leave that with me to sort out.'

Upstairs, Caroline found Trixie standing, bent over the washbasin. The water was pink. 'Trixie, get back into bed.'

'I just needed to wash my hands and my legs...' With dark shadows under her eyes, her face the colour of putty, Trixie groaned. 'The cramps, Caro, they're so bad...'

'Take some deep breaths.' Caroline stripped the bed and placed a wad of newspapers and an old towel over the mattress. 'Come, lie down.' She gently helped Trixie to lie down. 'Annie's made you some ginger tea. It'll help with the cramping.'

'I'm losing the baby, aren't I?' Trixie glanced at Caroline. 'This is my punishment for not wanting it. I've lost Jacob as well. I don't care if I die now.'

'Enough of that talk! Max has gone for Matthew. You'll be fine shortly.'

'Can you die from a miscarriage?'

'No!' She snapped not knowing if that was true or not. She'd never spoken about such a thing with anyone before.

'I'm bleeding so much.' Trixie winced.

'Sip the tea,' she encouraged, holding the cup to her lips. 'I'll get more napkins. Are they in this drawer?' Caroline thought she'd seen them once in a bottom drawer under the washbasin.

'Yes.'

'Right, let's get you cleaned up. I'll go and fetch a jug of warm water.'

'Just use cold, I don't care. The smell of blood is making me ill.' Trixie gagged, which made Caroline gag as well.

'Get Annie,' Trixie cried.

Without another word, Caroline once more dashed down to the kitchen.

Annie took one look at Caroline's face and dropped the pan she was holding onto the table and followed her out.

'I'm worried, Annie, there's so much blood.' Caroline fought back her fear.

'You need to sit down. You look as white as my apron!'

'No, I need to help Trixie.' Caroline forced her shoulders back.

In the bedroom, Trixie lay crying, her pale face blotchy. Annie washed her down and between her and Caroline they cleaned Trixie and made her comfortable as best they could.

An hour later, Matthew arrived and shortly afterwards, Trixie's body expelled the baby.

Caroline wanted to sit with her, but Trixie turned towards the wall and wouldn't talk to anyone.

'Let her sleep,' Matthew advised, closing his medical bag. 'I've given her a draught. She needs to rest.'

They went downstairs to the drawing room where Max waited. He took Caroline into his arms to comfort her.

Matthew sat by the fire and Max poured them all a brandy.

'I'd like Trixie to stay in bed for a few days, and then slowly start to get up and sit about. No lifting for a couple of weeks,' Matthew said. 'Although the foetus was tiny, her body still had to expel it, and it'll take its toll. Trixie is thinner than I've seen her before.'

'She's not been eating or sleeping,' Caroline told him. 'Thomas's death, finding out she was with child and then Jacob leaving has deeply affected her.'

'We need to keep a watch on her and not let her decline any further.'

'Decline?' Caroline stared at him.

'If the heart and mind shuts down, nothing a doctor or anyone can do. The will of a person can be very strong in surviving but also dying.'

'Trixie wouldn't give up. She has the girls.'

'She knows the girls would be cared for by you,' Matthew stated, sipping his brandy. 'I could be speaking of something that doesn't happen, and I pray it doesn't. But I've seen people lose the will to live.'

Caroline stood, frightened by his words. 'I'll not let her wither away!'

Matthew looked at her fondly. 'My dear friend, even you cannot always have the answer if someone doesn't want to receive it.'

Caroline's heart banged in her chest. A steely determination entered her core. 'You underestimate me, Matthew.'

Max sighed. 'Darling, no one would ever dare to underestimate you.'

'Trixie won't leave us. I refuse to allow her.' She stormed from the room.

CHAPTER TWENTY-ONE

*D*espite Caroline's intentions, Trixie ate little and slept even less. Three days passed since the miscarriage, and nothing would rouse her from the bed or excite her enough to talk. She lay quiet, staring at the ceiling, not acknowledging anyone. Food trays went back to the kitchen untouched. Elsie and Bertha would sit by her bed and read to her, and she gave no reaction.

Caroline spent hours by her beside encouraging her to eat, to sleep, to recognise her presence. She cancelled dinners with neighbouring farms, sending Max by himself, she didn't visit the village, or go shopping in Lincoln or attend church on Sunday.

'You cannot keep going on like this, my love,' Max said on the fourth day when Caroline declined going to a neighbours' child's christening. 'I want you by my side. We need to keep our friendships with the families of the area. It's important.'

Caroline fixed combs to her hair, pulling it up to secure it away from her face. 'Yes, I understand, and I'm sorry, truly, but I can't leave Trixie in this state.'

He stopped tying his cravat and turned to her. 'Do you think she would do something foolish?'

'I honestly don't know.' Caroline didn't identify with the silent Trixie. The person lying on that bed wasn't her best friend. They'd been through so much together since the day they met and never once had she seen Trixie simply give up. Trixie's spirit was eroding away and for all her talk, Caroline was at a loss as to how to make her well again. 'I've tried everything. Elsie and Bertha have tried, and Annie, and nothing works. Trixie has no interest in life anymore. Matthew is right. A person's will is stronger than we believe.'

'I do not want to sound selfish, darling, but my main concern is you. None of this has been easy on you and I can see how tired you are. There is our baby to think of as well.'

Suddenly, a tiny movement fluttered in her stomach for the first time. 'Oh!'

'What is it?' Concern made his voice high. 'Caroline!' He rushed to her.

'The baby moved, or at least I think I did. Oh, Max.' Her throat choked with emotion. The baby really was real.

He put a hand to her stomach, and she laid her hand over his when the flutter came again.

'There. Can you feel it?'

'No.' He waited but no more movements occurred. 'Soon, soon, I shall feel our child kick.' He kissed her. 'I love you so much.'

'And I love you.' She felt happy and sad. 'We get to share this excitement, but Trixie doesn't. It saddens me so much.'

'Trixie might meet someone in the future,' he said, returning to the mirror to knot his cravat. 'It does not seem as though Jacob is returning. Next week I must advertise for a manager.'

'I honestly thought he would come back to us.'

After breakfast, Caroline kissed Max goodbye as he left for the christening and she gave Jeannie her instructions for the day, before going upstairs to see Trixie.

On the landing she heard crying coming from Elsie and

Bertha's bedroom, Opening the door, she found Elsie sobbing on her bed. 'Dearest one! What's the matter?'

She pulled the girl into her arms and rocked her. Elsie cried so hard she couldn't catch her breath. 'Calm down, calm down,' Caroline soothed. 'Shh now.' She stroked the girl's head, holding her tightly until eventually Elsie hiccupped her last sob and shuddered.

'Goodness. What brought that on?' Caroline asked.

Elsie knuckled her eyes, and Caroline gave her a handkerchief from her pocket. 'Everyone is leaving.'

'No one else is leaving.'

'Yes, they will.' Fresh tears dripped over Elsie's lashes, her young face pasty from all the upset. 'Trixie will die!'

Caroline reared back. 'No, she won't. Don't say that again.'

'She's dying now. I can see it. She's worse every day. She's not eating.' Elsie was half angry and half scared.

'Listen to me.' She took the girl's hands in her lap. 'Are you listening? Now, I can't promise you that Trixie won't die, but I'm doing everything I can to keep her with us.'

'I don't want to visit her grave in the churchyard like we do with Mussy and Mr Thomas. Jacob has gone, too.'

'But you still have many people who care for you here. Me and Bertha, Mr Max, Annie, Doctor Matthew, Jeannie, Dickie, Nessie and even Rosanna. We all care about you, and you'll never be lonely or without a home. Do you trust me?'

Elsie nodded and sniffed.

'You're nine now, and you're clever. You've seen enough and lived through hard times to understand how the world works, how it can be challenging, how we have to be tough to survive. You have to be tough now.'

'I don't want to be tough.' Elsie's bottom lip quivered.

Caroline hugged her to her. 'It's difficult being strong, but we must try to be. Soon, we'll have a new little baby to care for and I'll need your help. That's something to look forward to, isn't it?'

Elsie nodded and wiped her nose. 'I'll try to be strong like you. I'm excited for the baby to arrive. But I'm scared Trixie will die.'

Caroline kissed her forehead. 'Perhaps you could go down to the library and make a list of girl and boy names you like? We can discuss them with Mr Max after dinner.'

'You mean you might pick a name I choose?' Elsie's puffy eyes widened.

'Maybe. It'll depend on Mr Max, and what he wants, but the name you choose might be the baby's second name.' She straightened Elsie's plaits, so they hung down over her shoulders.

'It might be a long list.' Elsie climbed off the bed.

'More the better.'

Elsie hugged her and left the bedroom.

Caroline stood. A sharp anger built in her. She marched straight to Trixie's bedroom opposite and flung open the door so forcibly that it swung back and hit the wall behind.

Trixie jumped in the bed, Caroline hadn't seen her move properly in days.

'Get up!' Caroline demanded, storming over to the bed and whipping the blankets off her.

'No...' Trixie winced and feebly tried to grab at the bedsheet.

'Oh, yes you are. I'm tired of you wasting away. Do you comprehend what you're doing to the girls? You're frightening them. Elsie's been sobbing, believing you're going to die. Well, I'll not have it, understand! Not for a moment longer.' She stood with hands on her hips over Trixie. 'How dare you! How dare you just wither away, wanting to leave us!'

'Caro...'

'No, don't Caro me. I'm ashamed of you,' she shouted at her. 'The Trixie I love like a sister wouldn't just die and leave me and Elsie and Bertha. Where has your fight gone?'

'I...'

'No, don't answer, for its plain to see. You're being a coward.'

Something in Trixie's eyes flickered.

'Never would I believe you to be a quitter, but you are. Giving up. Selfish!' She spat. '*A selfish coward!*'

Trixie flinched. 'Stop.'

'No, I'll not stop. You want to die and leave us, the people who love you? I thought you wanted to see Elsie and Bertha grown, married, with babies of their own?'

Trixie turned her head away. 'I'm tired.'

'Tired? How can that be? You've been in bed for days. Wallowing.'

'Stop, Caro.'

'I thought you were my best friend?' Her voice broke, but she strove on. 'A best friend wouldn't leave willingly. I want you here. *We need you.* The girls need you and I need you. I'm about to have a baby and I want you here to share this wonderful time with me. Only, I can't celebrate this baby because you have lost yours. I'm sorry that you did.'

'I lost more than a baby. I lost Jacob.' A tear trickled down Trixie's face. 'And I'm a nasty person because I grieve losing Jacob more than the baby. I didn't want it.'

Suddenly, the fight ebbed out of Caroline. She slumped onto the bed beside Trixie and took her hand. 'You've been through an awful lot, no one denies that.'

'I couldn't face the world outside of this room,' Trixie admitted. 'I've had enough.'

'We all feel like that at times. However, we can't give in, Trix, because there's a lot left to live for as well.'

Trixie heaved a long sigh.

'I can't be without you, Trix,' Caroline said softly.

'You've got Max.'

'Yes, I do, and I love him with my entire being, but you and me...' She smiled affectionately. 'We've been through so much.'

'Too much.'

Caroline nodded. 'Agreed. I wouldn't have coped without you. I need you in my life. I have done since the day we met.'

'And I you.' Trixie glanced down at their joined hands. 'I just wanted a rest from it all. It was easier to just not care.'

'And now?'

'Now I realise I was being selfish, as you say.' Trixie reached for the glass of water someone had put on the bedside table. Caroline helped her for Trixie's hands shook.

After she'd drunk most of the water, Trixie rested against the pillows, exhausted.

'I'll leave you to sleep.' Caroline stood.

'Only for an hour,' Trixie said. 'Then I'll eat something.'

'I'll have Annie make some eggs and fried ham for you, with toast and tea.'

'Get Elsie to bring it up, and Bertha. I want to hear what they've been doing in the last few days. I'm sorry I scared them.'

At the door, Caroline turned to speak again but Trixie was already asleep. She quietly closed the door.

Downstairs she found Annie alone in the kitchen, Rosanna was washing pots in the scullery.

'Tea, lass?' Annie asked, drying her hands on a cloth.

'Thank you.' Caroline sat at the table. 'I think Trixie might be over the worst. We've had a talk. She's drunk some water and is sleeping now.'

'My, that's a relief and no mistake.' Annie poured water from a jug into the kettle. 'She's nowt but skin and bones.'

'In an hour I'll wake her. I thought we could make her up a tray, a plate of scrambled eggs and so forth.'

'Nowt would make me happier than to cook for her.' Annie peered at Caroline. 'You look a bit peaky, lass.'

'I'm fine. It's been an emotional day, many days in fact. I thought she might die.'

'Once we've got some food into her, she'll perk up, you mark my words. We'll have the old Trixie back again soon.'

Bertha burst through the scullery from outside and into the kitchen. 'Look!' She pointed behind her, hopping from foot to foot.

Caroline glanced over her shoulder and nearly cried. 'Jacob!' She rushed to hug him. 'You've returned.'

'Aye.' He flushed, embarrassed at the fuss. 'I'm back.'

'To stay?' she asked.

'Aye, if that's all right by you and Mr Cavendish?'

'We couldn't be happier. You've grown a beard.'

'Aye.' He rubbed his whiskered face, the brown beard, trimmed short, suited him.

'Sit down, lad,' Annie said, 'and welcome home.'

Bertha stood beside Jacob's chair. 'Trixie might get better now you're back.'

He frowned and looked at Caroline. 'What does Bertha mean?'

'Trixie has been ill.'

'Nearly dying,' Bertha added dramatically as only a child could.

Jacob jerked to his feet. 'Dying?'

Caroline glanced at the scullery where she knew Rosanna had stopped washing the pots and was listening. The maid always wanted to know everything that was going on whether it involved her or not. Caroline stood. 'Jacob, come with me.'

In the drawing room, Caroline closed the double doors to give them privacy and went to stand before the cherry fire.

'Is she dying?' Jacob asked, his face showing his fear.

'Only a few hours ago, there was a very good chance she could have done,' she told him. 'She's been ill for days. She gave up wanting to live.'

'How? Why?'

'She lost the baby the day you left.'

His surprise clearly registered. 'Is that why she is so ill?'

'It was simply the start of her decline.'

'Decline...'

'She couldn't take anymore, Jacob. You leaving, losing the baby, and all that's happened. She'd had enough. She stopped eating and sleeping. I truly think she wanted to die, and she nearly succeeded.'

'Christ in heaven.' He sunk to a chair. 'If I'd known...'

'I thought to write to you at Sarah's, but I didn't know if that was the best thing to do. You needed to either come back on your own accord or not at all.'

'I've come back to be with Trixie. I was willing to accept the child. I want her as my wife. Being in York made me miss her even more than I expected. I spoke with Sarah about it. We had long chats, and my sister said I was a fool. A child is what you make it. Sarah said I should be the man Trixie needs.'

Caroline smiled. 'Sarah makes a lot of sense.'

'Aye, she always has done,' he scoffed.

'This morning I've finally managed to make Trixie see that she still has a life worth living, even if its only for the girls and me.'

'Do you think she'd accept me again?' Jacob asked with little confidence.

'You'll only find out when you speak to her.'

'What do you think?'

Caroline placed another log on the fire. 'She loves you and that's a good start.'

'My wish is to make her happy, Caro, that's all.' Jacob stood. 'Can I see her?'

'She's sleeping now, but I'll wake her soon. Give me some time to wash her and have something to eat. Why don't you go and unpack in your cottage?'

'Is Mr Cavendish at home?'

'No, he's at the Fulton's christening. He'll be relieved to see you've returned.'

'I'll make it up to all of you.'

'There's nothing to make up, Jacob, honestly. It's been difficult, but we'll get through it, together.'

'I'll go and unpack. Prince and Duke are sitting beside my luggage at the back door.'

'They've missed you.'

He smiled. 'I'm glad to be home.' He closed the door behind him.

Caroline watched the flames lick at the new log. 'Home.' She liked the sound of that word.

* * *

ALTHOUGH SHE'D ONLY EATEN half of the eggs and ham, and a few bites of toast, Trixie's stomach was full, fuller than it'd been in weeks. The news that Jacob had returned filled her with happiness and dread. What if he was only here for the position of farm manager and not for her as well?

Caroline had been tight-lipped about it, concentrating on making sure she ate the food brought up on a tray and afterwards Caroline had asked Jeannie to fill the hip bath. As Caroline washed her hair, Trixie sat in the bath, hugging her knees, enjoying the head massage Caroline gave her. The food and the bath tired her out, but she felt better than she had in a long time.

Jeannie changed her bedsheets and added more wood to the fire. Back in bed, Trixie accepted the cup of tea Caroline gave her and even nibbled at an oatcake Annie had freshly made, just for Trixie, knowing they were her favourites.

'Put up or left loose?' Caroline asked her, brushing her brown curls, which had been left to grow long and shaggy about her head.

'Cut it,' Trixie blurted out, surprising herself. She glanced in the mirror to peer at her reflection. 'I look terrible, Caro.'

'Yes, you do,' Caroline agreed with a grin. 'You need fattening up, colour on your cheeks, and a good haircut. I'm not used to seeing you with longer hair.'

'I can always rely on your honesty.'

Caroline laughed. 'Speaking of honesty, I'm so relieved you are coming back to us.'

Sitting on the stool by the dressing table, Trixie plucked at green ribbons threaded at the top of her clean nightgown. 'Well, your anger is enough to frighten anyone into bending to your will.'

Caroline grabbed a pair of scissors from Trixie's sewing basket. 'Do you blame me? We've had enough sadness in this house.'

Elsie and Bertha came quietly into the bedroom, their gazes full of worry.

'You're out of bed?' Elsie's surprise kept her by the door.

'Come here.' Trixie opened her arms to her sisters and held them close. 'I'm much better.'

'She's had a bath and something to eat,' Caroline added. 'I'm going to cut her hair, bring back those bouncy curls.'

'Untameable curls,' Trixie chuckled.

'Can we stay?' Bertha asked, leaning against Trixie.

'Aye, but sit on the bed so Caro can move about me.'

Like old times, the four of them chatted while Caroline snipped at Trixie's hair. The afternoon grew dull outside the window as rain softly fell, but inside the bedroom, warm and cosy from the fire, the four of them laughed and gossiped until Trixie grew tired.

'All done. What do you think?'

Trixie twisted to the mirror and smiled. She looked more like her former self. Her black hair shone from the wash and the cut had given her curls the bounce they'd been lacking of late. 'Perfect.'

'It's you again,' Bertha said with the truth of a child.

'Let's get you into bed.' Caroline helped Trixie under the blankets while the girls cleaned up the hair on the floor.

Trixie grabbed Caroline's arm. 'Soon, I'll be as I was, I promise.'

'Absolutely, no one doubts it.' Caroline kissed the top of her head. 'Right, girls, we'll leave Trix to rest now.'

A knock on the bedroom door revealed Jacob.

Trixie's heart swooped. 'Let him in,' she answered Caroline's quizzical glance.

'Five minutes,' Caroline warned him gently as she passed out of the room with the girls.

Self-consciously, Trixie put a hand to her shorter hair.

'You've got your curls back.' Jacob stood awkwardly at the end of the bed.

'And you've come back, too.' She pushed away her tiredness to take in his appearance. He'd grown a short beard while away. 'I like your beard.'

'You do?'

She nodded. It made him look older, more confident, or maybe that was the new light in his eyes as he stared at her. 'How is Sarah? And the children?'

'Amazingly well.' He took a step closer. 'She's met a new fella, an Irishman named Anthony. A cooper by trade. Sarah delivered his wife's baby, but they both died a month later, the wife and baby.'

'That's sad.'

'Aye, but Sarah and Anthony got talking, and apparently, after a few months, he asked her to marry him. She moved away from the yard where she was living and into his cottage at the edge of Walmgate. It took me a day to find her when I first got to York.' He stopped speaking and changed his weight from one foot to the other as though not knowing what to do with himself.

'Is that why you came back? Because Sarah has a fella?'

'No. I came back because I wanted to be here.'

'You've changed your tune then? You couldn't wait to go.'

'I needed to get away. I needed to sort out my head.'

Trixie watched him, saw his uncertainty. 'And did you? Sort out your head?'

'Aye.'

She gripped the bedsheet. 'You want to keep working for Mr Cavendish?'

'Aye.'

'Have you spoken to him yet?'

'Just now. Mr Cavendish has been kind enough to let me continue in my old job.'

'That's good news. So, you'll be moving back into your cottage then?'

'Aye.'

His curt responses annoyed her. 'I don't have the strength to prise out your every thought, Jacob!'

Swiftly, he was sitting on the bed beside her. 'It's been hell,' he announced. 'Total hell.'

'What has?'

'All of it. Everything. You, Thomas, being here, watching him, watching you, worrying constantly that he'd take you away. My head and heart have hurt like I suffered from some insane disease.'

'I'm sorry.' She took his hand. 'I never meant to hurt you.'

'But you *did*, Trix. You cut me in *two*.' He looked wounded.

'I'm sorry for that, I really am, Jacob. You're the last person I'd ever want to cause pain. Will you forgive me?'

'I've already forgiven you. That's why I'm back. I can't live without you. Every street in York reminded me of you, of where we used to pass each other and say good morning. Your presence was everywhere, down by the river, on the bridges, like a ghost. I walked past the First Water Lane, it's mostly demolished now. Our old tenement building is gone, but I still saw you there in the ruins. It made me miss you even more.'

She brought his hand up and kissed it. 'Promise me, you'll never leave again. I couldn't watch you walk away another time.'

'I'll only ever leave you when I'm in my coffin.' He smiled.

'We'll get married soon?' She hardly breathed as she waited for his answer.

'Aye.' He grinned.

Exhaustedly, she raised her arms up and he gathered her close against him to kiss her softly, adoringly.

* * *

OUTSIDE THE MORNING ROOM WINDOW, snowflakes drifted gently. October had been a month of rain and November had begun with days of light snow. The fire roared up the chimney, and Caroline was thankful to be inside and warm and not outside working as Jacob and Dickie were doing building Annie's new cottage. They'd already added two bedrooms onto Jacob's cottage in readiness for Jacob and Trixie's wedding, and for the girls to move in. Furniture had been carried over there for the last few days. She thought how quiet the bedrooms above would be with only herself and Max sleeping on that floor, at least until the baby arrived.

Last week Max had travelled to Oxford, to finalise the selling of Thomas's townhouse. She would have accompanied him but the weather being so treacherous had kept her home. In her condition, Max was taking no chances.

She ran a hand over her swollen stomach and the baby kicked in response. She grinned. Matthew reassured her that the baby was growing well. They were all counting down the weeks until he or she entered the world.

A slight knock and the door opened, and Elsie entered carrying two books. 'Caro, our Trixie says I can't take any more books to the cottage, but Jacob has built shelves in mine and

Bertha's bedroom, and I can fit a few more books on them. Can I take these from the library, please?'

'Which ones are they?'

'*The King from the Golden River,* and *A Child's History of England Volume Two.*'

'Where is volume one?'

Elsie gave a cheeky smile. 'Already on my bookshelf.'

'Then you'd better keep the two volumes together.' Caroline chuckled.

'There's a third volume...'

'Where is that?'

'In the bookshop in Lincoln,' Elsie said in a suggestive tone.

'Oh, is it now?' Caroline said in mock surprise. 'You'd better save up your pennies then, hadn't you?'

'I have been doing. I don't spend mine on sugared mice like our Bertha does when we go into town, as much as I'd like one.' Elsie headed back to the door. 'Will you tell our Trixie you allowed me to have these?'

'I will.' Caroline turned back to her desk, secretly smiling at the thought that the book Elsie wanted was already bought and wrapped ready to be given out at Christmas next month.

Focusing again on the letters on her desk, she answered the last invitation she'd received and then added the event to her diary. A dinner party on December first with the Cuthberts.

The bell ringing at the front door brought her head up. Only acquaintances, or strangers, rang the front bell, everyone else went around to the yard.

She groaned inwardly. She didn't want to entertain today. She and Trixie were to make the final preparations for the wedding. Trixie and Jacob were to be married on Saturday in South Carlton. Most of the village had been invited. The wedding breakfast afterwards was to be held at Grange Lea in the drawing room. A room which needed all the furniture removing and the carpet rugs rolled up, tables to be brought in and decorated.

The bell rang again. Rising, she wondered if Jeannie hadn't heard it.

A moment later the morning room door opened, and Jeannie entered. 'Madam, there's a lady here wanting to speak to Mr Cavendish. I told her he was away from home. She insisted on speaking with you. I've put her in the drawing room.'

'Thank you. Bring in a tea tray.' Caroline walked along the hall and into the drawing room, where a woman stood by the fire, wearing a long black cape trimmed with black fur. 'Good morning,' she said, walking into the room.

The woman turned and faced Caroline. She resembled someone faintly and Caroline wondered who it was. 'Mrs Caroline Cavendish?'

'Yes.'

'I am Lady Stockton-Lee.'

Shocked, Caroline stared at her. Max's Aunt Lucille. Wayland's mother.

'You are surprised to see me it seems.'

'Of course. We've had no word of your impending arrival.'

'That is because I did not send one,' she replied stiffly. She studied Caroline for a long moment.

Uncomfortable under the woman's scrutiny, Caroline moved to stand near the fire. 'Max isn't at home. He's in Oxford.'

'Oxford?' The older woman seemed to deflate in front of Caroline. 'I have been gathering my courage for this meeting for weeks and now he is not here?'

'Please, will you not sit down?' Caroline gestured to a chair by the fire. 'Can I take your cape?'

Her ladyship began to cry. Silent tears ran down her cheeks that she wiped away with a black-edged handkerchief.

Not knowing what to do, Caroline helped her to the chair just as Jeannie brought the tea tray in. Caroline lifted up the teapot. 'A cup of tea, your ladyship?'

'Thank you, yes. I need one.' Lady Lucille Stockton-Lee dabbed at her eyes. 'How humiliating this is for me.'

'You have nothing to be ashamed of, your ladyship. Milk or cream?' She poured out two cups

'Cream. I do not taste cream often in India.'

'Sugar?'

'None, thank you.' Lucille raised her face to Caroline. 'You are kind, I think.'

She handed a cup and saucer to Max's aunt. 'I try to be.'

'And you love my nephew.'

'With every part of me.'

'And you are with child.' The other woman dabbed her eyes again. 'Does Max hate me?'

'Not at all!'

'He should.' Lucille stared into the flames. 'My solicitors have given me a full report on my son's insalubrious activities, the corrupt life he led before he died. The damage he caused. The killing of dear Thomas…'

'You are not to blame for your son's actions.'

The older woman looked exhausted. 'Who else is there? I was his mother. I raised him. Perhaps that was the problem. I over-compensated for his father's lack of love. Wayland had my full devotion as a child. He was spoilt. However, I never expected him to turn into a monster. Only, the signs were there. His selfish ways, his coldness…'

'He was a grown man, responsible for his own decisions.'

'None of what you say eases my mind.'

Tea was sipped, the scones on the tray ignored. Minutes ticked by in uncomfortable silence.

'I should be going. I have booked a room in a hotel in Lincoln.' Her ladyship placed the empty cup and saucer on the tray. 'It is strange to have returned home after so long away. I was born in Lincoln.'

'You will see many changes, I'm sure.'

'Likely a great deal.'

'And you have come in the colder months. You must suffer the difference in temperature keenly.' Caroline smiled.

'I have not worn a cape as thick as this for many years.' She rose gracefully. 'I am told Wayland is buried at Misterton Abbey, the family seat.'

'That's true. Max arranged it.'

'With the understanding that Wayland would have hated to be buried there.' She paused. 'My nephew exacted his revenge.'

'He was grieving Thomas, wounded himself from the stabbings. Wayland nearly ruined us.'

'Oh, do not believe I am upset by Max's arrangements. They make perfect sense, and I bear him no ill will.' She walked to the door. 'I am travelling to the abbey tomorrow. My late husband's cousin's son now resides at the abbey. It is no longer my home, but I wish to visit the grave.'

In the hall, Caroline waited while her ladyship glanced around, taking in the library through its open door, the wide staircase.

'This house looks far more comfortable than when I last was here. Such a long time ago that was. When I was newly married… You have done a tremendous job of transforming it into a fine manor.'

'Thank you.'

'When do you expect Max to return?'

'He plans to return in two days. Friday. We have a family wedding on Saturday.'

'May I call again on my return south to see him?'

'Absolutely. He will want to see you. He loves you very much.'

Tears again sprang to the older woman's eyes. 'He is as much my son as Wayland was, he and Thomas both. I have missed them enormously.'

Jeannie came and opened the door.

Her ladyship hesitated, as though not wanting to leave. 'That you have received me and treated me well, despite the words I wrote to Max tells me a great deal about the woman my nephew married. Your letter to me prompted my journey here. A journey which is dangerous and arduous to undertake for a woman my age. However, I am grateful to have done it.'

'I look forward to seeing you again, your ladyship.' Caroline held out her hand.

The woman took it with a smile. 'Will you call me Lucille? There are so few people left in this world that can call me that now.'

'I'd be honoured, but I think I should call you Aunt Lucille, as Max does.'

'I would like that, and you are Caroline?'

Caroline smiled. 'Or Caro, as my family calls me.'

'Caro...' Lucille nodded. 'Good day then.'

When the door closed, Caroline sucked in a long breath. She couldn't wait for Max to come home.

CHAPTER TWENTY-TWO

*T*he voices rang out in the cold church as the congregation sang a hymn led by Reverend Trott. Outside, a light covering of snow had fallen overnight, covering the ground in splendid white but wasn't too deep to make travel impossible or difficult. Folk from the village, wearing their best clothes had come to witness Jacob and Trixie's marriage. Although Trixie wasn't as well known in the village as Jacob, who had spent many an evening with the men drinking ale and talking of farming. He'd made friends and they'd entered the church to support him, and also for the free food and drink back at Grange Lea afterwards.

Caroline blinked away her tears of happiness as she watched Trixie stand beside Jacob. Trixie had regained some of her lost weight and looked healthy once more. In fact, at the moment, she looked as lovely as Caroline had ever seen her. Trixie glowed from an inner contentment and joy like never before. She wore a soft pink dress with cream piping and lace overskirt. Her dark hair was held up with combs studded with small white roses.

The love Trixie and Jacob shared shone to all who witnessed their exchange of vows. Elsie and Bertha stood proudly beside their sister. They could barely stand still such was their excitement. Both girls wore dresses of white satin and lace with blue sashes and blue ribbons in their dark hair.

Caroline would have liked to have worn something pretty, but it seemed a waste of money to buy a new dress for the wedding when her shape changed nearly every week. The lilac-coloured bodice and skirt she wore was bought to last the entire pregnancy with a waistband that could easily be altered. She'd added white lace to the sleeves and collar, and a new velvet hat, with lilac flowers stitched onto it, completed the outfit.

'What a magical day.' Annie sighed contentedly. 'To see these two joined together.'

'It's about time,' Caroline joked.

'Indeed.' Annie sat beside Caroline, and on the other side of her the pew was filled with the female staff. Dickie stood up at the altar next to Jacob, as proud as a peacock in his new suit.

The baby kicked and Caroline rubbed the spot, bringing Max's attention to her. She smiled at him and his gloved hand found hers.

'I am freezing in here. Who gets married in the cold months?' he whispered with laughter in his blue eyes.

'We'll be home soon and by the fire,' she whispered back.

'I am thankful we were married in summer on a beautiful day.'

'So am I.' She squeezed his hand, remembering their special day. The warmth of the sun, the perfume of the flowers, the smell of fresh mown grass, the twitter of birds in the trees. It had been an enchanting occasion.

'I suppose it does not matter when a wedding occurs, it is still a happy event when the couple involved love each other,' Max murmured soberly. 'Happiness can never be taken for granted.'

She pondered on his meaning. She kept her gaze on the reverend as he spoke, but her mind wandered back to the day before when Max had returned from a successful trip to Oxford. Thomas's townhouse had been sold and the money would pay off

Max's loan and help towards rebuilding the livestock numbers. She had told him the news of his aunt's unexpected visit. He'd been surprised and then thoughtful, not saying much at all. She hoped he wasn't blaming himself for Wayland's actions, or his own responses, but she understood him well enough to appreciate he'd be feeling guilty for not preventing the chaos that Wayland caused, and his aunt's pain.

She shook all that from her mind as Trixie and Jacob were declared man and wife. Cheers erupted and Caroline felt a wash of joyful emotion come over her as Trixie and Jacob kissed. Arm in arm, the happy couple led their guests out of the church to the whiteness of the snow-covered countryside.

The sun peeked between grey clouds, dazzling on the snow to make it shimmer like crushed diamonds. Dried rose petals and rice were thrown over Trixie and Jacob, much to the Reverend Trott's dismay at the mess. Elsie and Bertha danced about with excitement.

A progression of farm carts and gigs followed the Cavendish carriage back to Grange Lea, though some people walked or rode on horseback.

The drawing room soon filled with guests. Caroline checked to see if Annie and Rosanna were coping with the array of food trays that was taken through to the tables by Nessie, Elsie and Bertha. Jeannie took coats and hats, while Dickie tied up horses and gave them a feed. Guests mingled and soon the house was full of chatter and laughter.

At first, Caroline wasn't aware of the new arrival until Jeannie found her and told her Max's aunt waited in the hall.

Surprised, Caroline rushed straight to her. 'Your ladyship. Forgive me, I didn't expect you today.'

'I am horrified at my own forgetfulness. I did not remember that you mentioned that there was a wedding here today until I saw all the vehicles.'

'You've had a lot on your mind, no doubt,' Caroline said kindly.

'I shall leave immediately.' Lucille took a step backwards.

'You're very welcome to stay.'

'Aunt Lucille.' Max joined them. He hesitated only slightly before kissing his aunt's cheek. 'I thought you to be in Melliton.'

'I did not want to risk being stuck there if the snow became worse.'

The three of them stood by the front door in awkward silence while behind them in the drawing room, the noise was of good cheer.

'I will leave you to your party,' Lucille said.

Caroline heard the reluctance in her voice and felt sorry for the older woman. 'No, please stay.'

'Is that what *you* want, Nephew?'

Max cleared his throat. 'I would not want you travelling in such icy conditions. You are welcome here.'

'Come through to the library,' Caroline suggested. 'You can talk in peace in there.'

With the door closed on the wedding, Caroline checked the fire was blazing nicely and then put her hand on Max's back. 'I'll leave you two alone to talk.'

'No, stay.' Max held his body rigid, as though expecting a battle.

'You expect my censure, do you not, Max?' Aunt Lucille spoke sadly.

'Whatever you feel, Aunt, I am certain it is justified.'

'Your wife's letter left me in no doubt that I had misjudged you, and ultimately my son.' Lucille glanced at Caroline. 'You were right to send that letter to me. Brave and honest. I admire you for it. I should have said so the other day when I called.'

'Thank you.' Caroline inclined her head.

'But you should have told me first, Max. Had you have done, I would have been on the first ship sailing from Bombay and been here sooner. As it was, I took the new overland route across Egypt which is uncomfortable but quicker than sailing the entire way.'

Max stood stiffly. 'I did not want to seem like a child telling tales, Aunt.'

'Such horrid tales that occurred needed telling, Max, especially when it concerned my son and his atrocious behaviour.'

'What would you have me do? Tell you everything and then what? Pretend everything was well? Ignore Wayland's behaviour and continue on with my life at the abbey?'

'No, absolutely not.'

'Then what?' Max held out his hands. 'You were thousands of miles away and Wayland was out of control and listening to no advice. I was ashamed to be related to him. What he did to Caroline.' Max grimaced. 'The trouble he caused to me here. He was out of control, Aunt. How could all that be put in a letter and you would believe it?'

Lucille crossed the floor and placed a hand on his cheek. 'My dear Max.' Tears welled in her eyes. 'What troubles you have had, and I have been miles away and of no help whatsoever.'

'I did try to befriend Wayland, at first, but it proved impossible.'

His aunt shook her head. 'Do not apologise for anything, Max, I beg you. I had no idea my son had become such a...' She stopped, trying to find the right words. 'That he was no longer a gentleman. He has shamed me and his father. I thank the Lord your uncle did not live to see the man Wayland had become.'

'Will you not sit, Aunt?' Max gestured to a chair by the fire.

'Shall I bring us some tea?' Caroline suggested.

'No, please, not on my account. Your maids are busy enough.' Aunt Lucille sat and turned to Max. 'I am most pleased to see you have married well. Your wife is charming and kind.'

Max smiled at Caroline. 'She is the reason my heart beats.'

Caroline melted at his romantic words.

'You will make a sweet family. I wish I could stay and witness it.'

'Why can't you?' Caroline asked, impulsively.

'My home is in India, dear.'

'Does it have to be?' Max said. 'Could you not stay with us for a year or so? Be here to see our child born?'

'Gracious. Such an offer.' Aunt Lucille blinked rapidly. 'You really wish for me to stay?'

'Only if it suits you, Aunt.'

'For as long as you want to,' Caroline added. 'Max has no family left except you. How wonderful would it be for him to have you living with us?'

'Guests can easily become a burden,' Aunt Lucille warned.

'You are family, not a guest.' Caroline smiled.

'And would you not like to spend some time in the town where you were born and grew into adulthood?' Max asked.

'Besides, it would give you and Max the chance to talk and become close again.' Caroline wanted Max to have that.

'Also, for me to become better acquainted with you, my dear,' Aunt Lucille replied.

'You do not have to decide right away, Aunt,' Max said.

Lucille thought a long moment. 'I do have a very good manager at the tea plantation. I could write to him and inform him I shall be extending my visit for longer. The mail only takes thirty-five days to reach India now. Such a marvellous thing, thanks to Mr Wagner's new mail route.' She looked up and blushed. 'I am rambling.'

Caroline touched Max's arm. 'I will fetch a tea tray. You both have much to talk about.'

Aunt Lucille rose. 'Please, if I am to stay, then I should meet everyone. May I join in the celebrations?'

'Are you sure, Aunt?' Max asked.

'I have neglected my kin for far too long, dear nephew. It is time I started to act as an aunt to you and be a member of your family. If you are willing to have me?'

Max kissed her cheek. 'Nothing would make me happier, Aunt. I have missed you.'

'And I you, dear one.'

While Max introduced his aunt to the people of the village, Caroline visited the kitchen to see how Annie was coping.

'Ah, I'm fine, lass. Go back in there and enjoy yourself,' Annie told her, taking another tray of almond biscuits out of the oven.

'Let me help.'

'In your condition? You've been on your feet all morning.' Annie waved her away. 'You'll have swollen ankles by tonight. Take a minute to rest. You've been organising this wedding for weeks.'

'A sit down would be nice,' Caroline admitted, pulling out a wooden chair and sitting at the table.

'Pour yourself a cup of tea, lass,' Annie advised, placing the biscuits on a cooling rack. 'Rosanna, take that pot of coffee through and check the milk jug and sugar bowls. They may need refilling. Bring back any empty cups. Jeannie is waiting behind the tables and can't do it yet.'

Rosanna looked to complain but glanced at Caroline and thought better of it.

Trixie came in as Rosanna went out. 'There you are.' She smiled at Caroline, looking radiant. 'I see her ladyship is here.'

'Yes, and she's going to be staying for some months.'

'Really?'

'It'll be good for Max to have her here.'

'What are your thoughts about it?' Trixie sat beside her.

'I'm happy about it, truly. She seems nice. I want Max to have some family about him, and I think his aunt is lonely.'

'Poor woman,' Annie said. 'She might have money, but nothing replaces loved ones.'

'Agreed.' Caroline poured out some tea for the three of them.

Nessie came in with an empty tray. 'The food is going quickly, Annie.'

'Aye, nothing moves faster than free food.' Annie gave her a tray full of plates filled with sliced meat and bread and butter. 'Take this tray and I'll follow you with that tray of cakes.'

'I'll take it Annie,' Trixie offered.

'You'll do no such thing on your wedding day!' Annie scoffed with a wink and followed Nessie out.

'Cheers.' Caroline held her teacup high towards Trixie and grinned. 'To the happy couple.'

'Cheers.' Trixie laughed. 'Who'd have thought this is where we'd end up, hey, Caro?'

Caroline wrapped her arm around Trixie's shoulders. 'It's been a long road, dearest.'

'A very *difficult* and *long* road,' Trixie added.

'We've lost wonderful people along the way.' Caroline felt the tears build. 'But found some new ones.'

'And look where we are now?' Trixie said, her eyes also full of tears. 'We are married, Caro, both of us, to lovely men who care for us. We're all healthy and have a nice home.'

'And we're together.' Caroline nodded, forcing a cheery note to her voice.

'And there's a baby to welcome in a few months. Imagine how perfect that'll be?'

'Who will be spoilt and loved.' Caroline rubbed her stomach. 'And who'll have the best aunty in the world.' She gazed tenderly at Trixie.

Trixie kissed Caroline's cheek in a rare show of affection. 'Have I ever told you how special you are to me?'

'Stop it, I'll be in a flood of tears in a minute and it's your wedding day.' Caroline laughed, squeezing Trixie's hand.

'It's true.' Trixie wiped her eyes and sniffed.

'Well, I wouldn't be here without you. Your friendship has been everything to me.'

Trixie raised her teacup. 'To us!'

Caroline clinked her teacup against Trixie's. 'To us!'

ABOUT THE AUTHOR

Author of over thirty-five novels, AnneMarie Brear has crafted sweeping historical fiction with atmosphere, emotion, and drama aplenty that will surely satisfy any fan of the genre. AnneMarie was born in a small town in N.S.W. Australia, to English parents from Yorkshire, and is the youngest of five children. From an early age she loved reading, working her way through the Enid Blyton stories, before moving onto Catherine Cookson's novels as a teenager.

Living in England during the 1980s and more recently, Anne-Marie developed a love of history from visiting grand old English houses and this grew into a fascination with what may have happened behind their walls over their long existence. Her enjoyment of visiting old country estates and castles when travelling and, her interest in genealogy and researching her family tree, has been put to good use, providing backgrounds and names for her historical novels which are mainly set in Yorkshire or Australia between Victorian times and WWII.

A long and winding road to publication led to her first novel being published in 2006.

She has now published over thirty-five historical family saga novels, becoming an Amazon best seller and with her novel, The Slum Angel, winning a gold medal at the USA Reader's Favourite International Awards. Two of her books have been nominated for the Romance Writer's Australia Ruby Award and the USA In'dtale Magazine Rone award and recently she has been nominated twice as a finalist for the UK RNA RONA Awards.

AnneMarie now lives in the Southern Highlands of N.S.W. Australia

You can sign up to AnneMarie's newsletter from her website. http://www.annemariebrear.com

Made in United States
Cleveland, OH
15 April 2025

16099460R00163